WHEN DAY IS DONE

WHEN DAY IS DONE

Elizabeth Gill

This first world edition published in Great Britain 2003 by
SEVERN HOUSE PUBLISHERS LTD of
9–15 High Street, Sutton, Surrey SM1 1DF.
This first world edition published in the USA 2004 by
SEVERN HOUSE PUBLISHERS INC of
595 Madison Avenue, New York, N.Y. 10022.

FIC
G47532 wh

British Library Cataloguing in Publication Data

Gill, Elizabeth
    When day is done
    1.   Durham (England) - Social life and customs - 19th century - Fiction
    I.   Title
    823.9'14 [F]

    ISBN 0-7278-6012-7

Typeset by Hewer Text Ltd.,
Edinburgh, Scotland.
Printed and bound in Great Britain by
MPG Books Ltd., Bodmin, Cornwall.

One

County Durham 1901

E sther Margaret had insisted on dying in her own bed. It wasn't too much to ask, Vinia thought, except that she was young, she shouldn't have been dying at all. The house was tiny, in the middle of a pit row, the little boy cried and there was nowhere to get away from his crying. He wanted his mother.

The cancer had eaten away at Esther Margaret's insides. Vinia thought of it like a gigantic worm that was always hungry. Esther Margaret had kept the little boy with her as long as she could and the doctor had been there constantly, relieving the pain to such an extent that after a time Esther Margaret did not know anyone, including her tall, dark husband who stood now by the kitchen fire.

Tommy clung to him and Dryden must be tired, Vinia thought, he had been standing there for hours with the child asleep in his arms. He had barely slept in a week, sitting by his wife's bed day and night.

It was over. Esther Margaret had taken her last breaths with her husband and child beside her and a lot of people would have thought it was a great deal except that Esther Margaret knew very well her husband did not love her. He had never loved her. He had been kind to her during the last four years. It wasn't as though he went out and got drunk every night or ran after other women and there were plenty of women who would have had him, Vinia thought, looking at him. He was what Mrs Harris, who kept the grocery department of the store, would have called 'the bee's knees'. When women conjured men in

1

their dreams he was exactly what they hoped for, young, quiet, softly spoken. He had a Durham accent that was as warm as honey, the darkest eyes she had ever seen, skin the colour of toffee, black hair and an air of what? She wasn't quite sure. He moved well. He hadn't moved at all for the past two hours after he had rocked Tommy to sleep.

'Shall I take him for you?' she suggested, holding out her arms.

Dryden shook his head. It was as though he thought something might tear if he let go of the child. Vinia had known him since he was eighteen and she had not seen him break down, not when his brother had been killed by a roof fall nor when his wife had lost their first child, so she didn't suppose he was going to do it now. He blamed himself for their loveless marriage, Vinia knew he did, even though for four years he had come faithfully home to his wife at the end of each shift down the Black Prince pit. She knew how hard it was for him because all that time he had been in love with another woman and never touched her. Vinia knew very well that he hadn't because she was the woman.

She had always hoped that Esther Margaret didn't know but during the past weeks, when the doctor had stopped the pain with drugs, it was as though he had freed her tongue. One cold, wet afternoon when they had been sitting over the kitchen fire before Esther Margaret had taken to her bed completely, she said into the silence, 'You'll be able to have my husband when I'm gone.'

Shocked, Vinia stared. They knew one another well. Esther Margaret had been her good friend for years.

'What?'

Esther Margaret stared into the fire.

'Oh, come on, Vinia, you've always wanted him. If you had to live with him as I do you might change your mind.'

Vinia was stricken with guilt.

'I never—'

'I know you never. Pity. I used to think that maybe if he'd put you down and had you a few times he might have got over it,' Esther Margaret said, her voice rough against emotion.

Vinia shook her head.

'Shall I tell you what he's like to live with?' She looked hard at Vinia. 'He makes love like an angel, so there. He's kind and funny and he makes me hope the neighbours aren't listening to me crying out with pleasure. He tips up his pay and never asks for a penny. He loves Tommy to distraction. He never complains. He's never late home. He never drinks. On Saturdays he takes me to the market and buys me pretty things and on Sundays he takes me out walking and helps me over stiles and lifts me over muddy patches in fields. Have you any idea what it's like living with a man who treats you like that when he doesn't love you? It's a perpetual courtship. You never get to the ordinary bit. It's like he's always making up for it. I've tried picking quarrels with him but he won't fight. I used to wish that just once he would come home drunk and belt me and then I could hate him for not loving me.'

Vinia also wished that Dryden could have been the kind of man who loved two women at once. It would have been so much simpler. Plenty of men did it. They had wives at home and somebody on the side but Dryden wasn't built like that. She was the only woman he had ever loved and they had never been free to be together. His experience of women was bitter. She had been very careful with him all these years because she had the uncomfortable idea that it was an impression of her that he loved, not herself. Maybe he needed an ideal whereas she could go home to Joe, her husband, who had no illusions about her whatsoever.

Joe was the practical type. He had set her up financially so that, having started with one shop, she now owned three. He had guided and helped her. Joe had married her, knowing what her relationship with Dryden was, and he had never since questioned her but he was a very intelligent man. He had given her status with their marriage because he was the pit owner and every woman cared for that. She had gained a big sprawling house on the fell. They did not have a lot of money compared to other people who were landowners and businessmen but there was enough to keep the house, buy what they needed and keep

3

the pit and the shops going. It was Vinia's great delight to sit down on the settee of a Saturday night – her husband didn't go to the pub either, his father had been a drunk – and talk about the business. She could tell Joe anything and he would understand. They drank champagne on Saturday nights and very often they made love on the rug in front of the fire.

The only thing they lacked was a child and so it was as if Tommy had four parents. Vinia was at work mostly but she had Wednesdays off and would spend them at Esther Margaret's or they would go into Durham on the train and have tea and on Sundays she would invite Dryden and Esther Margaret to Sunday dinner. She knew that being friends with the pit owner and his wife meant that Dryden and Esther Margaret had no other friends in the village, Dryden being nothing but a hewer down the pit, but she didn't think they cared. She and Joe adored Tommy. She had got used to the idea that they would not have a child. Already Joe talked of Tommy having the pit when he grew up. They made the best of things.

Now however there was no best to be made. She took the child from Dryden's arms without asking him again and put Tommy to bed. The boy did not wake up. She came back downstairs. It was a vile January night. Joe had had to go back to the pit, just along the road, to deal with some problem. The snow was coming down as though somebody had been storing buckets of the stuff above them. The wind was knocking it sideways so that it was piling up beyond the windows.

'Would you like some tea?'

He shook his head.

'Would you like something to eat?'

'No, thank you.'

'Why don't you sit down?'

'Vinia . . .' he said impatiently and then stopped.

'I know I'm fussing. I'm sorry. I don't know what else to do.'

'There's nothing more to be done. You should go to the pit and let Joe take you home.'

'And leave you here by yourself?'

4

'I'm not by myself. I'll go and sleep with Tommy. Come on, I'll see you to the end of the road.'

He walked her down the pit row. It was the one which bore the pit's name, Prince Row. Automatically they went out of the back into the unmade street beyond the yards and she could see the pit wheel, black in contrast against the white sky. The snow was sweeping its way across the open stretch of fell beyond the pit and the houses. Some way over was Stanley House where she and Joe lived. It stood all alone upon a great bare stretch of fell which was clear and open to the sky. Here there was nothing to stop the intricacy of the snow in play and as the hard pellets hit her face she thought gratefully of how much love she had found in this bleak village high up on the Durham fells which had always been her home. It had kept its promises, except that she had no child. As they reached the pit she turned around.

'You should go back. What if Tommy wakes up?'

'He never wakes up in the night.'

'Dryden . . .' She got hold of the front of his coat, clutched fingersful of it like he was trying to get away whereas in fact he stood like a wall between herself and everything else. 'Try not to blame yourself.'

Dryden smiled and he traced his fingers across her hair where the wind was making game with her hat.

'Joe and I will look after you,' she said. 'Anything you want—'

'I'm grand,' he said.

'I'll come over tomorrow and help arrange the funeral and I will take Tommy if you like.'

'That's fine,' he said.

Always he agreed. She had no idea how to argue with him. It was like Esther Margaret had said.

'You go now,' she said. 'Don't leave Tommy,' and she ran away, across the yard, out of the darkness and into the office.

Joe was waiting for her. One of the nicest things about her husband, Vinia thought, was his modesty. Cleverer than the rest of the district Joe would have died rather than let them know, and his office reflected this. It was no bigger than it

5

needed to be, no bigger than the empty office next door. His pit manager had left recently. He had too much work to do but he accepted it. Joe loved his pit as much as he loved his wife. The pit and the house and Vinia were his whole life. He didn't say stupid things like, 'Is Dryden all right?' and she was pleased.

She was almost crying. Joe understood, just as he always did.

They went home and once she was there she was so grateful that the odd tear broke loose upon her cheeks. Addy, who looked after the house, had left a stew to be heated and the house was warm and Joe poured out red wine and they ate in the comfort of the kitchen by the stove and when they had eaten Joe said, 'I thought I might take Dryden into the office once he gets past the funeral.'

'What, as a clerk? I don't think he's any good at things like that.'

'No.' Joe spoke slowly and looked down into his glass. 'As a potential pit manager.'

Vinia stared.

'You think he can do that?'

'I know he can, if he applies himself.'

'What about Tommy?'

'It would be better because Dryden wouldn't be on shifts and Mrs Thornton would look after Tommy. She's done it enough lately.'

Susanna Thornton was a widow who lived two doors down from Dryden and had been a big help. The trouble was, Vinia thought, with a pang of jealousy, that Mrs Thornton was pretty and Dryden was alone.

'You don't think it's a good idea?' Joe said.

'I think we can do better than that,' she said.

Dryden walked slowly back to the house. He was not anxious about Tommy. The boy was worn out. He was old enough to be told that his mother was dying, that she was not coming back, and to stay by her bed while she was still there and to remember her.

Dryden stopped suddenly. He knew from experience that the

minute you thought you were coping you weren't. He did not want to go back to the house where his young wife was lying dead upstairs. She could not have died. She could not have been so ill all these months, not while he did not love her. She deserved that he should and he had realized that one of the hardest things in the world was to watch the woman you loved go home with a better man than you. Joe was a better man. Joe was so bloody kind, as though he owed Dryden, not as though Dryden lusted after his wife and he did. He didn't know how he kept his hands off her. He didn't know how he existed without holding her. He did it because of Joe, because Joe called him by his first name in front of the other men and it was a lot, Dryden knew it was, a signal to the world that they were friends. It could have cost Joe the respect of the miners. Joe was prepared to take risks for him. Joe cared about him and about Tommy. There was something special about a man who loved your child. He was generous. Any other man would have said, 'Keep your bloody eyes off my wife,' but he didn't. Any other man would have got rid of him. Joe created the balance. Clever, clever Joe.

The tears began to rain. He had held them back for so long and now they would not be contained. The loneliness was like a big tide that you saw at the coast on October days, the waves coming over the pier at Seaham. He walked quickly back to the house and closed the door. Silence inside and out and the house was warm because for many days there had been fires in every room. It didn't matter how many fires they had how often because Joe provided the coal free.

Dryden locked the door and went upstairs into the back room where Tommy lay asleep in the double bed. Dryden tried not to think about Esther Margaret, still and white next door. He shed his clothes and got in beside the child, who sighed in his sleep and then turned over and said, 'Daddy?' as though he knew, as though he were awake.

'It's all right, I'm here,' Dryden said and Tommy sighed again and went back to sleep.

Dryden moved in against his small body but he could not drag his mind from his wife. None of what he had done during the past four years had been enough. She hadn't said that. She hadn't said anything. She did not reproach or question him. He had wanted to love her because she had given him his son and he was grateful. He tried to show gratitude but gratitude was not what marriages should be about. He liked having her and she enjoyed it, he knew. He could make her body rise and yield but it was not love and she would make scones for tea on Saturdays and eggs and fried bread for breakfast on Sundays and good dinners all week and send him to work with a kiss and greet him when he came back with smiles and food and warmth and comfort but it was not love. Love was watching Joe and Vinia dancing together at the annual party for the pitmen and having to sit there and listen to the music and pretend that he didn't mind, that he was glad.

Joe also made Dryden aware that he bedded his wife frequently and with style. Dryden wasn't quite sure how Joe got the message across but he did. He was the pit owner. He had the best hand in the deck. He had given her all the things that Dryden could never have given her. She had jewellery and furs and the great big house upon the fell. Had they not been such friends he would have been obliged to and indeed in public still did refer to her as 'Mrs Forster'. In public also Joe could call him by his first name but Joe was always 'Mr Forster' or 'sir'. In spite of all the Sunday dinners and Tommy there was no way past that.

The following Sunday Joe called on Dryden and Dryden could see that he had something important to say so when Tommy was happily playing by the sitting-room fire he and Joe retreated to the kitchen and Joe said, 'Dryden, look, I think you have a lot of ability. Have you considered moving up?'

'What, deputy?'

'No, manager.'

Dryden stared at him.

'Are you being funny?'

'Think about it,' Joe said. 'Walter has left. There's an empty office next door to mine.'

'But I couldn't do it just like that.'

'You don't fit any more below ground,' Joe said, green eyes frank. 'You know you don't. You could go to classes for qualifications and I could teach you everything I know. You don't have to decide now. I know you've got more important things on your mind.'

Dryden did think about it. He thought about it when Esther Margaret's coffin stood at the front of the church and Tommy clutched his hands. People had been shocked that he had taken the child to his mother's funeral. Tommy knew she was dead. Now he would see what happened to dead people.

Susanna Thornton had argued with Dryden about this. It amused him that she thought she could make the difference. He could see that she imagined herself in Esther Margaret's place. If only she knew. She was bonny. Her husband had been dead six months. Joe had let her keep on the house even though Jack Thornton had not had a pit accident. He had drowned in a pond when drunk.

'That bairn shouldn't be going to any funeral,' she told Dryden. 'He's been through enough. I could take him to Bishop for the day and buy him some Black Bullets.'

She went on and on. It had been rumoured in the village that Jack Thornton often got drunk and then came home and treated his wife to a hiding. Dryden wasn't surprised. She was a pushy little cow.

'Thank you, Susanna,' he said. 'I don't think so.'

'It isn't decent,' she said.

She had come in and cleaned the house and made food he didn't eat. He was going to have to find someone else to do it before she tried to take over completely and he offended her.

Vinia had offered to have the funeral tea at their house and Dryden was glad, not just because his own house was so small but because it got them away. He had spent so much time there recently he felt like he was going mad. Also somehow the idea that Esther Margaret would no longer be there came as something of a relief. She had been ill for many months, things had got worse each day. There had been no let up.

The day was bright. Some snow still lay on the ground but the sunshine improved everything. There were even a few snowdrops over by the far wall. Dryden could see them as he stood, cup and saucer in hand, by the window in the sitting room. A lot of people had come to the funeral. The women were gathered in the kitchen. Dryden heard Tommy laugh from in there. It was good to hear him. Joe came over.

'Will you come back to work tomorrow?' he said.

'I have to find somebody to look after Tommy.'

'Addy said she will have him for now, unless you'd rather Susanna Thornton.'

Dryden looked sideways at him.

'Don't you fancy it then?' Joe said.

'No, I don't. No wonder poor bloody Jack chucked himself in a pond.'

'He fell in,' Joe said.

'You sure?'

Joe laughed. Dryden liked the sound.

'You haven't had a drink,' Joe said.

'I don't need one.'

'Go on,' Joe said and he went off and found a bottle of whisky in the sideboard, then two large cut glasses, and poured generously. 'You could come and stay with us for a while.'

Dryden could not imagine anything worse than being in the same house with Joe and Vinia in bed together.

'No, thanks. I'm fine.'

'Addy has a sister, Meg, who would do your house for you. She's married. She's nice. You could see her, if you think she would do and Tommy takes to her.'

'Is that Meg Carter?'

'That's her.'

'That would be good,' Dryden said, sipping whisky slowly. He couldn't remember the last time he had had a drink and it was excellent whisky, single malt. Joe didn't drink much, he thought, but when he did it was the best.

'Have you got another suit?' Joe indicated Dryden's Sunday best.

'Yes.'

'So wear it tomorrow.'

'I don't know.'

'Look, Dryden . . .' Joe stopped. 'I need somebody I can trust. Running the place by myself is too much. You've been there since you were twelve.'

'That doesn't mean I'm going to be any good at it.'

'I'll pay you more money.'

'A lot?' Dryden said hopefully.

'Yes, a lot, but you'll have to study as well as work.'

'I can do that while Tommy's in bed.'

'And go to evening classes for a long time but I'll help you as much as I can and you can help me. I don't think you realize how much you know,' Joe said.

Dryden got back to find Susanna Thornton in his kitchen. There was the smell of dinner. The place was spotless, almost like it belonged to somebody else. Susanna was small and dark like Vinia and for a few seconds it was his best dream come true and then she turned around from the fire as he put Tommy down.

'You're later than I thought you'd be,' she said. Houses were never locked during the day around here. If he wanted rid of her he would have to tell her. 'I can put the bairn to bed and then we can eat.'

'No,' Dryden said. 'I'll put him to bed myself, thanks. I've asked Addy Robinson's sister, Meg, to come and see to the house from now on. Thanks for everything you've done.'

She looked hard at him.

'You don't want Meg Carter here. You'll have to pay her.'

'That's right. You've been very kind but you have your own house and I don't want to impose on you.' He went over and opened the back door.

Susanna flounced out. Dryden shut the door and took Tommy upstairs. He read his child a story and then glanced into the other bedroom, imagining his wife still there, both dead and alive, but it was completely empty, the bed changed and every clue to Esther Margaret's presence gone. He didn't really

11

want to sleep in there by himself. The bed looked like acres and he was aware of the wardrobe and chest of drawers full of her clothes. He wished he could have another of Joe's large glasses of whisky.

He went downstairs, sat over the fire and tried to read. The silence was irksome. He thought what it would be like the following day when he went to the office for the first time. People would talk but he and Joe had been friendly for so long, he didn't think they would be very surprised. Joe was right, he did know a lot about pits and what he didn't know he could learn.

He put off going to bed until late, convinced that he wouldn't sleep when he got there but eventually he was bored and tired and the strain of the day caught up to him so he went. He had not been long there when he heard the patter of bare feet on the floor. Tommy stopped short at the bed.

'Could I sleep with you?'

''Course. Climb in.'

'Thanks, Dad,' Tommy said cheerily and got into bed. He nestled in close. He was lovely and warm. 'Do you think Mammy's reached heaven yet?'

'Bound to have,' Dryden said, closing his eyes.

'Is it far?'

'About as far as Uncle Joe and Auntie Vinia's.'

'Now you're being silly,' Tommy said and he turned over and went to sleep.

Two

D ryden took to mine management as Joe had hoped he would but then apart from his work and his child he had nothing. Joe had thought he would marry. Dryden as a married man seemed to Joe a lot safer than he was as a single one though nothing appeared to have changed except that Tommy needed a lot more attention, at least to begin with. Meg Carter ran Dryden's small house as efficiently as she ran her own. Dryden worked. He spent five and a half days every week at the office, always went home to have his tea with Tommy and then spent time with his son except for the two nights a week when he went to classes. Joe and Vinia had Tommy then. Joe would have liked the child to sleep at their house but he was aware of Dryden's loneliness so he said nothing and when Vinia would have suggested it he stopped her.

'He needs his son there.'

'I know he does. I need Tommy here,' she said. 'He's the closest we're going to get to a child of our own.'

'You don't know that.'

'Two marriages, all this time and no child. I'm so sorry, Joe. I know what it meant to you and I . . .' He got hold of her.

'Tommy will make a fine pit manager. You watch,' he said.

After that their lives settled into routine and Joe was glad of it but he sensed a restlessness in Tommy who grew bored quickly. He hated school and did not learn to read and write. Joe wished he could have suggested to Dryden that Tommy should go away to school and he would pay for it but he did not dare. Tommy was all Dryden had. There were never any women, just himself and the child.

On Saturday afternoons Joe took Tommy to football matches or any other form of sport he could find. The boy liked sport and was good at it. On Sundays they got together for dinner but often as time went on Tommy was not content and as soon as he had eaten he wanted to go home to play with his friends – conkers, marbles, football, cricket, depending on the season. He would stay out later and later until one night the summer that Tommy was eight, Dryden turned up at their house long after Tommy's usual bedtime, an anxious look on his face.

'Is Tommy here?'

'No.' Joe brought him inside.

'Something's happened to him.' Dryden was trembling.

Joe tried to make comforting noises but it was dark, there were ponds and streams on the fell. He didn't like to say anything to Dryden but there were gypsies camped beyond his house. He had seen their fire at night lately.

'Where have you looked?'

'All over the village. His friends are at home. They said they left him in the back lane outside our gate and I've looked and looked. Where could he be?'

Joe offered to help and as they stepped outside he caught the glow of a campfire and Dryden saw it too and stared in that direction.

'Dryden . . .'

He waited until Dryden looked at him.

'There are quite a lot of them.'

Dryden went on looking at him for a few seconds and it seemed to Joe that his eyes glowed like embers and then he set off in the direction of the campfire. Joe went after him. He was worried. Gypsies travelled in groups. Sometimes they were harmless. Sometimes they were thieves. Sometimes they carried weapons.

As he and Dryden drew nearer the piebald thick-legged horses heard them and moved slightly. It was a big fire. They were not sitting around it precisely. It was not a cold evening. Joe could smell something cooking. The smoke from the fire rose into a clear sky and the neat vardas were well back as though there was nothing to harm them so that they did not need to huddle close. As Dryden drew near a boy broke away and came to him, not hurrying but as though he was greeting somebody arriving home. It was Tommy.

'Dad?'

'What are you doing here? It's late,' Dryden said.

The men were tall and lean. There were at least a dozen of them. They stared. Nobody moved, neither the women in their long skirts nor the men, who to Joe's eyes looked so exactly like Dryden and Tommy. Joe wanted to catch the child up into his arms and run like hell but he pushed down the feelings and waited. Nobody was holding the boy against his will. As Dryden stood unmoving a tall man, older, came forward and a jewel in his ear glowed red against the firelight.

'Is this your boy?' he said, holding Dryden's gaze.

'Yes.' Dryden's eyes were black liquid shine.

'He's one of us,' the man said.

'No.'

'Yes, he is.'

It seemed to Joe like somebody was casting spells, magicking curses. He didn't like it. He had never thought of Dryden as a traveller but he did it now because it was as though most of what went on was unspoken and he felt like he was the only one there who didn't hear it. He could feel Dryden threatening the older man as surely as though he had reached out and pushed him. By now Joe had seen him do this before. He could reduce the most aggressive pitman to silence without doing anything. It made him very useful at work. It took a brave man to argue but this man with his lined bronzed face smiled suddenly into Dryden's cold gaze and said, 'You can't stop what will be.'

Dryden didn't say anything, he drew Tommy back against him but Joe could have sworn he heard Dryden's voice say, 'If you come near him again I'll kill you.'

He didn't. He wouldn't have said such a thing with Tommy there but the older man's eyes narrowed as though he had and Dryden turned Tommy around and marched him off.

'I want to stay.'

'It's late.'

'Can I go back tomorrow?'

'It's school tomorrow.'

'After school? Can I?' He stopped and looked up.

'There's a football match after school. You said you'd come with me,' Joe said.

'Did I, Uncle Joe?'

Joe got down beside him. The child looked at him and Joe felt a rush of love. Tommy was more precious than anything in their lives.

'You did and you must keep your promises.'

'Yes, of course,' the child said but he was not old enough to quell the disappointment on his face and Joe felt pain. He and his football were no match for Tommy's ancestry. Dryden's father had been a Romany who had forced a village girl in the local church and never been seen again. You could not alter such things, the old man had been right. Joe panicked. What if the gypsies came to the house and tried to steal Tommy? He had heard tales of travellers who did such things.

Standing in the kitchen of Dryden's house while Dryden put his son to bed Joe tried in vain to be realistic and when Dryden was in the kitchen once more he said, 'What if they come for him?'

Dryden looked at him and grinned and Joe felt himself relax. Dryden might be half gypsy but he was the most stable person Joe knew and had lived here in the village all his life.

'What, surround the house, you mean?'

'I just . . .'

'I know.'

'I can't compete,' Joe said.

Dryden sighed and sat down by the fire, frowning. Joe watched him and then said, 'You knew that man?'

Dryden shook his head.

'You acted as though you did.'

'Did I?' The turn of the head and Dryden's blank gaze did not fool Joe. There were things going on here which he did not understand and once again Joe wanted to run upstairs and grab

16

Tommy, fold him into a blanket and tear across the fell towards home, bolt all the doors and never let another living soul inside. And Dryden understood so that Joe was embarrassed.

'There are things you can't protect people from,' Dryden said.

Joe remembered it. He wished he hadn't but he did.

The gypsies left. There was nothing on the fell but a scorched mark where their campfire had been and Joe was glad. He would take Tommy to football matches again but it was no good. The pleasure was gone. Tommy saw football now as two lots of men kicking a ball around a field.

More and more often he did not come home. During the summer months he slept outside. He would not go to school, he cared nothing for education and Joe tried to interest him in books but Tommy's dark eyes were continually searching at the light beyond the windows. He would not be contained.

'Have you considered beating him?' Joe said in exasperation once when Tommy had gone missing for three days and then come back home as though nothing had happened.

Dryden smiled at him.

'Is that what your father did when you weren't the son he wanted?'

'You treat it so casually, as though it doesn't matter.' Joe was almost shouting. And then he saw. 'You can't hold him.'

'No, I can't. With luck if I let him go he'll keep on coming back.'

Vinia tried to talk to Tommy and it was difficult. He was exactly like Dryden in looks. By the time he was twelve he was almost as tall as she was.

'Don't you know what you're doing to your father?' she said.

He no longer came to their house by then but for once Joe had persuaded him. They could not talk to him like this in front of Dryden. Tommy looked regretfully at her as though he were the adult. And he smiled, just like Dryden did, and then he said, 'I don't have time for this.'

'What on earth do you mean?' Vinia said.

'I'm going away soon.'

'Going? Going where?'

Joe had to stop her from clutching hold of Tommy. But they had already lost him, he could see by the look in Tommy's eyes.

'I wish I could have been here more,' Tommy said and then he left.

That night in the cold darkness while Dryden pretended to sleep so that he should not get in his son's way Tommy left for good. Dryden lay in his bed and listened. There was not much to hear but in his heart and mind Dryden could sense the piebald horses and the wagons, see the flash of gold upon honeyed skin. He knew when they paused to give the boy time to catch up with them.

Dryden heard him go down the stairs and through the kitchen. He heard the outside door and after that there was silence. It was not the same silence there had been when Esther Margaret died. In that silence he had held his child in his arms. Now there was nothing to hold. The father in Dryden told him that he would see Tommy again but the mystic in him knew that he would not. There would be no note, for Tommy could barely read or write, he would have taken nothing because he did not care for possessions. Dryden knew that the little house he had thought full of love had been nothing but a prison to his boy and that the only thing of any worth he could give Tommy was his freedom. He did not understand why Tommy wanted to leave, only that his child was a bird beating its wings against a small cage. Strange how we cannot have the things we want. All he had wanted was the woman he loved and a child and for that he would not have denied Tommy the cold night air under the varda, the stars above and the way that the road opened out before him in endless quest.

Always there was a new day. He would go to work and sit in his office. He was pit manager now officially. He went down the pit every day at least once and the monotony of it all was the saving of him. Stupid things like tea at eleven and sandwiches at one and the way that the winter day cut in so close upon the light and he was grateful. The long summer days were torture because each day was another to go through. The summer days went on forever.

It was the silence of the house which defeated him. He stayed at work until it was late, until he did not have to go there and watch the evening crawl past him on leaden feet. He could stay at work and drink tea. Paper and pen became his solace and the way that the pit was never done, never still. He welcomed intrusions and when there were accidents or help was needed in any way by the men and their families he was always first there. It was better than facing the house where Esther Margaret had died and Tommy had left without a word. Joe went home to his wife on Saturday afternoons. Dryden stayed at work, turning down invitations until nobody asked him anywhere and even Vinia had given up on Sunday dinner.

The war came. It was a hot summer. August was sweltering. Men left the village but at the pit everything was the same because they produced coking coal which was used for iron and steel and in war such things were necessary for weapons and transport so they worked on.

Dryden was glad of the work, he held to the routine until one day the following spring when he received a letter from France. It was from Tommy. A friend had written it. It was formal, stilted, but it was the most welcome communication Dryden had ever received. Tommy hoped that his father was well. He was a soldier and was fighting but he wanted to see Dryden. When he had leave he would come back to Durham. He was sorry he had left like that. He dreamed of the little house upon the fell, nightly he saw it.

Dryden was ecstatic. He had been wrong, his instincts had betrayed him but his common sense had been good. He had let his son go and now Tommy would come back to him. He carried the letter about with him, showed it to Vinia and Joe. He even went and had Sunday dinner with them. Each day was a delight. The world was a wonderful place. He enjoyed his work. He got up each morning and his first thoughts were of

Tommy. At night he lay with the windows open and listened to the wind sweeping across the fell. His son would come home. Would he have grown? Would he look different? Would he want to stay when the fighting was over? It could not last much longer.

The summer was almost here, and Tommy's leave, and Dryden was pleased with everything so it could not be on that bright morning when the ragged yellow flowers lifted their heads so bravely upon the fell, when the curlews flew low and the water ran clear and the sky was so blue that it hurt to look at it, it could not be upon that July day they brought a telegram to the office and it was for him.

Dryden thought it was just as well that he had no faith left because everything was swept away except himself. As though God had intended each man to be broken and no boy to remain upon the earth that was so beautiful. Every joy he had ever felt was gone. Were they not fit for the world, not good enough to stay there together? Around him things went on, he felt sure. Inside the cage of his mind there was nothing but the telegram informing him that his child had died. Tommy was almost eighteen.

Three

It was a pleasant summer morning and Dryden was convinced, just as he was sure every morning, that in a moment
he would awaken from the nightmare and Tommy would be
alive or it would be even further back and he would awaken by
his wife's side, Tommy safely tucked up in bed in the back
room, and the world would come together. Either that or he
would be dead and grateful for it.

Neither happened and he was not in bed. He was lying on the
hillside beyond the village and the morning sun was pouring
down on him just as though everything was all right. He had no
idea how he had got there except that he had been very drunk.
Drink was the only thing that kept the pain of Tommy's death
away. Vinia and Joe were all for having him at their house but
he could not bear their pale, shocked faces, he could not stand
their company, neither their presence nor their conversation.
He did not want comfort. He did not want to go on. He just
wanted to die.

The hours had crawled past, whisky-assisted. It was early
by the look of things. The dew had not left the grass and it
was a clear morning. Further over a bird flew up, singing.
Dryden was amazed that things went on as normal. As he lay
there a woman came into view, an old woman, her hair black
and white and her eyes so dark that he could not see into
them.

'You'll catch your death lying there like that,' she said.

Dryden ignored her.

'It's rained all night,' she said. 'You're soaked. How long
have you been there?'

It would, Dryden thought, save a whole lot of bother if he should catch pneumonia.

'My house is just over there,' she said, nodding, and in the distance he could see it, a low stone house with gardens around it. Smoke was rising in a straight line from the chimney. 'Come in and I'll make you some tea.'

'No, thanks.'

'It's just a step away.' She was in danger of becoming a nuisance. 'I've got the kettle on. It'll be boiling by now.'

He didn't answer. Maybe if he ignored her she would go away. He looked down to where the mist was rising from the valley, leaving behind the impression that Sweethope, in the bottom by the river, had nothing but roofs, silver against the morning.

'You're wet through.' She hovered over him.

'I'm not your problem.'

'You will be if you die here. This is part of my garden,' she said.

'It is?' Dryden looked around him at the field.

He got up. He was stiff from lying there. The woman picked up the empty whisky bottle. She was right, he was wet. His clothes stuck to him and his feet squelched in sodden shoes. He had no intention of going to her house except that it was directly in his path. He didn't remember having seen it before or her. They walked up a narrow track which went around to the front of the house and he thought it was one of the prettiest places he had ever seen. It was set back, halfway up the hill and the hills rose around it but there were gardens on every side. The gardens to the front were full of yellow and white roses.

She ushered him inside. Dryden was too exhausted to argue. It was dark in the hall but the room on the right was a big kitchen and from it he could see the fields which rose up to the top of the fell. Sheep were dotted here and there. Her kitchen was all white with white cupboards and a dresser and a big square table and chairs all painted white with tiny blue and yellow flowers, white walls, the floorboards scrubbed and a big black range, shiny with leading and she was right, the kettle was boiling fiercely.

She sat him down and took off his shoes and gave him hot tea thick with sugar, laced with whisky, mug after mug of it. Then she persuaded him up the stairs, he didn't know how and into a blue and white bedroom. The bed looked so inviting, the sheets smelled clean. From the open window there was the scent of herbs and flowers which made up the raised beds in the back garden. He could hear her singing in the kitchen. He went to sleep.

When he awoke there was the aroma of coffee and bread baking. His clothes had gone. The room was perfectly neat. He had not been awake long when she came upstairs with a tray. He told her he was not hungry. He never wanted to eat again.

'I want whisky.'

'You can have it after you've eaten,' she said.

The bread was warm and covered in thick, golden butter and raspberry jam and the coffee tasted fresh. Dryden watched her as he ate, tidying the room when it didn't need it, dusting carefully.

'I'm Dryden Cameron.'

'Yes, I know who you are.'

'Who are you?'

'Rowan Haversham.'

It was an unusual name and he had heard it before but the whisky and his state didn't aid his memory.

She went downstairs and got the whisky bottle without being asked and a glass and then she poured it out for him, a first glass and then another and then another until he couldn't remember anything and after that he slept and every time he slept he dreamed that Esther Margaret was alive and Tommy was a little boy. It was the sweetest dream of all. He could not think why he had ever imagined he could have more than that. He couldn't think that he had wanted more. It had been so much, the beautiful golden-haired girl who kept his house and looked after his child and yielded her body to him in the sweet darkness. And the small boy he had loved so much had been part of the day-to-day as though that would go on forever. He could not believe he would never see them again. He wished that he could sleep and dream and go on dreaming until the dreaming became all the reality there was. Every time he awoke they were dead.

Somehow it was Monday and Mrs Haversham was hanging out the clothes in the back garden, the white sheets and the white pillowcases were blowing in the summer breeze above the grass and from his bed he could see the hills and the blue summer sky and smell the cream and white roses in the garden.

She would bring him rosemary bread and lettuce, cheese which she made herself, white and sticky rich, freshly churned butter and tea which she poured from a white china teapot. At night the smell of the flowers seemed even sweeter after the warm summer day and she would report the fox that had walked along the hedgerow, the sparrowhawk that had clawed a mouse from the track outside the house, the squirrel which had scampered across the lawn and the doves which came into the garden to feed, flocks of them, grey and white, dainty, their necks iridescent in the sunlight. At night the crows nested in the trees and owls flew together in the orchard beyond the house.

Every day she would bring him a bottle of whisky and pour its golden contents into a short stout glass. Sometimes she would read to him, stupid things he didn't care about, poetry and essays from bygone days, her voice soft against the fading evening light. Sometimes he fell asleep while she was still reading to him. Sometimes when he awoke in the night he could hear her voice even though she was perfectly still so that he could not see her shadow in the corner. All he could see was Esther Margaret's face as she stood in the doorway of their cottage with Tommy in her arms. She was smiling at him. Everything would be all right soon. He knew it.

Joe had not cried. He had not cried in the office when the telegram had come. He had not cried when he had to tell his wife that Tommy was dead and he did not cry when every night his wife turned away from him in bed so that there was no comfort of any kind.

Dryden had disappeared. He had walked out of the office

before Joe could do or say anything. Joe assumed he had gone home but when he ventured to Dryden's house Meg said he was not there. The only other place Joe could think of was his own house but Dryden was not there either. Joe searched the pubs in the village. He thought Dryden might have put himself in front of a train or something equally awful but the police had no reports when Joe was brave enough to enquire. He went everywhere asking but it was only after three days that Arnold Smith, the owner of the off-licence, came to him and told him that Dryden had been into his shop the first day and bought several bottles of whisky.

'And you gave them to him?'

'He paid for them, Mr Forster. What was I supposed to do?'

'He could be lying dead in a gutter somewhere, you bloody fool,' Joe said, eager to blame someone.

'I didn't know what had happened then. I'm only trying to help here,' Arnold said.

Joe forbade himself the luxury of losing his temper further. This was not helping.

'I'm sorry, Arnold. I don't know what I'm saying half the time.'

Vinia did not go back to work for several days. Joe had no choice. The country was at war and there were no signs of it letting up. He was working seven days a week and working alone now that his pit manager had walked out. He should have been grateful for the work. It was the only normal thing left. If it had not been for Addy there would have been no food or order at home. Not that they ate anything, and Vinia said nothing. They lay a long way apart in bed in silence while the summer night fell heavy as thunder beyond the windows. A week crawled past and he had searched everywhere, asked everybody. Then another week and after it Meg came to him at work, her face white and pinched.

'My Earl says that he heard some man in the Bull last night who claimed he'd seen Mr Cameron.'

Joe drew her into the office and closed the door.

'Where, Meg?'

'Drunk in the field.'

'Where?'

'Up past the village.'

'When?'

'I don't know. Earl didn't know the man's name. He's stupid is my Earl. I've asked him 'til I was blue in the face but he was half-cut at the time, which he doesn't do often, mind you, and he doesn't remember anything.'

Joe thanked her and left the office. He went to the pub she had named but the landlord could remember nothing. Joe left the village. He walked up the main street and out towards where the road led across the moors and then plunged down into the valley towards Sweethope. There was nothing to be seen. It was too bleak once you got beyond the main road and the village for anything to survive, just a grown-over track and a ruined farm at the end. Here he hesitated, called himself silly, but did not want to go on any further. The local people wouldn't go near the place, claiming it was haunted.

Joe gazed back at the village and across at the well-kept farms beside the road. He enquired at all of them but nobody had seen or heard anything. He was about to leave and go back to the office but he didn't. He made his way a few yards up the old track and there he discovered an empty whisky bottle.

Joe walked the rest of the way up the track and tried to get into the garden of the ruined house. The gate was stuck fast halfway open and the garden itself, which had been left for many years, was so overgrown with weeds and brambles that he couldn't get in. The gate was rotten and eventually as he pushed, it splintered. The house must have been fine once but the windows were broken, the door was ajar.

He ventured inside, saying Dryden's name, afraid of what he might find but almost completely sure that Dryden would never have gone to such a place. It was dark in the windowless hall and smelled damp. The roof had fallen in and in the room which went off to the left there were rickety stairs leading away to the right. There was nothing and no one in there or in the room beyond, which had once been a sitting room, but when he ventured back through the hall into the kitchen there was glass smashed from what had been one and possibly two whisky bottles. The roof was open to the sky there, the ccilings had fallen in, only the walls were standing.

He went outside but there was no evidence anyone had been there. The view was wonderful, the moors and then the patch-work fields, the stone walls and the beginning of the dale itself. It was the kind of place where at the end of the day he could have imagined the family who had lived there, Bernard and Rowan Haversham, sitting outside at night, being glad that they lived in such a place, though farming was hard and Bernard Haversham had died before Joe was born. Mrs Haversham had gone on living there by herself for a long time. She had gone quite strange in old age. The locals called her a witch. He thought he could smell smoke and baking bread and even hear a faint sweet song somewhere nearby.

He went back inside and through once again into the room with the stairs. Broken glass littered the floor and the stairs themselves looked precarious. When he tried his weight on the first step it was rotten and cracked beneath his foot. Halfway up they had given altogether and he could see the room through them. They were steep, straight up. He half persuaded himself that no one could have reached the top, especially not a man, but he went up anyhow, trying not to lean on the bannister in case it broke. He tried to convince himself that, having got up, he would get back down, and was not reassured when at each step the wood groaned beneath him. He thought he could feel the stairs swaying as though the whole staircase would leave the hall and break around him like firewood.

He was midway up the stairs. If it gave now he would fall through. If he were badly injured would anyone find him? He called himself names for not having told anyone where he was going. Too late now. He made his way into the shadows on the landing and into the first bedroom, which was small and lean-to and angled. He felt stupid. What had he expected to find?

The bedroom next door, which looked out across the garden, was empty too, so was the narrow room next door and the one on the other side, almost as narrow, and then he came to a closed door, the last room in the house. He hesitated in front of it, thinking of all the awful stories he had read. In the pale light behind him Joe imagined whispering and the faintest of footsteps. Then he stepped forward and pushed down the sneck with his thumb. The door gave, creaking.

It was a huge room, enormous for a bedroom and high-ceilinged like a barn, and here again the windows were broken and let in the scent of roses gone wild and the ivy had pushed its tendrilled fingers inside and the roof was showing sky and there was a fireplace in which lay a dead bird, and there in the corner of the room quite still and surrounded by empty whisky bottles was Dryden, dressed appropriately in black, just as he had been the day he left the office. He was unconscious. And somehow he was not alone, though there was nobody else to be seen. It reminded Joe of the dark lonely nights when he had been a child and imagined a guardian angel at the foot of his bed. Someone to watch over me.

Joe would not accept that Dryden might be dead. He walked across and then got down beside him, glad to be able finally to say his name, and as he did so it was like a spell broke.

'Dryden?'

Joe wanted to cry. His throat and face ached with all the tears he had not shed for Tommy. He wanted Tommy back so much that every breath hurt. There in the stillness Joe felt the tears begin to spill down his face.

'Dryden?'

He could see his friend breathing. Joe pushed back his hair. Dryden opened his eyes. After a few moments they narrowed on Joe. 'What are you doing here?' he said, as though everything were normal.

'I've come for you.'

'Why?'

'Because I need you at the pit. I can't manage without you.'

Dryden lay there for a long time, saying nothing, and then he sat up and gazed around him as though noticing the room for the first time.

'Can you get up?' Joe said.

'What?'

'Can you stand?'

Dryden got slowly, carefully to his feet, taking in the room, turning a complete circle, watching.

'Come home with me now,' Joe said.

Dryden moved out on to the landing, hesitating at the top of the stairs.

'It doesn't look too good,' he said.

'It held us coming up,' Joe said.

It held them coming down, though they did it one at a time, and then they walked out of the gloom and into the sunlight. Dryden gazed around him at the overgrown garden and into the fields beyond.

'Come on,' Joe said.

He didn't know how they got home. Dryden was so weak that his walking was slow and it was early evening when they reached the house on the fell. Vinia had been at work that week but he knew she was finding it hard to concentrate and kept going home early. When she saw Dryden she came over, searching him with her eyes as though for clues.

'Where have you been?' she said. 'We were so worried about you.'

He looked blankly at her and then swayed.

'I think he should go to bed,' Joe put in.

Together they led Dryden upstairs. He looked around the blue bedroom.

'I'm not ill,' he said.

'But you're tired,' Vinia said, 'How about a bath?'

Joe showed him the bathroom and left him there, hoping he wouldn't pass out in the bath. Joe walked upstairs and into the kitchen. His wife was standing by the kitchen stove, crying, but when he would have touched her she moved away, clearing her throat and saying, 'How did you find him?'

'I followed a trail of empty whisky bottles to Haversham's old farm. He was asleep in the house.'

Some time later, just as Joe was getting anxious, Dryden

came downstairs, wearing Joe's clothes, looking tired and confused. They sat down to eat in the dining room but although Vinia kept putting food in front of him Dryden ate nothing and he seemed unaware of them. Joe tried to eat, he attempted to make conversation but all Vinia's mind was concentrated on Dryden, so after two vain attempts Joe gave it up.

When the meal ended Dryden got to his feet.

'I'm going home.'

'Why don't you stay here?' Vinia said.

'I don't think I will.'

Joe tried to talk to him but Dryden was insistent. Joe went with him. He wanted to sit down and cry like a hurt child when they got there, the emptiness filled the little house like soil filled a grave. Even the noise from the houses around it did not filter through, as though the grief was an extra wall. Joe stood in the living room and they heard somebody laugh next door. It was like an insult. He didn't know what to do or say. The house was so neat, everything clean and tidy, just as they had left it, and there was no clue that Esther Margaret or Tommy had ever lived there.

'Will you come in to work tomorrow?' Joe said. 'I need your help.'

'Can't you find somebody else to do it?'

'Like who? We're in the middle of a war. Besides, what would you do?' It wasn't the right question but then nothing was. He was going over everything in his mind before he said it and it was still wrong.

'You're my pit manager, Dryden. You're not just anybody and we've worked together all these years. Please come back to work. I need you there.'

Dryden agreed but Joe realized it was just to stop him from going on about it and then Dryden waited for him to leave. Joe went home. He and Vinia didn't talk either. There was nothing left to say. He wanted to make bright remarks but he was exhausted and all that night his sleep was interrupted by the stairs in the old Haversham house giving way, rotten beneath his feet.

Dryden did not go to work and when Joe went to the house it was locked, possibly for the first time ever, back and front, with no sign of any life. He called at Meg's house when he finished work, interrupting their tea. It made him heartsick to walk into Meg's house where everything was normal, where the children sat at the table eating ham and egg pie. The war had not affected the little pit village as much as it had done in other places. Many of the miners had allotments and grew all their own vegetables and they kept hens and pigs and were used to making the most of everything they had. Earl, Meg's husband, got to his feet and encouraged Joe to sit down with them. For the first time in almost three weeks Joe was hungry at the sight of egg custard, bread and jam, and then his hunger was replaced by envy. Earl worked at the Morgan steelworks, he was a moulder, making good money, and their little house was filled with all the things Joe had never known, children with shiny contented faces, Meg and Earl at ease with one another.

He said he didn't want to interrupt but Meg gave him tea and a plate with pie and salad and she told him how concerned she was about Dryden.

'Mr Cameron never came to the door even though I knocked and knocked,' she said.

Joe wanted to stay. He longed to be a child at Meg and Earl's well-filled table. There were books in a small bookshelf at one side of the room, it was crammed, the open fire was lit for cooking, though the night was not cold, and when they had finished eating Earl sat the little girl upon his knee for no reason at all. Joe knew that later Earl would go out for a couple of pints and his wife would put the children to bed but for all Meg grumbled she had a good man who rarely got drunk but on Saturday nights and he loved them. Meg's eyes were clear. She was the luckiest of women, feeding her younger child small pieces of bread and jam which he smeared across his face.

'Do you think I should try going again tomorrow, Mr Forster?' she said as she saw him to the back door.

'Don't waste your time – and, Meg,' Joe turned towards her at the door, 'don't worry about the money. I'll see you have it.'

'Oh no.' Meg blushed. 'I can find other work.'

'I know you can but I don't want to lose you. Please, just wait. He'll get better.'

'Do you think he will?' Meg followed Joe down the yard to the gate. 'He should get married and have other bairns,' she said.

Joe thought he couldn't have put it better himself.

Four

The view from the train when you come into Durham station is the most beautiful in the world. How could you learn to hate it, Roberta Grant thought, wiping away the tears. It was not like Darlington station where the rain fell on you through the roof and the pigeons made a nuisance of themselves, nor like Waverley, dramatic with rock. It was home and Bobbie had always loved it until last year when her brother, Charles, went away.

They had not been parted before. Other boys had been sent away to school but when it came time for the decision to be made her parents decided that it was more important for the twins to stay together and so they had had all those years, twenty-three, in which to be together. They could have stayed together after that. There was no reason for Charles to go to war. Their father owned a factory which made clothing and it worked full-time on uniforms and it was too much for their father to manage by himself but Charles would go.

'You can help,' he said.

Her father had raged. What did she know of factories? What did she know of work? What did women know of anything outside of houses, children and sewing? She knew that he did not mean it, it was only that Charles was his son and he was afraid that if he went to war he would die. Their mother had died some years earlier so her father knew what grief was like and was not eager to extend the knowledge but all Charles's friends were going, including his best friend, Forbes Stillman, and he did not want them to think he was a coward.

'It isn't cowardly to work towards the war,' her father said but Charles would not listen.

He joined up with his friends and Bobbie and her father went to the station to see them off, up the winding road at the top end of the city. When you got to the top the view of the little city was marvellous. From there you could see each rooftop individually, every church, the way that the six hills went up and down and best of all the cathedral and the castle that had been there for so very long, as though to say that everybody who ever left would come back, that things went on, but it was not true.

It was a very small station. You could not watch for long when the train left because it was out of sight within seconds and after that there was nothing to be done but go home. She did not want to go home. Her father pretended that his wife had not died. Each morning her clothes were put out just as though she would get up and put them on and nothing which was hers had been thrown away. Bobbie was not allowed to change anything so that it was as though her mother was perpetually about to come back and being held in that kind of suspension was torture. Nightly she thought her mother would come into the dining room, where her place was always set. There was food enough for four even after Charles went away.

In Bobbie's dreams she was always moving away from the station and Charles was waving goodbye and her father was driving back into the town and then through the streets and out to the other side, up Claypath and beyond into the country where he had built the house which had been her mother's dream. Did all dreams end like this, with reality, she wondered?

Forbes had been particularly sweet to her at the station, as though they were more than friends, which they had never been. His mother was long dead and his father had not been able to face the station so perhaps it was just that he needed somebody there, so she smiled on him, watched them board the train together, waving frantically, and when they were gone and she was left behind and the train was out of sight there was nothing to do but go home.

She dreaded it. All those empty rooms, all those meals to be got through with her father. Nothing and nobody to break the monotony.

Christmas that year was dismal. She found her father on Christmas Day standing over the grand piano in the music room and she knew that he was remembering the Christmases they had had in the past when they had all been together. Her mother had died when she was sixteen. His children were a disappointment to him, she knew. She lived only for the business and was not interested in the idea of marriage and children, whereas Charles was musical and cared only for playing the piano. Since he had been gone her father went in there often as though the piano might give him back Charles.

'I wish you played,' he said to her on Christmas Day as the evening fell and rain poured down the windows.

'I couldn't possibly,' she said, trying to sound cheerful for his sake. 'I can't even sing.'

'Do you think Charles will be all right?'

He asked her this often as though it were a talisman. Her reassurance would protect Charles from the German bullets.

They had seen Charles off from the station yet again recently. She had stood there with her father, trying not to break down in front of either of them. Early that morning Charles had been sick. She had heard him retching in the bathroom. In the beginning he had been eager to fight. A year and a half later, several of his friends were dead and the enthusiasm had gone. He was afraid. When he had come home he spent hours at the piano and she could judge his moods by the music he chose to play. The silence was therefore all the greater when he had gone.

She had not realized that she would like working at the factory. At first it was just a distraction from the difficulties of her life and there was no longer anything to do at home. They had a housekeeper and servants and Bobbie was of the opinion that they would work better if she was not getting in the way. She spent a great deal of time at work and the more she did the less her father did and the more he stayed at home but in some ways it was easier. In the early days when she had first started he interfered in everything she did, not trusting her to get it right and countermanding every decision she made but in the last eighteen months he had learned that she was perfectly capable of running the factory no matter what other people might think or say. She had surprised herself. Unlike Charles she was born to it and of late her father had been inclined to let her get on with it. She didn't mind. The factory had become her whole life and to know that she was doing something so useful towards the war effort made her feel good.

She had learned to dislike the house which her father had built for her mother when they married. Her mother had come from a rich family but was left alone in her youth and they had married for love. Whereupon her husband had built the house, huge and extravagant, half a dozen miles beyond the city.

It was a half-timbered brick house set dramatically against a hillside where rocks fell far below amidst a tumbling stream. There in two hundred acres it was a monument to their love. It had become a museum after she died. Nothing was altered, nothing touched, and in June forests of her favourite shrub filled high and wide the road which wound to and from the huge gates. Rhododendrons in pink and purple and orange were her father's delight. She had learned to hate June. Her mother had died amidst all that colour. It seemed to Bobbie like a sick joke.

After Charles went away she did not spend much time at home but every day she walked Charles's black and white springer spaniel, Smith, through the gardens to the two lakes which she and Charles always referred to as the ponds. It was her gesture to him. The last thing he had said to her before he got on the train each time was, 'Look after the dog, Bobbie.'

'Don't call him "the dog",' she said, trying to smile. 'He has a name. Don't worry, I'll walk him every day.'

'Make sure you do then,' he said.

She waved until the train was out of sight.

Five

The days scraped past as harsh as sandpaper. Three weeks, four, five and Joe reported that there was no change. Dryden had not come back to work and neither had he let Meg across the doorstep and though Joe had been there every day there was no answer. Vinia began to think that Dryden had left. It was one of her worst nightmares, that, and the possibility that he had killed himself, were the only unfulfilled nightmares she had left. Somehow it seemed possible they would come true. After all, everything else had gone wrong.

There came the day when she could bear it no longer, when Mrs Forster, the pit owner's wife, made her scandalous way to the house of the widowed pit manager and there she banged on the door.

Summer had edged its season into their lives without their noticing. The little front gardens were filled with vegetables instead of flowers these days. It was warm. For once the back door was open to the air. She pushed it open further.

She expected chaos but as she stepped down into the kitchen all was silent. No fire burned in the grate and there was a thick layer of dust on everything but it was undisturbed. No one had touched the fire since it died or a chair since they had last been there weeks since. The front-room door was closed and when she ventured inside there was a stale smell to it, a good stale smell of dust on polish. A fly was dead on the window ledge. She longed to open the window but didn't like to.

If he was there, which she had begun to doubt, he was upstairs. She went up the steep stairs very softly because she was afraid he had hated his life so much that he had ended it.

37

She had always thought that she would know when he died and so she almost believed now that he was alive, whether he was there or not.

She knew this house well, it had been the house where she and her first husband, Tom, had lived, the house where she had discovered her love for Dryden and when she had known the brutality of his half-brother.

Tom and Dryden had fought over her there and when Tom had died in an accident down the pit she and Dryden had lived there together. She had felt guilty over Tom's death, blamed herself for not loving him sufficiently and then lost Dryden to Esther Margaret. She had married Joe from there, partly to put Dryden at a distance and partly to sever for good the relationship with Tom. Tom had been bad-tempered and charming. She thought the only person he had ever loved was Dryden. She had come between them and very little good had come of that, she thought bitterly.

Tom was dead and Dryden was heartbroken over his only connection – the son he had named after the brother he had loved and never learned to hate.

She wanted to call before she got to the top of the stairs but somehow she couldn't. The windows were open here, she could feel the clean air. She made her way into the bigger bedroom, it was the room where she and Tom had slept, where Esther Margaret had died. The door was ajar. She pushed it further open and there he was.

The bed filled most of the room and he was lying amidst the bedcovers, most of them pushed back because of the heat. His body was slick with sweat, shiny like chocolate. His hair was a black storm among the white pillows and there was on his face several days growth of dark beard. His eyes were closed but when she said his name they opened and he regarded her uncomprehendingly at first and then his gaze rested on her in recognition.

'Vinny,' he said.

Her name sounded sweet on his lips.

'The door was open.' Suddenly she couldn't bear his pain, she couldn't stand what he was going through, on top of what she was going through. She put her hand over her mouth.

'I'm sorry,' she said.

She went to him and he pulled the hat off her head and his fingers went into her hair and down her neck and on to her body and she was close and he was kissing her as he had never kissed her before. Only he had, it seemed to her, it was the same kind of kiss that Tom had given her when they were falling in love and she had adored him but her memories of Tom were full of his hard words and hurtful hands. She struggled. Dryden let her go.

She sat up and then got up, recovered her hat from the floor, turned it around in her hands as though she were going to put it on again and then didn't. She sat down on the bed and looked at him.

'I taste like Tom to you,' he said.

She was about to deny it but she could see that it wasn't any use.

Dryden laughed.

'I thought you loved me all these years but when I kiss you I'm Tom.'

'I want you to come back,' she said.

'Whatever for?'

'Because I can't bear it without you. I really can't.'

'Oh, you've got everything,' he said. 'You have Joe and your work and your – your position in the village as Mrs Forster. What in hell difference does it make to you what I do?'

'Joe doesn't love me any more. He doesn't want me and I – I don't want him and it's all your fault, that's what it is.' She leaned over and touched his face with her fingers. 'Do you know what you mean to me?'

'Don't.'

'You have to hear it. I love you more than anyone else in the world and that's all right mostly but now . . . I want you to come back.' She was crying. She had told herself that she would not, and that she would not beg and plead with him but it was no use. She could not help it.

*   *   *

39

Dryden did not remember which day it was, he was unsure of the week. It was August. The heat baked the little pit houses and there was not even a faint breeze coming off the fell. In the bedrooms it was stifling. He opened all the windows upstairs and then he went down for cold water and opened the doors there too.

The wallpaper in the bedroom was peeling. Esther Margaret would have had that fixed long since. The house was nothing but a shell to him and in the quiet of the afternoons when he slept he thought he could hear the sweet sound of Rowan Haversham singing in the kitchen and when he awoke the smell of bread and washing and coffee wafted to him on the hot breeze.

Sometimes Ella from next door left food on the step, bread or cake covered in a tea towel so that the flies wouldn't get it. He existed on that and cold water, waiting until he was so hungry that he felt sick, and then he ate as much as he could bear to eat of whatever it was and then he went back to bed and slept or lay there and let the hot afternoons go past. He watched the shadows alter on the ceiling and he would hear Joe come to the doors, banging and shouting.

It was only when the little house turned into a furnace and he could bear the heat no longer that Dryden had opened the windows upstairs and the doors down. He feared that Joe might arrive but no one else. Ella would not venture nearer than the door. Married women wouldn't do such things without good reason and Ella's husband, Sam was a jealous bastard. The few times Dryden had spoken to Ella, Sam had watched him carefully. Dryden had laughed to himself afterwards, thinking that Ella was not his type and then, imagining her small round body, ample breasts and heavy bottom with lust, decided that the trouble was every-body was his type these days. At night sometimes he could hear Sam and Ella and she uttered sweet little submissive noises that made Dryden want to shout into the pillows. He was careful however to encourage no woman to think he favoured her. He did not want to marry any of them. He had been married once like that, he didn't want it to happen again.

He had not expected Vinia to come to the house. There would be a big scandal if anyone found out she had done such a thing and with no sense of decency she had come upstairs and into the bedroom where the place was like an oven and he had discarded any clothes except the sheets long since.

He always forgot how much he loved her until he saw her again. She was not the most beautiful woman in the world, he knew, except to him, but she was the neatest. Nothing was ever out of place and her clothes, which she had always made herself, were perfect on her. She wore a thin white summer dress, low at the front with a V neck and buttons, caught at the hips to show off her slender figure. She looked the epitome of breeding and good taste. She stood back for several seconds as though unaware that she should not be in the room and then her feelings bettered her guilt and she came to him as she had never done before and kissed him. That was all it took. Dryden got hold of her, put her down and kissed her as he had wanted to for so long.

At first she responded but after a few seconds she began to resist so he let go of her. The expression in her eyes was disproportionate to what he had done. It was fear, and since he did not think he had given her any reason to be afraid of him there was only one conclusion to be borne. Dryden could not believe that Tom, dead for so long, was in his way here.

The truth was of course that he might taste like Tom but it was Joe who was in the way, Joe with his gentlemanlike polite ways, with his intelligence and book-learning. This woman would never again let any rough pitman put her down on to a bed and take her and he would always be Tom to her, with hard hurting hands, and though she pleaded and cried he was not deceived. How strange when he had thought it the other way round. Wouldn't it be funny if Joe arrived and found them together like this? Joe would kill him.

Having thought of Joe, Dryden could feel his presence in the room. He wound the sheet around his body and moved back.

'You shouldn't have come here,' he said.

She had stopped crying. Her eyes were full of anger.

'What option did I have? How much longer are you going to behave like this? Joe is worked into the ground—'

'All you care about is Joe. That's all you ever cared about. Joe's pit and Joe's house and Joe's bloody money . . .'

She covered the small distance between them but stopped short at the bed, realizing, he thought, that she had lost her temper and was going to hit him and then she said, 'Oh God,' and stood, trembling, for a few seconds and then she bolted.

For somebody who had done nothing but lie in bed for weeks Dryden was rather pleased at how he got away from sheets and bed and reached the door before she did, pushed it shut with one hand and turned around. He could see by her eyes that all her mind was concentrated on Tom. They were dark with terror.

Dryden breathed carefully for a second or two.

'I wasn't going to hit you,' she said.

There she was, he thought, ready to make terms for her freedom. That wasn't right. Tom had done that.

'I'm not Tom, Vinny, really I'm not. I'm not going to belt you because you nearly smacked me in the face. There's no need to run. I'm not going to put you down on the bed and make you do anything.' He opened the door and moved away.

Vinia went to the door and she turned around as though she was going to say something and then walked out.

Dryden went back to bed but he couldn't stay there any longer somehow. He got up and washed and shaved and put on some clean clothes and then he stepped out of the house into the bright afternoon. He walked halfway down the bank to Meg's house and into the backyard, where she was bringing in the washing.

'Could you come and sort the house out, Meg?' he said.

She nodded.

'I'll come tomorrow.'

Dryden walked slowly back up the bank and past the row towards the pit. Nobody said anything when he ventured into the front office. Joe was too wise to say much when Dryden

reached his office. He looked up from where he was working at
the desk.

'Hot, isn't it?' Dryden said.

Joe agreed that it was and Dryden went into his little office
next door and sat down behind the desk.

Joe could not understand what had happened and since Dryden
offered no explanation he was left to make up what he thought
had happened. He had been there every day for weeks without
success. Had Meg somehow made the difference? He didn't
want to question Dryden, it seemed enough that Dryden was
actually there at work. Joe didn't want to cause problems where
there weren't any. The answer was provided for him when he
went home in the early evening and told Vinia that Dryden had
gone back to work.

'I don't understand it,' he said, 'after all my efforts. Did Meg
persuade him?'

'No, I did.'

She didn't look at him, she went on carefully dealing with the
dinner.

'You did what?' Joe said.

Vinia looked at him.

'What else could I do?' she said. 'I know I shouldn't have but
I was so bothered about him.'

'And what did you do to persuade him?'

'I talked to him.' She didn't look at Joe, which she should
have been able to, unless she was lying to him. Did she have
cause to lie to him, Joe wondered, and then realized that he was
full of jealousy and suspicion. Had she persuaded Dryden as
wife of the pit manager, as his friend's wife, or as something
more intimate?

'My talking all these weeks outside his front door didn't
make the difference.'

'I wasn't outside the front door, the doors were open, it was
so hot.'

She still didn't look at him. Joe's insides were going sick.
'And what was he doing?'

'I said you couldn't manage any more without him.'

'Vinia . . .' Joe said. 'That wasn't the right thing to do.'

'Maybe not but it worked.'

'People will draw conclusions.'

'I couldn't let him go on like that any longer. You wanted him back at work, didn't you?'

'Not at the expense of my wife's reputation.'

'I was prepared to take the risk.'

'For all of us?'

'You're being ridiculous, Joe.'

'Am I? Next time you want to do something stupid you might consult me first.'

'I knew you would say no.'

'Wonderful,' Joe said.

Six

D ryden had to go to the miners' annual Christmas party at the mechanics' institute and there watch Vinia and Joe dancing. It was all he could do not to get up and walk out and when the music ended he left. He could hear her voice shouting his name as he made his way out into the bitterly cold night.

'Dryden!' She ventured after him into the snow. He stopped and she came to him.

'You didn't even sit with us,' she said.

Who had he sat with? He didn't remember. She stood there in front of him, not saying anything, her eyes filling with tears.

'We miss him too,' she said.

Dryden didn't want to talk to her.

He looked up and down Ironworks Road. The pubs were turning out and he was desperate for a drink. There had been nothing but beer at the dance and beer was too much quantity and not enough alcohol. He watched the men spilling, laughing and drunken, from the Royal Hotel, which was just at the top of the bank and around the corner, and then from the Golden Lion and the Cattle Market, which were at the bottom of Oaks Row in the main street at either side, though the Lion was up a bit, beyond the railway gates. He thought he could smell the alcohol fumes and cigarette smoke through the open doors even though the pubs were all a good distance away.

'We miss you,' she said.

He tried to walk away and she touched him. It was strange. Nobody ever did that any more. She put her hands up to his shoulders and he had forgotten how slender her fingers were and now that they were close how small she was.

'Please come and have Christmas dinner with us,' she said. 'I haven't invited anyone else.'

'Don't mention the word Christmas to me.'

He would have left again, thinking of how the fire had been banked down in his house and how he would be able to bring it back to life and sit over it for a couple of hours, watching the flames through the whisky. It was Sunday tomorrow so it didn't matter how drunk he got or how late he went to bed.

'I have to go,' he said and tried to leave her for the third time. She clung and kissed him on the cheek. It was so sudden, so unexpected, that Dryden was surprised. He felt the warmth of her mouth and remembered for an instant how sweet a woman's lips were and how much he had always wanted her. Then he remembered the pitmen emerging from the pubs. This was not something he wanted them to see. She meant nothing by it in the obvious sense but they would read everything into it so he very carefully moved her and then he walked away.

By the time Vinia got back inside she was sobbing. Joe had stood in the hall and watched her. He went to her but she turned away.

'Why can't Tommy be here?' she said.

She didn't want to go back inside but she had to. They had people to talk to and smile at. They must be the last to leave and she wanted to go home. When they finally got there the old feelings closed around her heart and she did not want to go to bed.

She paused, looking at the stairs, and then she made her dogged way up them. The room was welcoming, the fire burned steadily. Addy must have gone home late, worrying about them coming in to a cool house, Vinia thought fondly. Joe hovered behind her. She ignored him until he said, 'Do you want me to go and sleep in another room?'

Vinia's insides twisted. They had rarely spent the night apart since they had been married and she did not understand why, having moved out of the way, Dryden should be more trouble to their marriage than he had been when they saw him almost every day. He had never hidden his affection for her. Perhaps feelings, like clothes, were the better for an airing. Joe had not had cause to be jealous and a potentially difficult situation had been easy. Her love for Joe somehow rested against the love that she had for Dryden.

Joe sensed that she wanted to go to Dryden and night after night they had lain apart as though Tommy's death had broken some bond between them, as though their love had died with him. Love was not the feeling she had now for Dryden. She wanted him. She wanted to run back to the village and into his house and up the stairs into his bed so that she could wipe out the hurts of his life. She knew it wouldn't work but her instinct was to do that and Joe knew it. She could see by his eyes.

'I don't want you to,' she said.

'Yes, you do,' Joe said.

'None of the other beds are made up and none of the fires are laid.'

Joe went into the first room. It was the least likely, she thought, if they were to sleep apart. It had been his father's room. What memories he had of it she was not certain but even though it was the best bedroom in the house, the biggest and the most elaborate, with a view right across the front of the house and the fell, he had refused to move into it when they were first married. He didn't talk much about his father but she remembered Randolph as a drunk and a bully. He had been feared and hated in the village and had run down the pit to such an extent that Joe had spent years making up for what his father had done both in his neglect of the pit and in the way that the people did not approach him for anything. Joe had changed all that. The pit was as safe as it could be, he had brought back all the old traditions such as the party tonight, which his grandfather had begun when the pit first opened and he was influential in the area. The people loved Joe for the good man that he was and so did she.

The room was clean and neat, Addy cleaned the whole house each week. There wasn't a speck of dust but it was freezing in there, whereas the bedroom across the landing had a fire which burned most of the day and night and was warm and comfortable with books and chairs and ornaments.

'Please, Joe,' she said, trying to drag him out.

He went with her on to the landing but only as far as the linen cupboard from which he began to extract sheets, pillowcases, blankets and a big pink quilt which she disliked so much that she had hidden it away there.

'It's too cold in that room,' she said.

Joe ignored her and went back into the room and began making up the bed.

'You aren't listening to me,' she said.

Joe stopped and looked at her.

'You don't want me any more, Vinia. You want Dryden.'

She denied it and too vehemently, she could hear her voice as it hit the air, explaining and pleading, but Joe just stood, not listening to what she was saying, waiting for her to stop.

'Nothing has changed,' she said.

Joe almost smiled. He looked kindly at her.

'You married me because you couldn't have him.'

'I did not!'

'Yes, you did. I kept waiting for you to go.'

'I didn't think of it.'

Joe said nothing for a moment. He eyed the bed like it was holding a gun on him.

'And now . . . how could you bear not to when he's so hurt? His life is in pieces. I've never seen him like this. How could you not go to him if you love him so much?'

'I can't leave you.'

'You have left me, Vinia, in every way but for your physical presence and I can't stand to sleep in the same room, knowing that you want him so badly. Go to bed, please.'

Seven

T he winter turned hard right after Christmas. Before then
the snow was only in rehearsal but somehow once Christmas Day was over it was a signal for all hell to break loose on
the tops, Dryden thought, battling with Joe's car as they went
down the valley side and into Cornsay and then to the bottom
of the valley at Esh Winning and along the main road towards
Durham. How had he let Joe talk him into going to this
wedding?

It was because they barely spoke any more. Dryden knew he
was not easy to be around and any social aspect of the friendship between himself and Joe had ceased. Joe had grown tired
of his grief. Dryden didn't blame him. Being around someone
who was constantly bitter and angry must be very trying
indeed.

Of late Joe had stopped bringing sandwiches to the office. No
doubt he could not bear the silence while they waded their way
through the food. Joe had started going home to Addy at mid-
day. It was a relief. Dryden liked the quietness at the office
without him. Perhaps Vinia went home at noon and they spent
the time together.

Since the night of the pitmen's party Dryden had not seen
Vinia. He tried to hold to him how beautiful she had looked, the
dress she had worn, the few seconds when they had been alone
in the street, the warmth of her, the touch of her mouth, the
whiteness of her hands. On his worse days he imagined again
the few times they had kissed and in the depths of the night
sometimes he thought he could hear her footsteps on the stairs.
In another moment she would open the door of the bedroom

49

and fling herself into his arms. There his desire stopped because his mind played him Joe offering him the running of the pit, being kind to Tommy, trying to persuade him to rent a better house and a thousand days when Joe had been there. Without Joe he would have been defeated long before now.

He was defeated, he thought, as the snow thrust itself sideways at the car. He felt as though he had put down all the good things life had ever had to offer and picked up every burden. There was a long and terrible silence and inside that somewhere were Joe and Vinia.

Joe was no longer a happy man. He grieved for Tommy but also for the way that Dryden had given in under the loss and perhaps for other things. Dryden didn't know. At one time they discussed everything. Now Joe treated him like an inferior, issuing instructions. So when Joe had come to him several days since, into the tiny office where Dryden was doing what he had been told to do and Joe had said, in a much more friendly tone than he had used in weeks, 'Dryden, would you do me a favour?' Dryden would have offered to walk barefoot in the snow to Durham if Joe had requested it.

Joe looked so tired, so white and thin, so cool-eyed.

'Tan Machin is getting married in a fortnight to a girl in Durham.' Tan was a deputy at the pit, a well-liked man. 'He's asked us to go and Vinia doesn't want to. Would you go instead?'

A wedding. Joe thought he wanted to attend an event where other people's happiness covered everything like icing?

'Yes, of course,' he said.

'You would?' Joe looked pleased.

Dryden wanted to say something that would soften the air between them, to ask after Vinia, to try to regain some footing which had been lost but it was no use. The space between them was like a stone.

Joe thanked him briefly, went to his office and since then somehow things seemed to get worse. The day before the wedding Dryden had tried to put an opposing view over something and Joe had said, 'When I want your opinion I'll ask for it.'

If this kind of conflict had been a daily occurrence between them it wouldn't have meant anything but Dryden didn't remember the last time Joe had pulled rank on him like that. He didn't say anything. He watched the small amount of colour die from Joe's face as the sentence seemed to reverberate around the room. Dryden had somehow got himself out of the office and into his own and he stood there before the fire, taking deep breaths until he recollected that his body knew how to breathe without him helping. They didn't meet again that day before it was time to go home and then Joe opened his office door and said, 'You haven't forgotten about the wedding? I'll leave the car here for you,' and without waiting for a reply he walked out.

Dryden cursed Joe now and that made him feel better but the snow began to lessen and finally died as he drove into the little white-covered city, down North Road, and turned up the cobbled street which led to St Margaret's Church. He had determined not to be early. He didn't like churches and even though St Margaret's seemed small and friendly he was glad that lots of other people had got there before him.

Tan's family turned and smiled at him and Tan's dad, Arthur, came over and whispered, 'We're so pleased you could come, Mr Cameron,' and Tan waved from the front and then there was a short wait during which Dryden hoped nobody noticed he did not get down on his knees and pray. God did not deserve his prayers.

The bride was a few minutes late but when she turned up Dryden remembered why he did not like weddings. The bride and groom were just starting out in life, whereas he felt that everything was behind him. Other people's joy was difficult to stand and it seemed so miserable to begrudge them such a brave attempt at happiness. The bride was a pretty, dark-haired girl who came up the aisle on her father's arm, smiling at her guests as though her whole life had been leading to this day.

The candles were a hundred dancing flames in the gold

fittings throughout the church. Dryden could smell hope, joy, innocence. They believed that if they made their vows today before God he would look after them. They trusted him.

Dryden felt old. He felt grubby and used-up and betrayed. He had no part to play here. Yet this was not true. They were glad he was there. After the service the girl's parents had put on a splendid meal, considering they were in the middle of a war. It was at a nearby pub and they came to him, the bride and groom and their families, as though it was important to them that he should be there. He fought down the bad feelings.

The snow had stopped and the dark day was brighter for it. There was laughter, merriment. As they sat down to eat Tan came to him leading a woman and said, 'Miss Grant, I would like you to meet Mr Cameron, who is my pit manager. Mr Cameron, this is Miss Roberta Grant. She runs the factory where my wife works.' He spoke those last words with a smile of pride and Dryden turned to find the most beautiful girl in the world standing beside him. He could not think how he had not noticed her even in the gloom of the church. She was young, about twenty-five, and well dressed. She wore expensive clothes and a frivolous hat and an air of confidence that only the rich had. She was smiling and offering her hand.

Dryden waited for a young man to appear beside her but nobody did. He took her hand and made polite remarks and so did she and as other people began to sit down at the table they sat down together. Her black hair was sleek and shiny, her eyes were like blue jewels and she spoke the kind of flawless English that was not often heard in Durham. She chatted to the people on her other side and across the table and made it so easy for him. He had armed himself ready for questions but none came. Miss Grant, he decided, had the best manners of anyone he had ever met and since it was unlikely they would ever meet again he sat back and enjoyed the experience, watching her pretty face and smiling at her witty remarks.

After the meal the bride's father gave a short speech, Tan said a few words and then it was over. It had been, Dryden thought, almost completely painless. He should have left, he had no reason to linger, except that other people drank tea, got up and chatted and he was alone with Roberta Grant.

'I don't know anybody,' she said.

'Neither do I. You run a factory?'

'I help my father to run it. My brother is in France, fighting. Do you have a family, Mr Cameron?'

Dryden didn't look at her. He concentrated on the door, wondering whether the time had come to leave.

'No,' he said.

'That's a beautiful suit,' she said. 'It was made especially for you?'

Vinia had had it made, from the finest cloth she could buy. It was dark, elegant and fitted him perfectly, had been made with love and skill.

'Yes,' he said.

What a long time ago it seemed, yet it was only last Christmas. A year ago. How strange that in those few short months he should have lost so much.

Music was starting up, musicians were playing a waltz and the bride and groom were dancing, so he could not leave. When the music ended everybody clapped and the musicians began again and Miss Grant suddenly looked to him like a girl waiting to be asked to dance. He thought that one of the young men there would ask her and then he realized that they would not because they thought they could not. She was too rich, too confident, too well dressed. She sat watching as the young people danced but no one came over. Dryden didn't understand it. A lot of young men were in France so there was a shortage. These men were in the kind of jobs which prevented their leaving but they were not educated, they were afraid of her. He was the nearest person to her social level.

By the beginning of the third dance the sparkle in Miss Grant's eyes was beginning to dim. He argued with himself that she would not want to dance with a gypsy who was years older but then she didn't seem to have much choice. He told himself that she probably went to parties and danced all the time but if her brother and his friends were in France there were no parties nor any dancing. If she turned him down then at least he had asked so he said, 'Would you care to dance, Miss Grant?'

The sparkle came back.

'I would like that very much,' she said.

Dryden hadn't danced in a long time and had little inclination to do so now but her manners were so good that he made himself be gracious. To his surprise it was easy and she was light in his arms and he was surprised at how pleasant it was. They danced the next dance and the one after that and then she asked if they could go outside because she was too warm so they walked the short distance down the street into North Road and on to Framwellgate Bridge.

The winter day was closing in but it was light enough to make out the castle and the cathedral and the houses across the river where lights were burning. There were two swans on the river, white blurs against the dark grey of the water. It was completely still and cold enough for Dryden to see his breath.

'This is the view from the station when Charles goes away,' she said. 'I've come to loathe it. I'm so afraid he won't come back.'

Dryden tried to think of something comforting to say that wouldn't insult her intelligence. She drew slightly nearer, as though his presence was a help, but her shoes slipped under her. Dryden caught her, very carefully, steadied her and she smiled into his eyes. When he let her go she said, 'Will you come back inside and dance again?'

'How long do you think it would be before people talked about you, dancing the evening away with an old gypsy?'

'How old are you, thirty-five?' she said and her eyes danced.

'I'm thirty-eight.'

'Dear me, such decrepitude,' she said. 'We won't go back inside then.'

Dryden was never altogether sure what happened after that because it could not be that a woman so young and so far above him would put herself into his arms and offer her mouth, people didn't do such things and he would never in a million years, however much he wanted to, get hold of her, but she was there

in his arms and he was kissing her and she seemed in favour of
the whole thing and it occurred to him that she had never done
such a thing before because she was hesitant and eager and her
lips were so warm and so cold all at the same time and then she
stood back slightly and looked at him. Dryden waited for
accusation, for blame, for indignation, instead of which Miss
Grant stood there, her eyes getting bigger and bigger, with her
fingers entrapped in his hair and her other hand about his neck
and she said, 'Do it again.'

'I'm sorry.' Dryden found his voice from somewhere.

'Oh please don't be sorry. I would hate that you hadn't meant
it.'

She looked sincere. Dryden was too old, too experienced, to
think that this was really happening to him, that a girl like this
wanted him to kiss her. Yet she allowed her arms to stay around
his neck and her fingers caressed his hair and he thought how
sweet it had been and he thought that she knew nothing of
kissing but she wanted to. It couldn't possibly have been the
first time, but she was all hesitation and need. He had been
wrong about innocence, it was charming. He drew back.

'Miss Grant . . .'

'I'm called Bobbie. What is your first name?'

'Dryden.'

'I love it,' she said and her eyes were like blue-black stars. It
made him smile.

He told her that it was too cold for her out here and they went
back in and danced and it became the kind of evening that you
hold in your memory because there are so few like it. Old people
when they danced were dry and formal, their steps matched too
nearly because they had been together for so long, there must be
no excitement left, but to dance with Bobbie was bliss, tempt-
ing, it raised a dozen different issues, a hundred possibilities.

He tried to talk sensibly to himself about this. It would be
madness to take it any further. She did not seem to know. She
would have danced every dance with him had he asked. Perhaps
it was just that she did not care. He had thought that he did not
but the naïveté in her was so beguiling that he wanted to be

careful so they talked to other people and only danced the last dance together but it was balm to Dryden, having watched Joe and Vinia over the years doing the last dance at various dances and parties.

Afterwards he saw her to her car and there she had already learned feminine wiles. She leaned back against the car and lifted her face in invitation so that even a man like himself who thought he was so much in love with another man's wife and grieving for his child could not resist her mouth. He would not see her again so it was not that great an indulgence except that it was.

Men were dying on the battlefields in France, they were sitting in wet mud, combatting not only the German army but fatigue, bad food, rats, lice, every discomfort possible, not least that they could be dead before morning, and here he was standing in the cold winter night kissing a girl who had rarely if ever been kissed before, untouched, beautiful and already, he could see, with regret and astonishment, half in love.

When he stopped and she opened her eyes, even though the shadows around were dark, he thought he could see a flame of desire burning there. It was inappropriate and it was his fault. She was young, innocent, vulnerable. She did not deserve somebody like him.

'When will I see you again?' she said.

'You won't.' Dryden tried not to look at her.

'So this is what you do?'

'What?'

'Go around kissing women at parties and then . . . Is it funny?'

He was smiling. He had just thought how lucky he was. She knocked a hand against him.

'Well, do you?'

'No, of course I don't.' He got hold of her in case she was going to keep on bashing at him and then somehow it turned into another kiss and this time she got as close as she could and her arms imprisoned him. He drew away. 'This is not a good idea,' he said.

'I think it's the best idea I've had in months,' she said.

'No.'

She stood back.

'You're married, aren't you, and pretending?'

'My wife died. Fifteen years ago.'

'And you couldn't find anyone in the universe who wanted you in fifteen years? I don't believe it.'

'I had a child.' As soon as the words were out he regretted them. He had barely spoken Tommy's name since Tommy had died, it caused him such pain, and in the years since Tommy had left he had filled the loneliness with memories and it had seemed to him that no woman could bridge the gap. He looked away. Suddenly he wanted to go home. If he said now that Tommy was dead it would be the more true, the more real somehow. It seemed to him that the more often he declared Tommy to be dead the further away his child's life was and the more unreal were all those precious memories that held his mind together during the cold reaches of the night.

'You should go. It's getting very late,' he said, having drawn back far enough to be sure that she would not touch him. 'It was nice to meet you.'

She stared at him.

'It was nice to meet you? Is that all? What is it? Does your son take up your whole life? You're just like my father. There is nobody in the world who matters except Charles. Whatever I do or no matter how hard I work I'm not Charles. I thought . . .' She stopped there because her voice quivered and then she turned to go and a better man than him would have let her, only he couldn't. He got hold of her and brought her to him and then he kissed her as he wanted to kiss her, without restraint, and after that her eyes were like blue stars and her mouth turned up at the corners with delight.

'You do like me,' she said.

It made him laugh. He couldn't remember the last time he had laughed.

*   *   *

Bobbie could have danced all the way home. As it was she was very late because she did not like to say goodnight and every time she said it he came back and kissed her again. So when she finally got back to the house her father had gone to bed. She danced all the way up the hall and all the way back to the front door and then she floated upstairs and sat in front of her mirror before an enormous fire, having apologized to Freya, her maid, for keeping her from her bed.

'Did you have a good time, Miss?' Freya said.

Bobbie let herself fall back on to the bed.

'I had a wonderful time,' she said.

She slept happily, turning over a couple of times in the night only to remember what she thought was the best day of her life. The following day was Sunday. She awoke late, Freya brought her breakfast in bed on a silver tray, and Bobbie sat, watching the snow fall outside and wishing that it had been herself and Dryden Cameron being married yesterday. Phyllis and Tan would be lying in bed together now. What bliss.

She lay back and imagined that Dryden was here and then she thought about her father and the kind of men that she had known before and she realized that her father would never accept Dryden and she could not believe that she had fallen in love with an unsuitable man. He had no money. He certainly had no background. He would never be acceptable. What was she to do? The idea of never seeing him again having found him was impossible, yet he could not be an official part of her life.

Her father would have welcomed any one of the young men she knew, because, like herself, they came from middle-class backgrounds, their fathers were in business, they had been to good schools and universities, he knew their families. How unfair that she should want someone as different from this as was possible.

When Vinia went into her shop on the main street that Monday morning she was interested to hear what Em Little who helped her in the shop and with the making of the clothes had to say about the wedding. She had not wanted to go. She did not know

Tan well or his bride and thought she had been asked out of courtesy alone. The idea of going anywhere with Joe when he was in a permanent bad mood was unreasonable, she thought, and when she had voiced her objection he had said only, 'I'll tell Dryden to go.'

He didn't say, *I'll ask Dryden to go.* She did not miss the difference.

Things were getting worse. Joe did not stay at home and eat breakfast with her, he went out early. She knew he was coming back at mid-day and having Addy prepare a meal for him but she did not see why she should go back, she had always stayed at the shop and eaten with Em. She thought Joe went home because he was sure she would not be there. The evenings were a case of who could get home the later. They were like two children squabbling over a toy.

Joe had not come back to their bed. What Addy thought she could not imagine. She tried to comfort herself with the idea that better folk slept apart but she and Joe had never been better folk. Part of Joe's charm had always been that he was a man on everybody's level. The evening's pattern had changed. The dinner would be at whatever time the later of them came in. It would be eaten in silence or near silence and then they would work, Joe would go off to the study and she would go up to her bedroom, which was almost like an office, she spent so much time there at a desk by the fire. Very often she did not see him again until the following evening.

The only good thing to be said for it was that Joe's bedroom – she now thought of it as his – was as warm and comfortable as her own, Addy had seen to that.

Sundays were hell. From getting up to going to bed she and Joe avoided one another. Having no excuse, they had three meals to get through but they read papers or looked at work and that afternoon, when the weather was vile, snowing and blowing across the fell, she had fallen asleep before a big log fire in the sitting room and Joe had gone out. He was gone so long that she began to worry, only being relieved when she heard the back door clash long after dark. Where could he have been all that time?

He did not come into the room. He went into the study and worked and she did not see him again. She lay on the settee and cried.

They were busy that Monday morning and it was only when the shop closed for an hour at mid-day that she and Em sat down by the fire in the back room and Em told her what a beautiful wedding it had been, how handsome Tan had looked and what a pretty-mannered girl the bride was. The food had been lovely, the church was like something out of a fairy tale and . . . Em moved closer, face pink with excitement, Mr Cameron had spent the whole evening dancing with Miss Roberta Grant.

'Not just once,' Em said, 'half a dozen times at least. Everybody was talking.'

Vinia could not believe this. His son had been dead for only a few months, he had paraded his grief before them to such an extent that it had ruined their friendship with him, and her marriage, but he was dancing at a wedding with some woman and he had not even the sense to be proper and discreet about it.

'She's very young,' Em said, 'and very bonny.'

This made things worse. Vinia was filled with jealousy, envy, anger, all the things she hoped not to feel.

'I'm sure it meant nothing.'

'Do you know her?'

'Know her? Why should I know her?'

'Her dad is John Grant. They're very rich. He owns a mill by the river in Durham and Miss Grant wore the most beautiful costume and a gorgeous hat and he couldn't take his eyes off her and she seemed so taken with him. I mean, she wouldn't have gone on like that otherwise, would she?'

'Like what?'

Em drew nearer.

'He took her outside and kissed her.'

Vinia's appetite, which had not been good to begin with, left. She put down the sandwich, which had been the pork from yesterday's roast. She could not believe that Dryden, having caused such problems, could have a wonderful weekend, dancing with a beautiful girl. Did he not know what he had done? Did he not care about her or Joe any more?

Em was describing Miss Grant in detail and how when the evening was late Dryden had kissed her again when he had walked her to her car. Did he not realize that people would talk? And what on earth did a rich beautiful woman want with him?

The moment Dryden got home he regretted what he had done. He was euphoric from kisses and dancing and Roberta Grant's smile but when he had driven across the snow-covered fell and pulled up outside the door of his house in Prince Row he thought about his situation and realized that he must not see her again.

He gave himself credit that he had not asked her nor let her arrange anything in the impetuous and no doubt inexperienced way she seemed prone to. Somehow he had avoided it, distracted her, put her off, though at the time it had seemed more than the unsuitability of the idea. He had wanted to see her again more than he had wanted anything or anyone in a very long time, possibly always. He called himself stupid and middle-aged and he thought that half the people at the wedding had been from Deerness Law, Tan's workmates, friends and their families. It would be all round the village by Monday that he had made a fool of himself over a girl twelve or thirteen years younger than he was and it had been unfair to her and he was angry with himself.

As though you can make up for such things he worked at home all day on the Sunday and was early on the Monday. He had grown used to Joe's silence. The trouble was that Joe had been his only friend. To be on the wrong side of Joe meant almost total isolation. There were however plenty of people to talk to at the pit and when he went into the pit itself he half expected sly comments. Nothing happened.

They had treated him like china since he had come back to work after Tommy died. Few of them had lost sons to the war because their sons were pitmen or foundry men and most of them, in fact everyone that he could think of, was married. The day went on as usual except that in times past he and Joe would have eaten their sandwiches together, whereas he ate nothing, saving his appetite for the evening and whisky and Joe would have come in and talked to him about the wedding, asking silly questions. He might even have confided to Joe that he had lost his senses and kissed a pretty girl. As it was he did his work, dealt with the usual problems and was so used to fending everything off Joe that when Joe came through mid-afternoon and accused him of not telling him about a delivery which had gone wrong at the end of the previous week Dryden merely said, 'It's all right. I sorted it out.'

Joe looked as though he was about to lose his temper. He didn't, though Dryden waited. He wanted to reassure Joe again but there seemed no point. He sat there and waited for Joe's wrath to vent itself on him and then Joe said, 'Yes, of course you did.'

Later Dryden blamed himself for what happened. Joe was in the doorway when Dryden heard his own voice.

'What have I done?'

Joe, holding on to the door with one hand, regarded him with a look that was as cold as the weather.

'What could you possibly have done?' he said.

'The coal wasn't late. It—'

'What in the name of God does it have to do with that?' Joe never shouted but he did it now. The door was open. Joe looked down as though the floor held answers. 'You're in the way,' he said, 'you've always been in the way.'

He went out. Dryden sat there for a few minutes and then he went and knocked on the door of Joe's office and, hearing his voice, went in. Joe was writing furiously and didn't stop until Dryden said, 'Do you want me to leave?'

Joe stopped writing, looked up.

'You think somebody else would employ you?'

This surprised Dryden. He had his qualifications. He was good at his job.

'I don't know.'

'They wouldn't. You're a gypsy, a different colour, a different race, and this is Durham. Tradition and the way things have always been is of the utmost importance to people here. Nobody would take you on. I am doing you a favour. You should think yourself lucky that you have such a good job, so why don't you go back to your desk and do it?' Joe launched himself from the office as though Dryden were contaminating it, so Dryden went back to his desk and got on.

Eight

B obbie lasted three days before she went to see Dryden. On the Sunday she had convinced herself that she must not see him again. By Monday she was reliving Saturday night several times an hour, by Tuesday she was bored with her life, hated everything and could have shrieked at the people at work for every small mistake. By Wednesday she was desperate to see him and could not imagine why they had not made a proper arrangement. She tortured herself with the idea that perhaps he had not really wanted to see her again.

She left the office early on Wednesday and motored out of Durham and up on to the fell. It was not the weather for such journeys and normally she would not have done such a thing. She had no idea where he lived, all she knew was that he was the pit manager at the pit in Deerness Law. Unfortunately she had not realized that the area was riddled with small pits, she didn't know what it was called so three times she had to get out of the car and make enquiries about him, to the huge amusement of the men she met. They whistled and shouted at her, grinning through their black faces but she did not think they meant any harm and even directed her to the right place, informing her that it was the Black Prince she wanted on the edge of the fell, at the far end of the moor nearest the village itself.

He had been right, she thought, as she drew up outside, it was not a big place though it looked neat for a pit as far as she could judge. She left the car and went into the offices and there a young man came forward, looking surprised to see her.

'Can I help you, Miss?' he said, with that note of certainty in his voice that she had heard a hundred times from men when they were sure your being there was not right.

'Is this where Dryden Cameron works?' She looked straight at him.

The young man looked nonplussed.

'Will you tell him that Miss Grant would like a word?'

'Would you wait here a minute, Miss?'

He disappeared, coming back within a few moments. He then showed her down a dark corridor and into the smallest office she had ever seen, where Dryden sat behind a very old desk. He did not look pleased to see her. Bobbie shut the door.

'What on earth are you doing here?' he said.

'Not quite the greeting I had in mind,' she said.

'This is not the place—'

'No? Was I supposed to wait for you to come to me? And when would that have been, some time after hell freezes?'

'Miss Grant—'

'How dare you "Miss Grant" me after the way you kissed me?'

He glanced at the door and then he got up and he said, 'Bobbie, I'm sorry.'

'Oh, I see. It was a mistake?'

Dryden Cameron, she thought, was not used to women speaking their minds. He didn't answer her straight away but that wasn't because he didn't have an answer, it was because he didn't want to say it to her, she thought, and he went on looking at her as though he was taking a photograph, something he would need to treasure and hide.

'You must have realized by now that there is no way we can have any kind of friendship. If I behaved badly I apologize. It was just that . . . you're so beautiful and . . .'

'And?'

He smiled at her. It was a gift, his smile, such a tentative effort, as though he was never quite sure how it would be received.

She didn't move.

'Tell me that you don't want me here and I'll go.'

He waited and then he said, 'Your mother is dead. Your brother is in France. Do you want to tell your father that you can't control your desire for a gypsy?'

'I can't control my desire?'

'What else are you doing here? I'm not your equal. You want what you see.'

'That is very crude.'

'I'm glad you think so. I don't want you here. You had no right to come and I have a lot of work to do. Please go.'

Bobbie went.

Dryden drank a whole bottle of whisky that night until he had brought some reason and some sanity into the darkness and even then much of it eluded him. He kept falling off the edge of the alcohol back into the space where he was alone. It was a space that was getting bigger every day, it took more and more whisky to keep the edges of it close enough for him to catch. He knew very well that one day soon he would lose it altogether and after that nothing would matter. He hated the place where Joe and Vinia had put him and he should not take Roberta Grant to that place. He knew what it was like when your child was your whole life and, though it seemed strange to him, to be able to give John Grant something as precious as his daughter was only right. It was the best thing to do he told himself before he lost consciousness. It was the only thing to do.

Nine

March came. You always thought March would be an improvement on the weather but it never was in Durham. Flowers might peep through the grass in other places. Here, just as you started to think it would get better there were heavy snowfalls. It melted a little quicker towards the end of the month but that just meant everything was dripping wet, and there were lambing storms, usually sideways across the fells, small hard flakes with a low wind behind them in case anybody thought spring might be in the offing. The old people would shake their heads and say the snow was always the worst in March.

Bobbie worked. She tried not to think about Dryden Cameron and the way that he loved her because she was sure he did. It was the only comfort available. The war went on. The need for uniforms went on. The lists of the dead grew longer and each night she prayed for Charles and Forbes and each day she hoped for no bad news. Her father was desperate for Charles to come home.

The middle of a war was the place where there were few parties, no social respite. All they did was work and day by day she longed for a man she had met only twice, the second time to quarrel. She told herself that at least he was not at war. He lived in some scrubby little house with his son and pulled coal out of the ground daily for the war effort.

Bobbie had never been so aware of other women, in particular she noticed those who were married and had small children. For the first time in her life she wanted that. She had not realized that you had to have the right man to imagine yourself in such circumstances. Day after day she ran the factory, took care of the problems. Bobbie, swamped with work, tortured by the idea that she could have gone back to Dryden Cameron each night, that he would have taken her into his arms, that she might have had his child.

His words came back to her again and again so that she knew it was nothing but a dream. He was right. Her father would never have accepted him. She would have lost everything and she could not put such a burden on to her father when Charles was away. All he had was the hope of Charles returning. She could not hurt him further. She was glad that Dryden knew such things and sorry for it because it meant that she did not see him.

There was a faint glimmer of hope in her mind. When Charles came back and took over the business . . . She could almost hear him laughing. Charles hated the business. He had wanted to be a professional pianist. Her father thought such ideas were ludicrous but she could see her own dreams being sacrificed for Charles's. He would have his heart's desire. She would be on her own for the rest of her life, running the business, and other women like Phyllis would have husbands and babies and she like many others would have to smile and pretend that she didn't mind. And then the telegram came. Until then the worst days of her life were those when Charles and Forbes left and the day that her mother had died and the day that Dryden Cameron had ordered her out of his life, but they were small beside this. The one thing which she had gone through in her mind a million times and hoped and prayed against happened. It came to the house and was brought to the office. Her father called her into his office. It was a lovely room, it looked out over the Wear. In the old times when she had been younger, before the war, university students rowed in the regatta on long warm summer days, schoolchildren were given the afternoons off and people sat on the banks and shouted encouragement, they had picnics and ate ice cream. Now there was nothing on the river, the water was dark grey from all the cold rain and the towpath was deserted in the bad light. The winter trees were dark and bare so that she wished her father's office looked out over something else.

He held the letter in his hand.

'This has arrived. I can't open it.'

She thought she had never seen him look so pale and his eyes were those of an old man who had seen too much.

Bobbie went over and took the letter from his hand and opened it in trembling fingers and picked out the words.

Missing. Believed killed.

She handed it back to her father and his eyes fixed on the words and she thought he was going to pass out.

The day ground endlessly on. The problems did not stop, they did not even lessen. One of the machinists hurt her hand and had to be taken to hospital. A consignment of uniforms was lost en route, and the noise of the machines and the operatives went on and on. Why had she thought they would not, as though everything had to have respect for what had happened? She tried to persuade her father to go home but he wouldn't.

Her whole body ached and then the light faded, the relief of evening arrived and she and her father were at last able to leave the factory and go home to the house her father had built so optimistically for her mother so long ago. She could not believe they had been happy then, yet they had been. She and Charles had had an idyllic childhood, prosperous, filled with laughter, tucked up in bed each night, read stories by their parents. Her mother had bought her pretty dresses and she had gone to parties and their father had bought Charles a grand piano even though he didn't want his son to be a pianist and scoffed at the idea. There had been Sunday walks by the river and toasted crumpets by the fire and holidays where at one time they had owned a house on the Northumberland coast in Beadnell. She remembered the long wide beaches, the buckets and spades, the castles they had built and decorated with shells, the long summer evenings where her mother would come down and call them in from the beach and they would go to bed before the night came and be safe and loved.

It was all gone and she was trapped. All she had to look forward to was the business and going home with her father each evening and day after day going to work and taking the responsibility for everything and Charles not coming back.

Her father would not accept that idea.

'He's missing.'

He picked up on the only ray of hope and why should he not, how could he not when he had sent his only well-beloved son to war? He would not accept the idea that Charles would not come back. Throughout the evening he talked about how they could not know and if they did not know . . . He was ready to be glad, ready to believe that Charles could be alive and she could not make him give up hope, she could not take from him the only crumb left upon the table.

In the middle of the evening Hector Stillman's Bentley appeared on the drive. Hector himself, Forbes's father, who owned mills and department stores and lived in a grand house at the far side of Durham, was grey-faced and looking old for the first time that she remembered. He came to comfort her father and to tell them that Forbes was coming back. He could no longer fight.

'He's hurt?' she said as they sat down by the drawing-room fire.

Hector didn't answer. Perhaps Forbes too was dead and it was only that Hector could not face the idea.

'They're taking him to some hospital near Dundee.'

The two men huddled over the fire. Bobbie knew they would not miss her. She could not bear another second of this. The evening had turned cold and rainy. She got the car out and drove as fast as she could out of Durham, through the little mining villages and across the fell, past the Black Prince pit, then stopped outside the first row of houses. She banged on the door of the first house and after an interval a skinny little woman wearing one of those pinafores which crossed at the front and fastened behind, encompassing most of her body, came to the door, whereupon Bobbie said, 'I'm sorry to bother you. Do you know where Dryden Cameron lives?'

'Four doors up, pet.'

Bobbie was astonished. He lived in a little house just like these other people? She thanked the woman. She went over and banged on the door. She thought she could see a line of light from inside but it took some time before the door opened and he stood there.

Bobbie had never thrown herself into a man's arms in her life and her upbringing stopped her from doing so now but only just. He didn't ask her what she was doing there, he merely drew her into a chilly dark sitting room and then through into the kitchen of what was by far the smallest house Bobbie had ever seen. A huge fire blazed there in a black shiny range and horse brasses at either side reflected firelight. There was a table and chairs and to one side a small sofa. He sat her down on a little stool before the fire.

'You thought I wouldn't come back, didn't you?' she said.

'Why, you're frozen,' Dryden said, getting down beside her, taking off her gloves and rubbing her fingers.

He didn't ask her whether she wanted tea, he got up and busied about making it and she had not the energy to tell him that she didn't take sugar, because he poured the tea out of a big brown pot and ladled spoonfuls into it and milk and then he gave the cup and saucer into her hands, only asking first, 'Can you hold it?'

'Yes, yes,' she said. She couldn't. Her hands shook so much and she began to cry. She looked about her and, struggling for something which seemed sensible to say she said, 'I thought you had a child. Isn't he here? Is he in bed?'

'My child was a soldier. He died last summer in France.'

If she could have put down the cup and saucer she would have but they seemed glued to her hands. She stared at Dryden.

'He died?'

'Yes.'

'Oh God,' she said.

Dryden took the cup and saucer from her hands and some-how she found his shoulder and she realized then that was what she had been searching for all day. Her father had offered her no comfort, she had had to be strong for him but this man could shield her from the awful things which threatened her and at the same time she could stroke his hair and whisper idiotic words into his ears and then she wanted to kiss him. She wanted to kiss him more than anything in the world. Her fingers found his chin and her mouth found his lips and he didn't stop her. He didn't tell her all those sensible things he had said to her the last time they met, until the ferocity of her kiss threatened to make him overbalance back on to the multi-coloured hearthrug which graced his floor and he moved, grasping her forearms and looking into her face.

'Charles is missing,' she said. 'They think he's dead. My father will never believe it. He will go on hoping and hoping. My mother has been dead for years yet every morning her clothes are laid out on the bed and a table is set for her at each meal and paintings of her are all over the walls and . . . She isn't dead to him, you see, and he can keep her alive with these things. Nobody ever dies in our family, they aren't allowed.' She smiled at this witticism. 'Charles will live forever and I will have to . . . I will have to . . .'

She kissed him again even more fiercely than before, fought him down on to the mat and he let her. She looked at him.

'You are so . . . I didn't like to tell you. You are so graceful and so perfect.'

He said nothing. Bobbie laughed.

'That's what men usually say to women, isn't it? I've had it said to me dozens of times. Don't you think it's strange that people want perfection? Flawless?'

'I have marks all over my body.'

'You do? From what?'

'From working down the pit and from an accident I had, blue marks which never come out and scars from fights. It's only my face that's all right.'

'It certainly is all right,' she said and traced a finger around his mouth. 'I would like to see.'

'Yes, I thought you would,' he said. 'Might I suggest another time?'

'No. I want you.' She undid the buttons on his waistcoat and then on his shirt. He didn't stop her but he said, 'It isn't the right time.'

'Will there be a right time?'

'I don't know.'

'I think I'll take now just in case there isn't.' Her fingers found the belt at his waist. 'I don't know what to do.'

'You've got the idea,' he said and then he pulled her down on top of him.

She had had dreams of what this would be like. She would be married but to no one she had ever met and he would be rich and handsome and they would be in Italy and the windows of the room would be open and her father and Charles would both think he was right for her and he would be a businessman and he would help run the factory so that Charles could go off and play the piano to his heart's delight. She and the man would go home and they would attend Charles's concerts because by then he was a world-famous pianist and her father would be so proud of both of them and he would be able to retire. They would live with her father and Charles, they would meet for meals and exciting conversation and she would wear wonderful dresses and he would adore her and they would have children and her father would be so proud of her.

The trouble was that the man had remained cloudy and indistinct in her dreams. There was nothing cloudy or indistinct about Dryden Cameron or his kitchen floor. So much for white snowy sheets and Italian hotels but she wanted him more than she had ever wanted the man in the dream and if she hadn't wanted him when they first began she certainly would have done by the time they got to the serious part because he knew exactly what he was doing. She had never seen such confidence. The young men she knew were the sort who barely knew how to kiss a girl they had just met but he had no difficulty with her clothes, her body or the fact she knew nothing about men. She had heard stories about this, that women spent all night crying on the stairs because of what men did to them, that it was brutal and hurt, that it was disgusting and respectable females didn't want to but she did want to and it didn't hurt and his body was exquisite in the firelight despite what he had said and it was just so normal, it was exactly right as she had known it would be from the first second she set eyes on him. She would never stop wanting him. She would never stop loving him.

He carried her upstairs and put her into bed. It wasn't very warm up there but he put a match to the fire and held her close and all the demons that had pursued her that day fell away beyond the bed and then beyond the door and beyond the house and beyond the village, they went into the cold darkness of the fell and were lost. She didn't care. All she cared about was to sleep close in his arms and to think that she would not leave him. When she turned in the night he was there and everything was warm and comfortable and even the sounds from the other houses were a murmur against the night.

When she awoke it was morning and he was lying there, looking as though he had been waiting for her to wake up.

'You have to go back,' he said, 'and I have to go to work.'

'Not yet.'

'Meg comes in to do the house.'

Bobbie reached for him, kissed him, drew him down to her.

'Tonight then?'

'If you can.'

'What makes you think I can't?'

She could not let him go and yet she had to, lay there watching him sluice his body in water and he had been right, his back was a mass of blue marks. He dressed and went downstairs for fresh water for her and then she got out of bed and reluctantly washed and dressed. She kissed him at the doorway and then he walked her out to her car and she had no option but to get into it and go back to Durham.

Ten

F orbes Stillman went to the hospital in Dundee and after that her father and his father were rarely apart. Hector asked her to help. She called herself stupid for caring, because she had enough to do. Her father did not go back to work though she realized that he had been doing less and less, as more and more often the managers and the top people at Stillman's were getting in touch with her, firstly because they assumed she knew where he was and what he was doing and more importantly what he wanted them to do and then because she had tried to help them in the first place.

Hector lived by the river in Durham but he deserted the loneliness there and came to live with them. She wished that Forbes would come back. Older than she was, he had been a good businessman. She badly needed his help.

The two men did not seem to notice anything that she did. Most especially they did not see that night after night she left the house after dinner and did not return. She tried to be subtle, to leave her car away from Dryden's house and sneak up the backyard, but cars were few in pit villages and there was always somebody about.

It had not occurred to her that she could be the subject of a serious passion. Marriage, though this was not that, among her friends, unlike the working classes, was a much more civilized arrangement and seemed very often to be the work of fathers who thought that land and businesses were the important part, though if they threw their sons and daughters together suffi- ciently usually they took a fancy to one another and things worked out just as well as if it had been formally arranged.

This was different. It wasn't a meeting of minds. In the first place she didn't want to talk to Dryden about the problems she had. She wanted to leave those at the factory. Their personal problems were so awful that they couldn't discuss those either. In the beginning she had the feeling that this resembled – how awful – what men went to brothels for in that she wanted his body and didn't care very much about anything else and that was enough for a while.

It was tempestuous, exciting, almost frightening, the amount of feeling, just short of violent. She went home bruised and dazed with smarting lips and always that feeling of security which he gave her but she realized as the weeks went on that Dryden Cameron was prepared to play this game any way she wished and she had no doubt that if she had come to him in a different kind of mood he would have accommodated that too.

It changed. She would make excuses not to go home and she would drive up to Deerness Law in the early evening. Sometimes she even went to the pit and caught him unawares. She knew she shouldn't have, that people would talk, but she was beyond caring and besides, the danger was part of the fun. Sometimes they made love in his office.

Throughout that summer she saw him almost every day and on Sundays would spend the afternoons with him. She liked best those afternoons in the early autumn when the wind drove the rain across the fell and she and Dryden would sit over the kitchen fire and make toast and drink tea. Her burdens at work were so heavy by then that she was forever falling asleep in his arms.

One day in October she awoke and he was sitting, smiling at her. She closed her eyes and then opened them again to make sure he was still there and then she said, 'Do you love me?'

'Of course I love you. I thought you knew.'

'I just wanted to hear you say it.'

'I said it earlier.'

'I know you did but we were making love and that's different.'

'Not to me.'

'You never say things you don't mean, do you?'

'No.'

'Have you been in love often before?'

'Only once.'

'Once?'

'Would you like some tea?' he said and got up.

'I didn't mean to pry.'

He didn't answer that. She went behind him and put her arms around him and her face against his back.

'You are all that keeps me going. I couldn't manage any of this without you.'

He turned around and kissed her.

'It'll be all right,' he said.

It was the end of October when Forbes came home and it was a bitter day for her father because Hector's son came back and his did not, but by then the house had been turned into a sort of shrine for Charles, his likeness everywhere, his piano locked and silent and the music room locked and silent too. Her father would not even allow the maids in there to dust and nobody but himself was allowed into Charles's bedroom. He spent long periods of time in there.

Hector seemed to cope better. He was outwardly cheerful and from time to time would go into work but he could not face going back to his own house. They huddled together like frightened children.

Bobbie scarcely recognized Forbes. His beautiful brown eyes were like stones. He did not seem to recognize her either, stumbling as he got out of his father's car. He had been tall and athletically built. Now he was bent and so thin that his cheekbones were prominent over sunken flesh. His clothes were much too big. She did not think he recognized her either. He said nothing and no light flickered in his eyes. He did not seem to know where he was and even when Smith, Charles's black and white springer spaniel, sidled across he did not put out a hand to the dog. Smith stood for a long time and then Forbes noticed him and stared.

Bobbie's father went back into the house. Hector was jolly. He pursued Forbes with questions. How was he feeling? Was he glad to be back? Did he remember this house as well as his own and would he mind living there, for a while at least?

Forbes went to bed. Bobbie sent tea upstairs and had to put up with Hector in the drawing room.

'They told me he was much better. He's not.'

'At least he can't go back,' John said. 'We must be grateful for that.'

'Grateful? When my son has lost his mind? Whatever will I say to people? That he was weak? That he's gone mad?'

Bobbie couldn't stand it. She wanted to go to Dryden but somehow she couldn't desert Forbes in this house where dead people reigned and those who were still alive had no joy. When she ventured into his bedroom, having knocked and had no reply, he was lying in the darkness except for the firelight, on a day bed by the fire, wrapped in a huge dressing gown and managing to look like a child. He did not acknowledge her.

She went across and sat down on the edge of the bed. Still he didn't move, gazing into the fire.

She said, 'Do you know me?'

He turned and said abruptly, 'You haven't got a cigarette, have you?'

'Oh, yes.' She found her cigarettes, lit one, handed it to him and he smoked it quickly, gratefully, saying only, 'Turkish, is it?'

'Yes.' She put the rest of the packet and the silver lighter down beside him. He picked up the lighter and turned it over.

'You gave that to me.'

'Did I?'

'For my eighteenth birthday.'

'It's pretty,' he said.

'I always thought so.'

'You're very pretty too.'

Bobbie smiled.

'Is this my home?' he said.

'No.'

'I thought I didn't recognize it.'

'You used to spend a lot of time here. You used to come and stay when you were little.'

'Are we related? We aren't married, are we? I would feel such a fool.'

'No.'

'Or in love?'

'No.'

'And those men downstairs . . . the one who asks all the questions, is he my father? I keep thinking he said he was . . .'

'Yes.'

'Lord!' Forbes said and made her laugh. 'Is the other one yours?'

'Yes.'

'Thank God they don't both belong to me. I don't think I could stand it.'

That made her laugh too.

'Are you planning to go out?'

She was astonished.

'How did you—'

'You've got your outdoors shoes on. Don't worry, I won't tell.'

She was surprised. She had not thought that he would be charming. She didn't think of him like that but then Charles had always guarded his friendships jealously, had always been between them that way somehow.

'Will you be all right?'

'I'm starting to be glad I came here,' he said. 'Don't worry about me, I'm fine.'

She drove to Deerness Law, where Dryden was sitting over the kitchen fire, and for the first time somehow she was irritated with him.

'Do we have to sit in here?'

'I'll put a match to the fire in the other room.'

She caught hold of him before he went through the door.

'That isn't what I meant. I wish it wasn't like this.'

'Like what?'

79

'Secretive. Deceitful.'

'It doesn't have to be.'

She eyed him.

'So it's for my benefit, is it?'

'What happened?'

She didn't answer. She went through into the cold dark front room. Dryden went after her but he didn't offer to light the fire.

She put both hands on the back of the sofa and stood beside it, glad of the cool darkness as the tears fell.

'Forbes came home,' she said. 'He came home and he didn't know who I was and he isn't Charles. I want my brother. I want him to come back. Do you know what my greatest fear is? I'm afraid that there is nothing after this damned awful existence and I will never see him again. He was my twin. I feel as if I've been cut in half.'

Dryden drew her away from the sofa. She buried herself in him.

'Forbes doesn't remember anything,' she said, wiping her tears against his shirt. 'I'm stuck there with those two old men and a man who has lost his mind and one of the biggest businesses you've ever seen, a factory, three mills and four department stores. What in the hell am I going to do? Make love to me.'

'What, here?'

'Right here, right now.'

She stayed. It was cold and dark outside. Her father did not notice what she did and neither did Hector and although the few servants they still had must be well aware that she came back in the morning in time for breakfast they were far too well trained to say anything and too old to care. Also they must have been aware that she would brook no opposition. The more work she had to do the less reliable her temper was and the more she wanted Dryden. She could not bear to think of a single day without him. She knew that she was demanding and difficult but she knew also his tiny house was a haven. Here she did not have to pretend she was things she was not. She did not have to be strong and capable, make any decisions. She could lie in his arms for hours by the fire, fall asleep there. She liked that best. He would carry her to bed and the fire was always lit in the bedroom. She loved the little black half-moon fireplace.

If she wanted he would make extravagant love to her. If she didn't he would hold her close. It was the only place she felt safe, the only time she could be herself and he was the only person who was not afraid of her moods and tantrums. She could go there and scream and shout and cry. Dryden was impervious to it all. To her he was always the same. There was food and tea and whisky and a warm fire and a warm bed and his warm body.

'I do love you, you know,' she said, one night when it was late and she judged that her behaviour had been worse than usual. He said nothing. She pushed him further down into the pillows. 'Why are you smiling?'

'How do you know I'm smiling? It's dark.'

'I can hear you. Tell me that you love me, gypsy, or I will beat you until you're unrecognizable.'

Dryden laughed.

'Come on then,' he said.

She kissed him all over his face.

'I love you more than anything in the world,' she said. 'More than anything or anyone. I always will.'

She didn't know whether over the next few weeks Forbes remembered anything. She didn't think that he did. She thought he took what she and their fathers said as true and accepted it so it was difficult to tell. Day after day as the winter went on and then the spring rain poured down the windows and the wind bashed the life out of the daffodils, he sat by the fire on the day bed in his room and then by the window until it grew dark. He would not go anywhere or do anything and declined all invitations to move from that room even on Christmas Day, while his father became more depressed.

'I don't believe he remembers anything,' Hector confided to her on one occasion when they were having breakfast alone together. Her father very often ate breakfast in his room. 'I don't think he ever will.'

In a way Forbes's presence cast a blight on the house, his father so upset, but to her it was almost like having half of Charles at home, they had always been so close. She began to go home in the early evenings. Dryden was so busy at work that he was always late back and she had taken over her father's library at home. She could work there if necessary. It made a change from the office.

As the evenings grew lighter and the old men were out playing golf she would pop up to visit Forbes before getting down to a couple of hours before she went to Deerness Law. She didn't know whether or not Forbes was pleased to see her. He was seemingly absorbed in what passed beyond his window. She could never see anything in the garden but he was fascinated.

The gardeners had long since given up their jobs and gone off to war along with the chauffeur and all the other male servants other than the odd-job man, Terence. Her father did not think the garden was his territory so it had become a wilderness, the grass long like a meadow, the flowers finding their way as they lived. Smith, the old spaniel, was always with Forbes. Sometimes he would take himself for a short walk in the garden but his back end was almost gone so he didn't venture far. He was a worn-out gun dog, having gone into ponds in bad weather for dead ducks and cut his face a hundred times on brambles during rough shoots up on the moors. Now he lay by the fire, his head moving sometimes, his legs working. He was probably dreaming of the time before the war when Charles and Forbes had taken him with them and he had loved the sound of a pheasant calling in the sweet morning air.

Her father still talked about 'when Charles comes home' as though it was all he had to cling to, that and his friend, Hector. Hector had nothing left. Weeks went by when he did not venture into Forbes's room as though he could not bear what the war had made of his son. The two men were lost to the tragedy of war and so were their fathers. Perhaps we all are, she thought, one June evening as she walked wearily up the stairs. There was one saving grace. Within two hours she would be in Dryden's arms.

Forbes rarely ate much. The tea tray was left, the tea unpoured, the cake untouched, and he was as usual staring from the window. She greeted him, kissed his dry cheek and sat down. He didn't move his gaze from the scene outside and Smith didn't even raise his head. He was starting to go blind and deaf so little disturbed him.

Bobbie was too weary to make conversation. She sat down in a chair nearby and contemplated the garden.

'It's full of rabbits,' Forbes said.

'That doesn't surprise me.'

As they sat there in the early evening and the shadows lengthened, the rabbits came skipping on to the lawn from the trees at the far end and to her astonishment two half-grown foxes ventured out into the full light and began playing like puppies, amidst the grass. Bobbie had never seen such a thing but Forbes showed no surprise.

'Have you seen them before?'

'When the evenings are fine.'

'Do you read?'

'Can't.'

She looked at him.

'You can't read?'

Forbes smiled patiently at her.

'Of course I can read. I mean I don't want to. How's work?'

'You wouldn't be interested.'

'I might.'

So she told him all the things that had gone wrong that day. He frowned.

'You're in charge of it all?'

'Yes.'

'Including all my father's business?'

'He won't go any more since . . .'

'Can't you put managers in?'

'All the best men are . . .'

83

'Dead?' Forbes suggested.

'Fighting. And yes, many of them have died. I'm perpetually short-handed, with inexperienced people.'

'Sounds like a nightmare. Are you seeing your lover tonight?'

Bobbie looked at him. She didn't know what to say.

'How did you work that out?' she said.

'It wasn't difficult.'

'Don't say anything to anyone.'

'Who could I talk to? You're the only person I ever see.'

It was then that she realized he looked forward to her coming home, he valued the short time she spent with him. She tried to speak to her father and Hector about going upstairs to see Forbes but all his father said was, 'Let the blighter come down. How much longer is he going to stay up there?'

Her own father said nothing.

Eleven

T he talk was all over the village that Mr Cameron had a
fancy woman. Vinia had been of the opinion that anything other than talk of who had died and whether enough coal
was coming out of the pit for the war would be a relief but it
wasn't. The talk did not stop. She cursed Roberta Grant,
having never met the woman. Had she no more sense than
to have an affair with a man in a pit village, or were men in such
shortage that she had no choice? Everybody knew the big shiny
car and the local women gossiped about her beautiful clothes
and how young and bonny she was and how disgusting and
scandalous and why Mr Cameron hadn't got married to some
nice woman on his own level. It seemed to them twice the sin,
because there were so many widowed and unmarried women,
that a rich independent young woman should have him, and she
was obviously having him. Not that anybody said that but
Vinia thought it. It made her wince.

Strange. They never met and although Dryden had someone
else it was making things worse. Joe perpetually complained
about Dryden as though he did something wrong every day so
she could not understand why on that Wednesday afternoon –
it was half-day closing – she, knowing that Joe had business in
Durham, locked up the shop in the early afternoon and made
her way down to the pit office.

There was nobody about. Maybe they had broken to eat their
sandwiches. It was a lovely spring day, the first soft day of the
year. She walked along the corridor from the main office and
there Dryden was, a half-eaten sandwich on his desk, and he
was rifling the drawers for something. She stopped in the

doorway and without looking up he said, 'Bill, have you seen the—' and then he looked up. 'Why, Vinny . . .' he said.

Nobody had called her that in such a long time it made her throat constrict and her eyes fill. And she thought how could he look like that? He had gone through hell, they were in the middle of a war, he was overworked, often now they were there seven days a week yet he looked . . . goddamn him, she thought, he looked young. Was that what bedding a girl did for you? Men. But her name on his lips echoed in her mind again and again and the way that he looked at her, that soft look as though he had searched the empty horizon for sight of her day after day did the same thing to her insides as it had always done.

'Joe's not here,' Dryden said. 'He's gone into Durham to a meeting.'

'He actually told me,' she said. 'He doesn't tell me much these days but he did.' She moved into the office and she thought she had been wrong, he did look older, it was his eyes, careful, guarded.

'Can I help?' he said.

'Why bother when you've already done so much?'

Dryden didn't answer that.

'And how is Miss Grant?' It had not occurred to Vinia that her anger was veiled jealousy. She had not realized she was the sort of woman who would attempt to hold such a man to her in spite of tragedy and with nothing more than offers of Sunday dinner and the memory of a few embraces. He did not deserve that, however badly he was behaving.

He didn't smile but the amusement reached his eyes and Vinia wanted to be glad that he had found some kind of happiness in such awful times no matter how short-lived it might turn out to be but she could never cease to think of him as hers. He looked even younger like that and she thought of how he had been after Tommy died and she wanted to be glad that he could find anything to give him joy but she wasn't. The prim bit of her told her that a man who was grieving shouldn't look like that and the lover in her wanted him very badly. She had forgotten how important he was to her.

'I expect you know all about her,' he said.

'Oh, I do and so does the rest of the village. What on earth were you thinking about? She's rich and years younger than you and . . . the one saving grace, I suppose, is that she isn't married. Do you expect to marry her?'

He reacted as though she could have questioned a dozen people in the room.

'Who, me? No.'

'Then what are you doing?'

His black eyes took on guile.

'You don't really want me to tell you.'

'Now you're being obtuse. You know exactly what I mean. Her family would never stand for it, surely. What if she had a child?'

He didn't answer that and she realized he was the last man who would ever worry about such a thing. His wife and children were dead. If Roberta Grant were to have his child, no matter what the circumstances or the cost, he would be glad.

'She would lose everything,' Vinia said. 'Is that what you want? You want a woman like that to be reduced to waiting at home for you?'

'You don't understand,' he said, very still. 'The only thing that any man really wants is to put in a good shift so that his pockets chink with money and when day is done to go home in the gathering dusk to his wife and his child and his dinner. It's all there really is.'

'And do you expect to have that with Roberta Grant?'

'No. She'll get tired of me and besides . . . she couldn't take me anywhere.'

For a few seconds Vinia imagined what he would look like in evening dress in a ballroom, how he would stand out among all the fat, self-satisfied, rich middle-aged men and then she realized.

'You love her,' she said.

'I'm sorry, Vinny,' he said.

Vinia had never had a rival before. He had always loved her alone. The awful woman in her was glad that to Esther

Margaret, during the latter part of their marriage, he had been faithful and loyal but in his heart he had betrayed her every day with his regard for the pit owner's wife. This was different. She could never compete with Roberta Grant and in a crude sense she could not hope to. He was bedding this woman. He had that shiny look about him. He was in love and night after night Roberta Grant, who was so far above the rest of them that she didn't care who saw her come here and leave, who noticed the big silver car, came to him in a house she should have been too proud to go to and there she gave herself to him, like any whore, Vinia thought.

'It's not respectable,' she said and he laughed.

'Why should I care?'

'Because you are the pit manager, because you're supposed to set an example, because . . .' She couldn't say to him that she wanted him to lie alone in a little house that her husband owned for no better reason than because she loved him. She could not say to him that she and Joe no longer loved one another and that it was his fault. He had destroyed them all, he and his child who had died. Every day she missed Tommy, every day since all those years ago when he had left. That was where it had all started, when there had been nothing they could do but let Tommy go and he had never come back. She could not accept that. Some stupid part of her waited always for Tommy to come home.

'I didn't mean to say those things to you,' she said. 'I do understand and I . . . It's just . . . I just wish Tommy was here, that's all.'

It was a very small office and her words went round and round the walls like a children's fairground ride.

'Aye, he's bad like that,' Dryden said.

Twelve

That summer the sons of two of her father's best friends came home on leave and Bobbie and Forbes and their fathers were invited to dine. Her father did not want to go but thought the invitation kindly meant and since Hector agreed she talked her father into it.

'What about Forbes?' her father said.

She said she would talk to him. It was a lovely summer's day but she was surprised and rather pleased when she got home to find that Forbes was not only outside but had gone for a short walk as far as the big ponds, some way from the house. She strolled over. He was lying in the grass on the bank, asleep with Smith beside him. As she approached he made a little noise of panic, his eyelids flew back and he turned face down in the grass for a few seconds. Bobbie waited.

'Bad dream?'

'No.' He turned over, looked at her, smiled.

'I didn't realize you were downstairs, never mind all the way out here,' she said, sitting down.

'It's amazing what I can do when I try,' he said, with a little curl of his lips.

'How about dinner?' she said.

'What?'

She explained about the proposed evening.

'My father thinks I want to go there when all the other men will be in khaki?' he said.

'No, he doesn't think you want to go but he wants you to. Might you consider it?'

'If you wish.'

She was about to say that it wasn't what she wanted that mattered and then didn't.

'Do you want to?' he said.

'Why not?'

'Well . . . what about this chap you're seeing? Is he going to be there?'

Bobbie didn't answer.

'Sorry, old thing, I didn't mean to be inquisitive.'

'He's a miner,' she said.

'They're very good, you know. Having been in the collieries, they have such hard lives the war is no shock to them.'

Bobbie said nothing. Forbes eyed her.

'He isn't a suitable person then?'

'No, he isn't. Also he's . . . he's . . .'

'Married with half a dozen children?' Forbes said lightly.

She laughed.

'He's . . . coloured. I think his father was a gypsy. We haven't talked about it. What about the party?' Bobbie tried to be brisk. 'Will you come?'

He said he would think about it but on the Saturday evening when she put on a grey silk dress and went to see if he was ready she was surprised and rather pleased to see how good Forbes looked in evening dress. He was not bent any more, he had put on a little weight, his eyes were clearer.

'You look wonderful,' she said as she stood up.

'What a beautiful dress,' Forbes said.

His hands shook when she gave him a cigarette and he turned white when he got into the car. His father drove and her father sat in the front. She put her hand through Forbes's arm for reassurance but she wanted to be with Dryden. She would have given a great deal to have gone to dinner with him like that, all dressed up.

The family who were giving the party were old friends, she had known the boys when she was a little girl. She hadn't seen either of the two young men in many months. The host complained bitterly about the quality of the food having gone down since the war began but nobody else seemed to mind. It was such a rare occasion for them all to be together.

Bobbie took the opportunity to go out into the garden halfway through the evening and one of the men, Thomas Maugham, followed her out, saying,

'Sweet on Forbes, are you?'

She laughed.

'No.'

'There's still a chance for me then?'

'I thought you were engaged to Lottie. I shall tell her.'

'How is he?'

'Better, I think. This is the first time he's been anywhere. Do you know what happened?'

'Not exactly. The men say there are two kinds of officers, those who get you killed and those who look after you and he was one of the best. Sometimes it's just an accumulation of events. Keep an eye on him, won't you? Freddie Brough came home like that and when everybody thought he was better and they tried to send him back he hanged himself in the butler's pantry.'

Back inside somebody was playing the pianola and they had rolled back the carpets so that they could dance. Forbes was avoiding it. She went to him.

'You're supposed to ask me to dance,' she said.

So they danced. Their steps matched.

'Have we done this before?' he said.

'Many times. You taught me to waltz.'

She had been sixteen. What a long time ago. It was one of the few times when Charles did not come between his twin and his best friend. He was content to play the piano. If she closed her eyes for a few seconds she could imagine herself back then, with Charles's exquisite playing and Forbes, little more than a boy, noisy and given to daring exploits, and a superb dancer.

For the last hour before they went home he sat in the garden and smoked cigarette after cigarette, and she knew that he had had enough but the older men wanted to linger so it was very late by the time they arrived home. He said goodnight briefly and went to bed.

Bobbie couldn't sleep. She turned over dozens of times and the things that Thomas Maugham had said went round and round in her mind until there was no chance of sleep. She ventured along the warm dark hall to his room, telling herself she would just check and make sure he was all right. Quietly she opened the door.

The curtains were pushed back and the windows were open. It was not a dark night. The bed was empty, covers thrown back. She imagined him having nightmares, leaving the room, going downstairs. She panicked. She fled back along the landing and down the stairs and began searching the lower part of the house. She was already crying. What had he done? She skidded into the library and there he was, sitting with Smith at his feet, wearing a silk dressing gown and looking out, as the dawn began to break through the night.

'What on earth are you doing?' she said and made him jump. 'You frightened me. You should be in bed. You should . . .'

Forbes looked at her.

'Jolly pyjamas,' he said.

It was so warm she had not thought to put on a dressing gown.

'Were you having nightmares?' she said.

'No, I was bored with being upstairs.'

'I could . . . you could . . .'

'What?' He looked harder at her and smiled bitterly. 'Get in with you? I'm not a child, you know. I'm not much of a man any more either though so it wouldn't matter. I'm like Smith, I'm just about finished.'

'You shouldn't say things like that.'

'Why not? Isn't that what Porky was saying to you?'

She wanted to smile at this reference to Thomas Maugham's childhood nickname. He had been a large child. He wasn't any more, he was as skinny as the rest of them.

'He said you were one of the finest officers he'd ever known.'

'If I were I'd still be there,' he said.

The evening had been too hard for him, she felt guilty, as though she ought to have known it would be. She wished she could be angry with him. She did not want the responsibility of him on top of the work and the two old men and the blasted household and . . . She wanted to go to Dryden. He could bear her anger. He would hold her in his arms while she ranted. He was strong and capable and . . .

'Are you going back to bed?' she said.

'Are you going to tuck me up?'

He didn't mean it, she knew but she went with him anyway. Smith followed but he had such difficulty with the stairs that she picked him up and carried him.

'This disgusting dog doesn't actually sleep on the bed, does he?' she said, when they reached Forbes's room.

'There speaks the housekeeper. No, he doesn't, mostly because he can't reach and I don't offer. Why don't you go? I can get myself to bed, I've been doing it ever since my mother died and I went to boarding school.'

She didn't answer. Forbes understood.

'Don't worry about what Porky says. I'm not going any-where.'

'You have bad dreams though.'

'They aren't all bad,' Forbes said, taking off the dressing gown and getting into bed. 'I love France, the little white villages, the children playing in the streets, the roads bordered with poplar. I love the food and the people and . . . but so many of the towns are deserted and quiet and the people are so . . . so hurt, to have your country invaded and the Flanders sky is clear and unrelenting somehow. It's just the noise at the Front that gets to me. When I sleep I try to think of it without war, like it used to be, the people at work there on the land, the wonderful food and wine . . .'

Bobbie sat down on the bed.

'You dance beautifully,' she said.

'I didn't know whether I could dance at all, I couldn't remember having done it but somehow when the music started it all came back to me. I wish other things would, or maybe I don't.'

'What do you remember?'

'Most things I think, now, certainly my childhood and leaving here and most of the war, there are just odd gaps. It's more a physical thing really. All the time I'm exhausted and I think about going to bed.'

She leaned across and kissed his forehead. Forbes winced.

'Don't do that,' he said. 'That's what my mother used to do. I'm nearly thirty.'

'What shall I do then?'

'I'd rather you didn't do anything, thanks. Save your affection for your miner.'

'Goodnight then.'

'Goodnight.'

Bobbie didn't think either of the old men had noticed this interlude during the night but Hector came to her at breakfast the next morning and said into her ear, 'When young women spend half the night in young men's rooms it's usual for them to be engaged.'

Bobbie was startled.

'I'm only teasing you, my dear,' he said. 'I'm sure you need a man with at least half a mind. He is a very elegant dancer still and I'm sure that counts for a good deal and he wears a decent suit so well.'

'You shouldn't.'

'Sometimes I wish he had just died,' Hector said and he left the room.

Bobbie grew very tired over the summer. She told herself that it was because she was working too hard and had nothing to look forward to but to go home to the three men, none of whom, she was convinced cared anything about her welfare. Sometimes she could not even be bothered to go to Dryden and they restricted themselves to Saturday nights and Wednesdays but that was not enough. Her business life threatened to swamp her. She was so desperate to see him that they spent all their time together in each other's arms.

'I wish we could go away somewhere,' she said, 'so that we could do normal things.'

'We can if you like.'

'Could we?'

'Surely we could have a weekend.'

'Where would we go? It wouldn't have to be far or we would spend all the time travelling.'

'We could go to Scarborough.'

'We could pretend we were married. We could go dancing and have dinner and . . . I could wear a pretty dress.' Somehow she needed to wipe out the night of the dinner and dancing with Forbes. She wanted that but she wanted more. She wanted Dryden in the role. 'Would you really like to go?'

'I would love to.'

'Let's then. I shall devise something and I could take the Bentley and we could go walking on the sands and . . .'

'You're going away for the weekend?' She had told lies to her father and his father but Forbes's clear brown eyes were undeceived. 'With him?'

'Yes.' Somehow she didn't want to tell him and it was because he had nobody, because she knew that he would spend the weekend by himself because he could not bear to go downstairs and hear his father who these days continually carped at him and her father who said nothing because he was not Charles.

'Have a good time,' Forbes said.

'Shall I?'

'Of course. Have the jolliest time ever.'

'You don't mind?' Guilt had made her say that.

'Oh, Bob . . .' He hadn't called her 'Bob' since they were children. 'All you have is now. Don't ever think there's any more. Take what you can and run with it. I'll be fine. I have Smith to look after me and besides . . . I'm not your responsibility.'

That was progress, she thought.

'Are you sure?'

'Damned sure. I'll be here when you get back and you'll be cursing me within days.'

'I never curse you.'

She was so excited. The drive to Scarborough could be gained two ways, both of which were beautiful, there was the road over the moors and the road by the sea so they decided to go there over the moors and come back by way of the cliffs. She made plans and changed her mind again and again and worried that a single weekend meant so much. She was afraid that because it was rare and precious it could easily be spoiled but she looked forward to it very much over the next few days. A whole weekend of Dryden all to herself.

Thirteen

D ryden told himself that it couldn't last. Every day he threw up defences against the idea that Bobbie could leave him the very next day, to protect himself against being so hurt that he could no longer function. Because it was all he had. Joe was making his life a misery at work. Nothing he did was right and there was no longer any kind of relationship between them. Joe only spoke out of necessity and criticized him very often in front of the other men, so that Dryden ceased to have the kind of authority which ensured that the miners took heed of what he said, and behaviour at the pit was not the standard it had been. Twice lately he had found men smoking and Joe had heard about it and blamed him.

'The men are getting slack,' he said. 'What the hell are you doing?'

It was clear Bobbie wanted to be with him, to escape from the overwhelming difficulties of her life, and gradually there was born in Dryden's mind the possibility that she wanted him more than she wanted anything else. She was running the whole business herself. Her father could not have any power over her nor exert any influence, he needed her too much. There was also another reason why Dryden thought she might marry him. He was half convinced that she was pregnant. She hadn't said anything so he couldn't be sure but when she suggested they should go away for the weekend he went into Durham and bought a ring, sapphire with diamonds, and that week, sitting in his office, he took the ring from his desk drawer every day and gazed at the possibilities.

He had asked Joe if he might leave early on the Friday and have the Saturday off. He had never done such a thing before.

'What, the whole weekend?' Joe said, from behind his desk, Dryden standing in front of him.

'It's only one day and an hour or two.'

'We're in the middle of a war. What on earth would you want a full weekend for that's so important?'

Joe, Dryden reflected, must be the only person in the entire area who did not know he was having an affair. Didn't Joe and Vinia ever talk about anything?

Joe was giving him a very straight look.

'I'm going to ask Roberta Grant to marry me.' Before the words were out, unable to stop them, Dryden regretted it. Joe would laugh at his pretensions, would say savagely funny things and Dryden would be terribly inclined, as he had been so often lately, to hit him, thereby losing himself his job, his house and the best friend he had ever had, except that he feared his perfect weekend was about to be torn from his grasp by a man who was his boss and no longer liked him. Joe would never let him go now he had told him the reason.

Joe said, 'What?' and stared.

Dryden took the little square box from his pocket and flipped open the lid. The jewels glittered in the strong summer light.

'My God,' Joe said, 'that must have cost you three months' wages. How long have you been seeing her?'

'Since Tan's wedding last year.'

'Doesn't her father own the clothing factory in Durham? I have got the right one, haven't I?'

'Yes, he does.'

Joe looked at him and Dryden waited for the derisive laughter and the cutting remarks.

'And you think she'll marry you?'

'Probably not. It just seemed like the right thing to do, that's all.'

'I see,' Joe said.

'Can I have the weekend then?'

'Take it,' Joe said and waved him out of the office.

*   *   *

They stayed at a hotel on Blenheim Terrace in the North Bay, only a short walk from the castle. Their room looked out across the sea. Dryden had never stayed in a hotel before and he liked it, in spite of the fact that it was obviously somewhat run-down due to the war. Scarborough had been shelled just three months after the war began and buildings were damaged and everything was secured, the inhabitants nervous. Who knew when it would happen again? He liked being away. He liked the idea of having her to himself. He enjoyed the journey – she let him drive her father's Bentley and it was a joy – and he liked the idea that she was completely his. There were no distractions. They walked late as the sun sank beneath the horizon and slept in a big double bed with the windows open to the wash of the tide.

They went into town the next day and walked and shopped. The small box in Dryden's pocket distracted him. There did not seem to be a right time to introduce such a difficult subject. After dinner, however, the sun set splendidly once again and they stood in front of the hotel and looked out across the bay. There was nobody about. He turned to her.

'Bobbie . . .'

'Oh, I wish we could do this often. We will be able to surely when the war ends.'

It was everybody's favourite saying. When the war ended they would have their heart's desire, whatever it was. Would she make him wait however long that was for marriage? He wouldn't mind.

'Bobbie . . .' Dryden said again and he took the small square box from his pocket. He had her complete attention now. She watched in fascination as he opened the box.

'I've never loved anyone in my life as much as I love you,' he said. 'Will you marry me?'

Bobbie went on staring and then her eyes filled with tears and she clutched at the front of her jacket and said, 'Oh my God.'

'I know that you have your father to consider but the war won't last forever. Surely then you can decide what you want.'

'I know what I want,' she said. 'I want you.'

They went back to the hotel and made love and when it was

late she said, 'I can't wear a ring. We'll have to wait. After the war things will be different and – and my father may see it differently.'

'Can we do that?'

'What?'

'Wait.'

'Why not?' Her eyes were so clear.

'I'm wrong then. You're not having a child?'

The disappointment was already felling him. She sat back and one of the thin silk straps of her cream underwear slid off her shoulder so appealingly. Her skin was so soft, so . . .

'A child? Is that what this is about?'

'No . . .'

'It is. Oh, Dryden, I'm not pregnant. Were you worried? Did you think you had to do this?'

'Are you sure?'

'I would know. My body would tell me.'

'I don't mean to be blunt but . . . you haven't bled in months.'

'I don't.' She turned aside for a few seconds and avoided his eyes. 'What an awful subject. I never have much. My chances of being pregnant are extremely slight. I'm sorry if that's a disappointment. Do you want this ring back? How noble of you.'

'Look, Bobbie . . .'

'No, no. Here.' She held out the ring. 'I'm grateful for the favour.'

Dryden cursed himself for a clumsy bastard.

'Did you think a pregnancy would secure me?' He had seen her get angry before but not with him.

The question bounced off the walls and came back upon him a dozen times and even then she wasn't content. She called him names. It wasn't anything he hadn't been called before a hundred times but that didn't make it any easier to bear and when he tried to touch her she got off the bed and started putting on her clothes.

'I didn't mean to hurt you, Bobbie. I'm sorry. Please, just

wait until it's light and then if you hate me the same I won't stop you.'

Her hands moved ineffectually but she didn't cry. He wanted to go over and touch her. She threw the ring into the middle of the bed, and then she did start to cry.

Dryden put the ring back into its box and the box into the drawer of the little bedside table. She came over and got into bed and turned her back. Dryden couldn't sleep. Scarborough had lost its charms. He lay awake and waited for the dawn to arrive.

For the first time in many months Bobbie was glad to go home. Forbes was lying on a rug beneath the trees in the garden. It was early afternoon.

'He asked me to marry him,' Bobbie said and burst into tears. She was horrified at herself. She hadn't intended to tell anyone what had happened in Scarborough.

'And you said no?'

'What else could I say?' Bobbie pushed her fingers across her eyes as she subsided from her knees on to her side. 'I can't marry him, can I?'

'What happened?'

'He seems to think I'm having a baby. I wanted to be asked because he cared.'

Dryden had been completely silent since then as only he knew how, and nobody had spoken even when she dropped him off in Deerness Law. The problem was that she had the awful feeling Dryden's sixth sense was right and she was pregnant. Before this it had not occurred to her. The very idea was appalling.

It was years since she had been told by doctors that the likelihood of her ever conceiving a child was remote, since her menstrual cycle was almost non-existent, but this weekend, coupled with how strange she had felt lately, was upsetting. She was not going to be pushed into marriage by her body or by a man suggesting to her that he was acting out of respectable motives. Dryden's very attractiveness was that he was the part of her life which was secret, stolen, sweet, the only part of her life which was completely for her alone. It did not involve other people, decisions or visits to the doctor.

'If you love him there's no reason why you shouldn't marry him,' Forbes said.

'I am not having a baby,' she said.

Later, when the two older men came back from playing golf, they had tea in the garden. Forbes went off to lie down in the early evening and his father, who would never stay in his presence for long, had gone off somewhere too. She was left sipping tea with her father.

'Nice weekend?' he said.

She had told him she was going to friends in Newcastle though how he imagined she had the time or the energy to remain friends with anyone she didn't know.

'Have you given any thought to the future?' he said. 'Forbes is a lot better, don't you think?'

'I think he pretends he's better than he is. I don't think he actually remembers much, he just takes note of what we say.'

'Not well enough to go back then?'

'I don't think so.'

'Neither do the doctors. We had Dr Hazlitt and another here last week, he brought a specialist, spent time with him.'

'You didn't tell me.'

'There's nothing to tell, nothing positive. When he is a little better than now, I thought he might go into the office with you. He used to be a brilliant businessman.'

She didn't like to think about how different Forbes had been before the war. The truth was that she hadn't liked him as he got older. He was very brash, very daring. What they called a man's man. She had almost forgotten what he was like. How awful to know that you preferred a man damaged, hurt, compliant. Forbes, rich, young, handsome, had been the kind of man that mothers in the area would have loved as a husband for their daughters. Not that anybody would take him now. Nobody wanted to marry a madman. However, if he was shown to be better, they would want him all over again for his money and status.

He had gone out with lots of girls, driven around in a two-seater, had his clothes made in Bond Street, cared nothing for anyone and run his father's business with the kind of slick insincerity which was the very opposite of the way she ran it now. He would have called her sentimental because she cared for and looked after the people who worked for her, paid them well, shortened their working hours so that they were more efficient.

As it was he applauded everything she did but she thought that was to do with the fact that she was his only company. Her father barely spoke to him and even at tea that day his father had not been content until he had told him of the brave exploits of other soldiers in France. He bore it very well because he knew that his father could not stand him for long and that half an hour or so of this would be his measure for the day and then his father would lose patience and go off into the house. But Forbes would be white and tired by the time it happened and she would have spent the time not telling his father to leave him alone. It was exhausting.

'You're fond of him, aren't you?' her father said.

She was fond of him like she was fond of Smith but she couldn't say that Forbes inspired similar feelings to Charles's old spaniel.

'He has to be looked after,' she said.

'Does he?' Her father looked enquiringly at her.

'I don't know what you mean.'

'You're mollycoddling him, my dear. What man would want to go back to war when a beautiful woman spends most of her free time with him and –' he coughed – 'very often most of the night in his bedroom.'

'I do not!' Bobbie declared, hotly.

'Don't you?'

'He has nightmares.'

He did. She hadn't thought about it but somehow his nightmares could not be allowed to govern him and even though she should not have been able to hear his distress through the thick walls she did and was not averse to going to his room, tripping over the old dog, throwing back the curtains to any light and sitting on the bed, very carefully not touching him because she knew with sound instinct that he could not bear to be touched but needed her close. She could tell by his very breathing what state he was in and sometimes in the darkest hours she knew he could barely remember her name.

'His nightmares are becoming very convenient, don't you think? He's a man, not a child. Have you seen the way that he looks at you?'

'He has nobody else.'

'Oh, I don't think it's a question of numbers, my dear, I think it's something a great deal more intricate than that. I think he's in love with you. If you don't return the sentiment then you must try to put a little distance between you.'

'That's difficult, living in the same house.'

'I agree but you must try.'

That night Bobbie awoke and was fully aware that Forbes had awoken shouting but she didn't go to him. Silence descended, so some time later there was no excuse for her to put on a dressing gown and venture into his room.

It was light by then. He was not in bed and but for the dog, who lay on the rug, she would have thought that Forbes had gone downstairs and was probably in the drawing room by the window, smoking a cigarette, but Smith would not have stayed while his idol went into another part of the house. She said Forbes's name into the silence and then she saw him, crouched in the shadows in the corner with his hands up to his face.

'Forbes?'

As she moved towards him he drew back further.

'It's me, Bobbie.'

He very slowly took down his hands from his face and then recognition dawned, Smith got up and came over and went to him, snuffling into his face until she heard a chuckle of comfort and relief from him.

'That smelly old dog,' Bobbie said.

Forbes put his arms around the dog, who licked him appreciatively all over his face.

'You shouldn't come in here.'

'My father's been talking to you, hasn't he?'

Forbes's silence confirmed her suspicions.

'The old bugger!' Bobbie said.

'You shouldn't call him things like that.'

'What did he say to you?'

Forbes unwound slightly from the corner and was almost smiling.

'He questioned my manhood. Mind you, if he only knew how right he was . . .'

Bobbie got down beside him.

'Stop it,' she said. 'You'll be all right. It takes time. Come on, get up.' She moved the old dog as best she could.

'He's so fat,' she said.

'Walking hurts him,' Forbes said and got to his feet.

Dr Hazlitt looked gravely at Bobbie that Monday afternoon. He had known her since she was a child and used her christian name. She had not resented it before now but then she thought she had never liked him, he was self-satisfied, smug, sure of himself and superior.

'I never thought I'd say this to you, Bobbie. You're having a child.' He tried to smile. 'In war these things happen.'

'It's nothing to do with the war,' Bobbie said. 'I don't want it.'

He said nothing to that, as though she had blasphemed, and then, 'It could be your only chance. Think of it as luck. Surely . . . it wasn't lightly done.'

'No.'

'Well then?'

She said nothing.

'He isn't married? Because you could—'

'I'm not going to sneak off somewhere and have it and give it up to other people,' Bobbie declared and soon afterwards she was walking out of the surgery into a bright September day.

It was almost four o'clock when she got back to the office. She couldn't work. She couldn't understand why she felt no different, even the tiredness had passed. She turned around as the door opened and Phyllis came in. She was pale.

'Are you all right, Phyllis?'

'Are you busy?' Phyllis said.

'No, not if there's something wrong.' Glad of distraction she smiled and waved Phyllis into a chair.

'I thought I should tell you this even if you get angry and ask me to leave . . .'

'Ask you to leave? I wouldn't do that. I couldn't manage without you.' She came and sat down across the desk. 'What is it?'

'You'll think I'm interfering.'

'No, I won't. What?'

'It's about Mr Cameron. I didn't know . . . I mean, I did know that you were seeing him. Everybody in Deerness Law knows . . .'

'You haven't told anyone?'

'I wouldn't speak a word to anybody,' Phyllis said. 'Nobody in the factory knows or in Durham but up there everybody knows everybody's business. I didn't think too much about it. He's – he's very taking is Mr Cameron. A lot of . . . of women think so but last weekend . . .' Phyllis stopped as though Bobbie had silenced her and then she said, 'He went away for the weekend and I thought . . . for the first time I thought it was serious between you.'

As though a seaside town could make some crucial difference, Bobbie thought bitterly.

'The thing is . . . I said to Tan you would never consider marriage with a man like that but war does funny things to people . . .'

'You don't like him?'

'I think he's very . . . attractive. There's many a lass in the village who's set her cap at him and he's never noticed them and there was always a good reason for it. He was . . . he was always sweet on Mrs Forster. I'm not saying there was anything going on. In the first place Mr Forster wouldn't stand for it and Vinia Brown, for all she was a working man's daughter, is as close to being a lady as she could be with her origins, but everybody always said that she was the reason he didn't have anybody else.'

'He was in love with her all those years?'

'Since his wife died, presumably. I don't know. All I know is his behaviour was very proper, a lot more proper than some lasses would have liked, if they'd been in her shoes. Until . . . until the wedding. I wish . . . I wish Mr and Mrs Forster had come instead and you might never have met him. I feel like it's my fault.'

Women always thought everything was their fault, Bobbie thought tiredly. Why do we do that?

'I'm not saying Mr Cameron has treated anybody badly all these years but then some men are saints when they aren't married.'

Bobbie stared into Phyllis's white face.

'He treated his wife badly?'

'It was a long time ago but I don't think folk change much. First of all he got her pregnant so they had to get married . . .'

Bobbie's heart thumped.

'And then they had this awful marriage. He had other women and there she was, pregnant with his bairn, my mam told me all about it, it was one of the biggest scandals of the village. He drank, they never had any money, no decent food, no furniture and then she fell downstairs, lay there all night. The baby was born dead. He had been with another woman, a slut whose husband was working away. He treated his wife so bad she lost her mind and ran away from him.'

Bobbie couldn't think of a thing to say.

'Are you sure it's true?' was all she managed.

'As true as I'm sitting here,' Phyllis said.

Bobbie didn't wait. When Phyllis had gone and the shift was over she got into her car and drove much too quickly into the country, past Esh Winning and up beyond the allotments and gardens, which were in full use, it being summer, they were all growing vegetables, and across the fell to the Black Prince pit. She drew up in front of the office, got out, walked straight through the main office and there he was, office door open, working away at his desk. He looked up when he heard her. Bobbie went inside and slammed the door.

'What a nice surprise,' he said.

'It's not meant to be nice.'

He didn't say anything for some time and then he got up.

'I don't understand what I did . . .'

'Tell me about your marriage.'

'What?' His dark eyes were, she thought, instantly defensive.

'Tell me about it.'

'What does it have to do with anything?'

'Tell me about it,' she said again.

'Esther Margaret died. Tommy was . . . Tommy was almost five. She had cancer. It—'

'Before that.'

Dryden looked down at the desk.

'I see,' he said. Then he was silent.

'You had to get married. She was pregnant.'

'I was very young.'

'Oh, don't let's have "people change". You went with other women . . .'

'No . . .'

'Yes, you did. You slept with other women, you drank and on the night your wife had your child she had an accident, the child died and you weren't even there. Go on, tell me I'm wrong.'

Dryden wasn't even looking at her any more, as though the pens on his desk held fascination.

'You were bedding another woman at the time.'

She waited.

'You were, weren't you?'

'Yes.'

'And then she left you?'

Bobbie could hear people talking in the outer office through the silence which followed.

'She came back,' he said, 'and we had Tommy and . . . I paid for it over and over . . .'

'And you think I should take a chance on you now? Do you really?'

'I think you're having my child.'

'I am not and never will have your child,' she said. 'I don't want anything else to do with you. Don't ever come near me again,' and then she tried to walk out of the office.

He put both hands down on the closed door, one at either side so that she couldn't open it. Breathing very carefully Bobbie turned around, looked into his fathomless dark eyes.

'Let me go.'

'Not yet. Why did you come, if you thought such things about me?'

'I wanted to hear you say they were true.'

'This happened twenty years ago. Do you think I haven't changed with all the things I've been through? Do you think I'm going to treat you like that?'

'You're treating me like that now.'

'You can't come in here shouting the odds and expect me to accept it. You're having my child and you're frightened. There's nothing to be afraid of. I am not going to treat you badly.'

'No, you're not,' she said, 'because I'm not going to give you the chance.'

'You don't want me,' he said. 'Why don't you just say it?'

Dryden moved back so that she could have walked out. She didn't want to leave him. She wanted somebody to magic him into the kind of person she wanted him to be, with a family, a place in society, a skin that didn't look as though he'd been sitting in sunshine for weeks. She wanted him to be respectable, the kind of man her father would be pleased to have in his house. But he wasn't. He never would be.

'I don't want you,' she said.

Joe sat in his office and thought back to however many hundred times he had wished Dryden would find another woman. And because his father had put up this bloody wooden shack and called it an office and because he had spent money on safety measures, men's wages, renewing housing, and he had never spent money on this, Joe could hear every word through the walls. Roberta Grant slammed the door when she left. Joe's office shook with the impact. He didn't know what to do.

He listened to the door and reflected that by morning the news would be all over the village. Roberta Grant had a voice that carried and the walls between the various rooms at the pit office were thin. He and Dryden were no longer friends, nor did he want to be. His marriage had ceased in everything but name and there was no guarantee that this latest event would not make things worse. On the other hand could things be any worse?

He waited. No noise came from the other office. Dryden didn't leave, he didn't move, and when Joe ventured through some time later he was sitting working as though nothing had happened.

'You all right?' Joe said.

'Fine.' Dryden didn't even look up.

The truth was, Joe thought, that Dryden didn't trust him any more, not with confidences, but he had a horrible picture of Dryden drunk and lying in the old ruined house that had belonged to the Havershams. He didn't want that again but he couldn't bring himself to be anything more than civil.

Joe went home. He hadn't thought in months how he hated going home. He had forgotten what his wife felt or tasted like. He didn't notice what he ate or what she said, which was very little. They didn't have any conversation and that night it was the worst it had been. He tortured himself with thoughts of Dryden making his way through the darkness in a drunken haze to that house and up the stairs in hope or vision of what? Dryden would fall through those bloody stairs and break his neck. And he, Joe, would be to blame for not caring enough to offer help or comfort and his wife would break her heart over a bastard gypsy. Joe told himself that he didn't care, that it was not his fault or his concern, but he couldn't sleep. He was beginning to think he would never sleep well again. The worst of it was that he wanted Vinia like he might have wanted a whore and that was so undignified, so pathetic. His body craved and ached for her but he would not give in. He would not go to her, not while Dryden was continually in both their minds. It was not right. He did not care if Dryden . . . He did not care.

He got out of bed and went downstairs and in the darkness of the sitting room he went to the cupboard and found the whisky bottle but when he took it out of the cupboard and opened it and the smell of malt whisky flooded his senses it was not his wretched drunken father who governed him, it was he and Dryden drinking together after Esther Margaret had died. He wanted to weep. He thought of Dryden making funny remarks about Susanna Thornton. Their lives had parted since then. The chasm was so wide that he could not go to Dryden. Nor could he go to his wife for comfort, succour or any baser things. He put the bottle back into the cupboard and returned to bed to try and summon sleep from whichever dark corners it had retreated to.

Fourteen

T he old dog was getting slower and slower, Bobbie thought, as she watched Forbes come back from his Sunday morning walk. He walked a lot further now and Smith, though obviously finding it difficult, trailed after him. Forbes was losing the grey look. He was beginning to seem as young as he was, as though he had put down several burdens on his journey back towards the house.

He saw her standing in the drawing-room window and waved his stick at her. He didn't need a stick, he just carried it as countrymen do. It had a duck's head carved on the top of it and made her think of Charles and how in the old days the two boys went fishing and shooting together here at the grounds of their house and of Forbes's old house. She could almost see Charles beside him. She had to look away.

All that week she had tried to get used to the idea of living without Dryden. It was to her as though he had died too. For the past few days she had stayed at the office until late, avoiding the three men, but this was Sunday, she had no excuse to be anywhere else. Her father and his father were in the library, reading newspapers, sipping sherry and anticipating the meal to come. She went outside and met him halfway down the path. The lawns were soaking and the hair on Smith's long ears had curled in the wet. She smiled brightly.

'You look well.'

'You look tired,' Forbes said.

'I'm fine. Just too much work.'

He didn't say anything though he clearly didn't believe her. They went back into the house, though not to where their fathers were sitting, into the small room which looked out across the side of the house and towards the ponds. Two ducks flew down, braking before hitting the water. Smith settled himself beside the fire with a grunt of satisfaction.

'You've hardly been here all week. Even your father thinks you're working too hard.'

Bobbie studied the fire.

'I'm not seeing that man any more,' she said.

She didn't look at Forbes even though he was watching her.

'I found out what he's really like. If I marry him I'll lose everything and . . . I could see myself, poor and helpless, with a child, stuck in a little cottage and him . . . treating me like he treated his first wife.'

'I thought you loved him.'

She told Forbes then what Phyllis had said and how Dryden had reacted.

'Wasn't this a very long time ago?'

She looked wildly at him. Forbes waited until the silence made the sparks from the wood fire seem loud and then he said, 'What about the child?'

'I don't know. I've lain awake thinking about it night after night.'

'You could go away and—'

'How could I leave the business?'

'I'll manage the business.'

'You think you could?'

'I could try.'

She didn't like to tell him that she didn't think he was capable of very much. Even now he would spend hour upon hour gazing from the window. All he did was go for walks and sit by the fire. Running a big business was too much to leave to a man like that.

'I would have to give the child away if I did that.'

'If it's dark-skinned what alternative do you have?'

Bobbie's throat closed.

'The doctor says I was lucky to conceive at all. That's not

how I would have put it but . . . he says it may never happen again and . . . I want my child.'

'There is another way round it though it's hardly to be greeted with joy.'

'What's that?'

'You and I could get married.'

He said it so flatly as though no woman in her right senses would consider him and she thought how he had been, how girls had pushed themselves at him at parties, how the prettiest, most charming women sparkled to get his attention. It was like a fairytale, or a dream they had woken up from. She remembered watching him play cricket at school when he was seventeen and she was very young and thinking even then that men looked their best in white. What wonderful days, when the summer had seemed to go on forever and there was tea and diamond-shaped sandwiches and people wore hats to shade their eyes and the women wore summer frocks and sat around in deckchairs. Cricket was such a wonderful, silly game.

'It won't always be like this,' she said. 'The war will end.'

'And I'll go back to being who I used to be? I doubt it.'

'You'll be able to run your father's business and then you'll – you'll fall in love with some nice girl who'll stay at home and look after you and . . .'

'Bob, you can't have a baby when you haven't got a husband. What are you going to do, conjure one from thin air?'

'All I know is every instinct tells me I can't marry him and I'm not going to marry you because you happen to be the most generous man in the world. It wouldn't be right.'

'Then what are you going to do?'

'I don't know. Stick a knitting needle up myself!'

He smiled a little over that. Smith snored gently at his feet.

'You have to make a decision soon.'

'I know. That's why we couldn't get married. Your father and my father, they would think that you'd . . . that we'd . . .'

'Strange. It's every young man's idea of hell but somehow I'd be quite proud to think I could do such a thing now. Just think if it was a boy. Once they got over their initial reaction they'd both be so pleased.'

'And you'd have to pretend you cared about another man's child and accept it as yours. How awful.'

'I might look at it differently.'

'How do you mean?'

'I've been so involved in so many people dying I would like to be around somebody being born.'

She put herself into his arms at that point, the memory of Charles saying goodbye for the last time at the station rushed before her eyes and she missed him, his khaki figure, his smiling blue eyes, his long slender pianist's hands. He had waved and she had stood on that stupid platform and the train had been nothing but a blur through the wet mist and the rain had poured beyond the station roof.

The door opened and her father stopped instead of coming in.

'Now then,' he said briskly, 'what's this?'

She was about to say that it was nothing but she didn't. She wanted to stay there in Forbes's warm embrace for the next hundred years. She moved back, saying nothing. His father too appeared in the doorway.

'Are we going to eat or aren't we? The gong went ages since,' he said.

Her father moved into the room.

'You wouldn't be taking advantage of the situation, would you, Forbes?' he said.

Why did men get the blame, Bobbie wondered.

She was about to object strongly when she remembered that she couldn't and then she said, 'Please don't be silly,' and she got up and walked out of the room.

The problem seemed to have no solution. She did not want to be influenced by Forbes trying to offer her what seemed like an easy way out and when they had eaten she retreated upstairs. She didn't think he would follow her into her bedroom though in some ways her father had been right, she and Forbes were more familiar with one another's bedrooms than people who weren't married had any right to be.

The truth was that she did not think of him as a man. He was a substitute for Charles, not quite as high in her affection as Smith. That was not true, she thought, as the rain poured down the windows, obscuring her view of the garden. She cared very much about him, had learned to do so since he came back, tamed, and yet what she had loved most about Dryden Cameron was that he was the opposite. And look how that turned out, she told herself.

When she went down for tea, as she must unless she wanted her father asking questions, she wasn't altogether happy at the atmosphere. She had the awful feeling that one of their fathers or both had been bullying Forbes. Not that he said anything, but mid-evening he tried to excuse himself and go upstairs and his father said, 'I see no reason for you to leave the general company. You're obviously not ill any more. You could be better altogether if you tried, I think, you just don't want to.'

She had to stop herself from defending him, waited to see if Forbes would put up with this and sit down again but he didn't and for the first time since he had come back she thought she could feel anger coming off him. He didn't say anything, he just went, and left his father glaring after him.

Bobbie wanted to follow but she thought that would occasion even more remarks so she stayed where she was. When it was a decent time to go to bed she went into the hall to find the old dog standing behind the front door, whining, scratching at the woodwork.

She put on a coat and, pushing him back inside, she ran out and across the lawn, shouting Forbes's name, but the wind took away the sound and swallowed it. Searching in the darkness in such weather was difficult. She ran all the way to the ponds and there she found him, a still figure, standing on the edge.

'What are you doing?' she said.

He looked like somebody waking up.

'I thought I saw something.'

'Come back inside. There's nothing to see, it's dark.'

She took him by the arm and urged him into the house. Smith's tail was wagging, he was so pleased. She took Forbes's coat from him and took off her own and they went upstairs and sat on the rug by the fire in his room. His hair was so wet the water ran down his face. She found a towel and rubbed his hair and his face and then she gave him brandy from the decanter which he kept in his room and she drank some herself and the fire warmed her through.

'What did you see?'

'I can't remember. It's so frustrating. It's like I'm almost there but there's a thick fog around it.'

'And it was outside?'

'I thought it was. I'm obviously quite mad.'

'No, you aren't. You're getting better every day, though not like your father thinks.'

'He used to like me, when I was like him.'

'Thank God you aren't like him. He's incredibly objectionable.'

'You didn't like me much before, did you?'

'Of course I did.'

'No, you didn't. You put up with me for Charles's sake. You didn't even notice when I was desperately in love with you.'

She laughed.

'You were never in love with me, Forbes Stillman. You are a liar.'

'Yes, I was, when you were eighteen. You had a big party, you wore a gorgeous dress and you wouldn't dance with me, even though I asked you several times.'

She remembered him vaguely at her eighteenth birthday party. She had been beautiful then, surrounded by young men. Two had proposed that very evening and she had turned them down without a thought. They were both dead.

She got up and went for the brandy decanter and poured out more for Forbes and then for herself and, with nobody saying anything, they sipped at their brandy and by and by his body began to sag with weariness. He fell asleep, leaning towards her, and then his head brushed her shoulder. She gathered him to her and with a sigh he moved closer until his head was in her lap. She sat there, quite comfortable, for about half an hour, stroking his hair and drinking her brandy. After that he came to, apologizing, and she poured some more brandy and took it to bed with her.

He came to the office. She was surprised and not very pleased. He looked strange without the dog and more official somehow. He was wearing a new suit and was as slender as he had been at eighteen. His eyes were unsure.

Bobbie got her secretary, Rosa, to make him some tea. He asked polite questions about the business but when Rosa had gone he said, 'I think we should get married.'

He got up from his seat across the room and came and sat down on the side of her desk so that he was close. 'I think we should tell them,' he said.

To shut him up she showed him around the factory. He was so nice now, she thought. He chatted to all the girls. The older women smiled on him and said behind their hands what a lovely lad he was. Forbes looked like a boy and reacted like one, as though everything was new and he was pleased with it. Halfway through the afternoon he went home but not before he had said, 'I think we should do it tonight.'

She stayed at work until she risked being late for dinner but when she came in out of the cold dark night he had the two men assembled in the drawing room and he said, 'Are you going to do it or do you want me to?'

Her father was looking worried.

'Bobbie?' Forbes prompted her and when she hesitated yet again he said, 'We're getting married.'

There was silence.

'No, we're not,' Bobbie said.

'Yes, we are. We're going to see the vicar on Saturday. I've talked to him.'

'This is nonsense,' Hector said.

'No, it isn't,' Forbes said and, having given her time to butt in, he said, 'We're having a baby.'

The silence went on for so long that Bobbie thought it might never be broken and then his father started to laugh. It wasn't a nice laugh, it was heavy and strained and John went white and said, 'Is this a joke?'

'No,' she said.

His father laughed even more after that but Bobbie was equally concerned about her own father, who was white-faced and silent. Hector's eyes glinted.

'I don't believe it,' he said. 'You can barely walk across the lawn, never mind father a child.'

'If you managed it I'm sure I can.'

Hector looked at him as though he wanted to hit him. Bobbie ran over. Hector had learned to hate his son. He had adored the bright, brittle person Forbes had been.

'Hiding behind a woman,' his father mocked, and walked out.

Bobbie stood in front of Forbes, waiting for whatever happened next. In a way it was worse.

'You want to marry a man who has lost his mind?' her father said.

'He hasn't.'

'No? What use is he? We needn't ask, need we? What are you going to do, carry him, the child and the business? When I think of all the opportunities you had to marry well and you end up with a wreck of a man like him. I'm so very disappointed in you,' he said. 'I was doing you a favour –' this to Forbes – 'in having you here. You have abused my trust and my hospitality.'

Bobbie almost said that he hadn't but Forbes got hold of her arm at that point and squeezed gently so she stayed silent. And then her father too left the room. When the door was shut she let go of her breath.

'I was so looking forward to dinner,' Forbes said with a rueful smile in his voice and it was only when she turned that she realized she was crying.

'He was right,' she said, 'you are a complete imbecile. How could you do that?'

'What can I say? I'm in love.'

'You are rubbish,' Bobbie said and laughed a little through the tears.

She could not bear to let her ideas roam about in her head. She could not tell herself that she did not want to marry him, that what she wanted was some evil gypsy who had treated his wife badly.

They went together to see the vicar. There was nothing else to be done. She asked Phyllis to come to church and be a witness. Phyllis seemed surprised but said nothing uncomplimentary. Neither of their fathers went. Forbes asked Thomas Maugham, who was at home recovering from a wound, if he would be a witness, and so one cold wet February Saturday afternoon they went to church, the four of them.

It was one of the most awkward situations she could remember, when they met outside the church before the ceremony. They were polite and Phyllis laughed nervously.

It didn't take long. It had not occurred to her that she could be married in such a way, with neither her parents nor her brother in the church. Afterwards they stood about in the rain for a few minutes. Thomas suggested a drink. They went to the nearest pub and over a smoky fire she and Phyllis had sherry, the men drank beer.

The conversation was virtually impossible and all the time she wanted to run away, to get into the car and drive to Dryden Cameron's office or his tiny house where they had spent so many nights in one another's arms and beg him to take her back. She thanked Phyllis, they said goodbye outside and then she ran to the car and drove home.

Nobody offered congratulations, nobody said anything. It was as though nothing had happened except that when she went to bed Bobbie thought she should offer to share her bed with him. She thought he might even mention it but he didn't.

When the house was quiet and the fire had died down she

ventured through into Forbes's room, thinking for the first time that she didn't have to be quiet, and he was standing over the fire, fully dressed.

'Aren't you going to bed?' she said and then he heard her and looked around.

'Aren't you?'

Bobbie had not wanted anyone before Dryden or after him but she did not want to hurt a man who had done so much for her and the truth was that she loved him for his kindness to her.

'Just come and sleep with me,' she said.

'You don't mind?'

'Come on.'

They left Smith asleep by the fire and went into her room. She sat Forbes down on the bed and undid his tie and then she said, 'You can hold me if you want to.'

In answer to that he leaned forward and kissed her and to her surprise it was sweet and gentle and brought back memories of Dryden in certain moods. She put her arms around his neck and drew him close.

Vinia heard the shocking news from Em, that not only had Miss Grant given up Mr Cameron but she was going to marry Mr Stillman, the poor gentleman who had gone mad and had to come back from the war. Vinia asked Joe when he came home that evening, 'Did you know about this?'

The silence had gone on for so long in their house that she was almost surprised when Joe answered.

'She came to the office some time since. They had a blazing row.'

Vinia tried not to ask him any more and Joe didn't offer. He left her in the kitchen, heating the dinner, and went into the sitting room. Vinia hurried after him.

'About what?'

'It's not our business, Vinia.'

'About what?' she said again.

Joe didn't reply for a minute or two and then he said, 'Dryden asked her to marry him.'

'And that was what the row was about?'

'That was weeks since. He asked me for the weekend off and when I told him he couldn't he . . . he showed me this . . . this incredible sapphire and diamond ring.'

'And what did she say?'

'I don't know. I didn't ask and then she came in the other night and said she wasn't going to marry him and Dryden said . . .'

'What?'

'He said she was having his child and they had this row and then she went.'

Vinia tried to say something but the words stuck to her lips like wet blotting paper.

'Do you think he knows she's going to marry another man?'

'The whole damned village knows. Major Stillman was a very successful businessman and an excellent soldier. He's been decorated for bravery.'

'Did you say anything to Dryden?'

'Not much.'

'Don't you care about him at all?'

Joe was going to a meeting in the village. Vinia couldn't rest. She walked about the house for half an hour after he had gone and then she went to Dryden's house. It was empty. She stood and gazed down at the backyard and there was no light and though she went round to the front no light burned either upstairs or down. She walked the short distance to the pit. The lights were on though there was no one in the main office. In Dryden's office too there was a light and the door was closed to keep in the warmth. She tapped lightly on the door and heard his voice but when she went in she didn't know what to say. Should she pretend she didn't know anything?

His face did not betray him and she thought of how much she missed him. He was like someone unused to conversation, he greeted her very softly as though the space between them might break in two from the very sound of their voices.

'It's Saturday night,' she said. 'Should you be working so late?'

'I'm fine.'

'Joe went to a meeting.' Vinia moved closer. She wondered whether he did know about the wedding and if she should tell him. If he knew, it didn't matter that she told him and if he didn't surely it was better she told him than he found out from other people, at least she thought so. 'I didn't know until today that you and . . . you and Miss Grant weren't seeing one another any more.'

'That's right,' he said.

Vinia sat down on the back of the desk next to where he was sitting.

'Dryden . . . I would do anything not to hurt you but . . . she got married today.'

'Married?' He said it as though it didn't matter, as though he had come through so many hard schools that nothing mattered. His face didn't change, there wasn't a flicker of emotion. Nothing.

'She married Major Stillman.'

'Oh,' Dryden said.

'You asked her to marry you because she was having a baby?'

'Yes.'

'Could it be his?'

'I suppose.'

'I'm so sorry. Will you come and have Sunday dinner with us tomorrow?'

'Joe doesn't want me there and I wouldn't either if it was the other way round and he'd spoiled my marriage.'

'It isn't spoiled.'

'Vinny, your marriage is wrecked and you know it. Joe's so bitter he can hardly breathe.'

'That's not true,' Vinia said but her insides were asking why other women could have children who caused them problems and she couldn't and it was the cause of hers. She so often thought of herself and Joe sitting over the fire in the evening with children. It would not have been like this. There was not even a gravestone for Tommy. He was buried in France. 'I'll talk to Joe.'

'Leave it. It'll only make things worse if he thinks you came here when I was on my own.'

'But . . .'

'Leave it. Please.'

Fifteen

J oe's body got the better of him. There was no other way to describe it, he thought. He ached and burned for his wife and the more she didn't want him the more he wanted her. He couldn't sleep. He lay awake in the bedroom that had been his father's and began to understand what Randolph's life had been like. His mother had, from what he could understand, been the kind of woman who was habitually unfaithful. He could not accuse Vinia of that, or perhaps he could, that in her mind she had always been unfaithful to him. She would allow him neither contact nor comfort. Joe had never felt so little in control.

Always he had been the pit owner, the person in charge. Now he felt as though Randolph had been waiting inside him to make him the kind of person whose wife did not want him. Randolph had gone to drink and Joe's childhood memories were vague but he knew there had been other women at the house from time to time. Randolph had tried to keep this part of his life from his son but Joe could remember perfume, laughter, the colours of pretty dresses.

There was none of that in his own life. All he had was his work and because Dryden was the cause of his misery Joe no longer knew what to say and when they did hold conversation it was only about the pit. He could not bring himself to be civil to Dryden and although he told himself that none of it was Dryden's fault and he was being unjust Joe could not stop himself. In the evenings he was inclined to go home and drink and several times lately had downed a couple of glasses of whisky before Vinia got back.

Joe had never been ashamed of himself before. It made him bad-tempered and she was silent and distracted and shrugged him away like a dog she no longer had any affection for.

It wasn't that Joe decided to do something about it, it was that he got to the point where he could bear the situation no longer. There were various women in the area who did such things for money but Joe could not be seen to go there and, indeed, he didn't want to.

There was a young woman who lived on the very edge of the village who the villagers had nothing to do with. They called her a witch but Joe knew from his various acquaintance with the local landowners and businessmen that from time to time she took men to her bed for money. He had the feeling it was a great deal of money but his choices were few.

He didn't go. He held the idea in his mind as a last resort but having lain awake for weeks, having talked to and touched no one, without thinking about it one evening after supper Joe walked back through the village and out to the far side towards the moors and there he saw a light burning in the house which stood alone and apart from the other side of the village. Joe nearly went home but he wouldn't let himself. To complete his misery it began to rain so he went up to the front door and banged hard with his fist.

After a short interval a light came on in the hall and then the door opened. Joe had never met Sadie Haversham. She was the granddaughter of Rowan and Bernard who had lived in what was now the ruined farm. Their daughter had not married but she had had this child illegitimately to one of the local land-owners, a rich, married man. The disgrace had torn the family apart. Sadie's mother was dead but she went on living in this house, apart from the village, occasionally giving in to the demands of various well-off men, presumably because she no longer had the means to support herself or the house without.

The pitmen called her various vile names when they spoke of her but Joe thought this was because they could not afford and would never have her. He did not remember her mother, other than the fact that she had carried on the same trade, taking up

126

with a wealthy man from time to time and the rest of the time brewing various potions and making spells as far as the villagers were concerned. Rumour had it that she could have married but never had.

Sadie opened the door. She was very pretty but all Joe saw was the surprise. He stood there, waiting.

'Why, Mr Forster,' she said. 'Come in out of the wet.'

Joe went inside. People always associated sluttishness with loose morals, he thought, but Sadie's hall was bare and clean and the sitting room she took him into gleamed with polish, smelled of flowers, was painted white and almost empty. A large fire burned in the grate. Logs. Joe was astonished. She lived in a pit village but she burned wood.

'Don't you have any coal?' he said.

'Is that what you came for, to sell me some coal?'

Joe turned from the fire. Sadie was not a skinny girl, she had the kind of figure which men loved, generous and curved and she had golden hair and large blue eyes.

'I just . . .' Joe said and then couldn't go on. He wanted to run out. This had never seemed like a good idea. It had seemed possible but now that he was standing in the house and Sadie was flesh and blood it made him feel dirty and stupid and low and all those things which Randolph had been that he had so despised.

'Why don't you come upstairs?'

Joe didn't want to but he went. It reminded him of the house which her grandparents had owned, where Dryden had gone and the stairs were falling through. The stairs here were solid and carpeted beneath his feet but they felt just as fragile to Joe. She took him into another bare room where there was nothing but a big bed, white sheets. Joe had never wanted a woman less in his life than he wanted her now.

Sadie put a match to the fire in the cold stillness and Joe listened to the rain and wondered how he had come to this.

'Would you like a drink?' she offered, indicating a row of decanters on a table in the corner.

'No, thank you.'

'Your father used to like a drink. Isn't it funny, you coming here to me like your father did to my mother?'

'Did he?' was all Joe managed.

'We had coal then, lots of it.'

'Do you remember him?'

'Quite clearly. He was very like you.'

This was the first time Joe had been likened to his father and it didn't please him and then he thought his father had believed Joe was not his son so it was strange.

'I'm said to favour my mother.'

'I didn't know your mother. She died long before I was born.'

'I can . . . I can send you as much coal as you want,' Joe said.

'Something told me you would,' she said. 'And what do you expect for it?'

'I think I might have a drink,' Joe said.

She went to get it and when Joe smelled the sour sweet fumes of the spirit he was reminded of Randolph drunk on Sunday mornings when Joe came back from church, one booted foot on the hearth and a glass, well used, in his hand, a coal fire roaring up the chimney and the rest of the house dirty and neglected and himself ignored and that was what he was doing here. He did not want to go back to being ignored again. It was the darkest area of his life and he couldn't stand it.

He wanted to kiss Sadie but he didn't think she might like to taste the alcohol and when she handed him the glass he looked at it and put it down.

'So, you're not like him,' she said.

'I hope not.'

'My mother was in love with him.'

'Was she?' Joe could not imagine anybody ever falling in love with Randolph.

'I think it was because of him that she never married.'

Joe couldn't think of anything to say to that. Sadie laughed.

'Don't worry,' she said. 'Lightning never strikes twice in the same place. If you tell me what you want I'll tell you whether you can have it.'

Joe considered.

'I want not to have to go back outside in the rain,' he said. He didn't say *I want not to have to sleep by myself. I want not to be here. I want not to have my wife shun me. I want not to have learned to hate my dearest friend because my wife wants him. I want Tommy not to be dead. I want everything to be different. I want to be some other man but this one who can't control himself when he has responsibilities. I want to be better but what I want most of all is you.*

'I want to kiss you and I want to have you,' he said.

She came to him and put her arms around his neck and Joe kissed her.

There had been a time when he had not imagined he would ever kiss a woman other than his wife. He could not believe now that they had been happy. Was it all an illusion? She had always wanted Dryden. How had he lived with that and why?

Sadie tasted fresh and sweet and he could not think why he had hesitated for so long. This was not difficult. He was not confused either, as he had thought he might be. She was nothing like Vinia or did his memory betray him and it was just that he was hungry, needy, not quite confident? Perhaps it was all the same thing. She had married him for who he was and he was paying Sadie. Maybe this always had to be paid for, one way or another, and that made it very much the same thing, trading favours, everybody selling something.

The more he kissed her, the nearer Joe wanted to get. It was like having a drink of water when you had thirsted for years. You needed more and more. There was also an element of novelty. It had been many years since Joe had touched a woman other than Vinia and he could not help enjoying that he did not know Sadie. Perhaps he was more like Randolph than he knew.

He liked the mystery of Sadie's body and that she did not draw back or hesitate. He kept waiting for her to do that or for a husband to walk in or for her to say that she did not like him or that he had to go or that she had to go, but she didn't. Joe took her to bed and had her and somewhere about it there was an element of revenge, a paying back to life for the way that he had been treated. He liked that it was a deal, that she was not going to get up and flounce out, that there were no complicated issues such as there usually were with other people. She would not object to what he did after they had agreed, he did not even have to worry about whether he was pleasing her. Nobody interrupted, nobody pushed him aside. She made no sound and Joe liked having her in the cool silence with only the noise of the wood fire, which crackled and shifted. The wood smelled sweet, of apples or pears, and even the grey smoke coming off it was pleasant.

From time to time rain fell down inside the chimney and altered the sound of the room and the wind raced about the house, which stood quite alone.

Joe, being a patient man, took his pleasure slowly, because even though he had touched no one in so long he was used to women and for years and years had had his wife's body readily available. He was not about to rush anything. He was aware that this might not, should not, happen again, so it ought not to have been his fault that he felt afterwards like an over-indulged child, a greedy man. He could not understand what had driven him here, but he only knew that when he was satisfied. It seemed so trivial and stupid, so disloyal. He had been unfaithful to his wife for the first time and it did not sit easily. It had taken a whore to make him understand that no matter what she did he would always love Vinia and that was worse somehow. He thought about leaving but he didn't want to. Sadie might have other ideas. He looked across the pillows at her.

'Do you let people stay?'

'Were you thinking I might turn you out into this?' The night had grown worse, as though the wind were throwing rain at the house. She gathered him into her arms.

'You can have coal for the next hundred years,' Joe said, settling himself against her.

She laughed. He liked her laughter. He remembered what it was like to sleep close against someone and then he was only aware of her near as he drifted off.

*   *   *

Vinia had not liked the storm. Long after she had gone to bed she lay awake, listening to it crashing around the house, and to the silence within. It always was silent at this hour, only the two of them in such a big place, but somehow it felt different tonight. She didn't understand why. She had grown used to being alone at night. At first it had been a relief because she did not want Joe to touch her. Tonight it was lonely, worse in the storm.

In the end she got up, put on a dressing gown, ventured across the landing and opened the door of what she still thought of as Joe's father's room. Somehow she was not very surprised when it was empty.

She had not been in there since they had started sleeping apart. There was not a thing out of place. The fire had died hours ago so Joe must have left in the middle of the evening. There must have been some reason for him to go back to the pit but no one had come for him that she had heard. Perhaps he had gone there on a whim and stayed. It didn't seem like him not to tell her that he was going out.

She sat down on the bed and waited while the storm raged but he did not come back. She didn't sleep as the rain lashed the dawn and when it was a respectable hour she went to the pit office but it was Sunday and nobody was there. She did not understand what was going on. Joe's office was empty and in its own way as clean and tidy as his bedroom. She was about to leave when Dryden appeared, papers in his hands.

'Vinny?'

'I thought Joe was here.'

Dryden opened his office door. She followed him inside. He put down the papers on the desk.

'Not that I'm aware of, unless he's below ground.'

Vinia returned to the house and there he was, making tea in the kitchen, since Sunday was Addy's day off.

'Wherever have you been?' she said.

Joe considered her briefly.

'Nowhere,' he said.

'But . . . you weren't in your room and then I went to the pit and you weren't there either.'

131

Joe looked almost amused.

'You went into my room? Whatever did you do that for, you haven't before now.'

'It was . . .' She felt the need to apologize. 'It was the storm. I couldn't sleep. Where were you?'

'What does it matter to you where I am?'

Joe sounded tired. She wanted to say of course it does, you're my husband, but it sounded too strong a claim. What he did was no longer her business. Joe was too much of a gentleman to say so but if she pushed him much further she felt he would. It was like being shoved into the sea in a boat that had no oars, as though Joe was standing on the shore, watching her. She realized that, no matter what, he had always looked after her, she had always come first. Joe had left her all night alone in a storm in a remote house on the fell. He was not thinking about her any more. He collected his tea and went off into the study and shut the door and Vinia could not think of a good enough reason to go after him.

Sixteen

B obbie had not thought she could be happy without Dryden. It was not the kind of happiness which knew no bounds, it was more the sort of thing which learned to be content with so much less. Some of it was increasingly difficult as the baby got bigger and she had to cope with the day-to-day business and the idea of giving birth and it was not as though Hector or John was of any help. Forbes was no help either but she had not expected it. He was, however, there when she got home at night and if it was late they would sit by the fire in her room and she would have something to eat and he listened to her problems and their marriage had improved everything between them, best of all she liked sleeping with him. It was good to turn over in the night and not be alone.

As time went on there was so much to do that occasionally Bobbie gave way to tears in the late afternoons. Knowing that she would need at least a few days off after the baby was born she tried to make certain the business was structured to go forward without her. In the autumn her body seemed to be becoming alarmingly large and she was aware of being clumsy and of everything taking longer to do and Forbes went into his own room to sleep so that she could have the bed to herself but they still sat together late in the evenings and talked.

Smith became increasingly frail as the weeks went by. At first he could not get up the stairs without help, though that wasn't a problem, Forbes carried him. Then he was uncomfortable in the night and wandered the floor. Then he stopped wanting to go for walks. He began to cry in his sleep.

'Don't you think he's in pain?' Bobbie said one June evening when Smith was lying by the fire in her room.

'I don't like to think of it.'

'I think he is.'

Forbes looked down at the old dog for a long time and then he said, 'Do you want me to shoot him?'

'Could you?'

'Sometimes we go out with the gun, just for rabbits.'

Bobbie didn't like to suggest to Forbes that he might not manage something so emotional.

'Terence could do it.'

'Smith would know then. He would sense something wasn't right and he's been a good friend to me. I don't want to let him down. I'll do it tomorrow.'

'Don't commit yourself. Just do it without thinking about it if you can.' She tried to distract him with talk of other things but he kept watching the dog as though Smith were about to disappear.

They went to bed and the next day she worked but she couldn't concentrate and in the end she drove home early, only to find that her father came hurrying along the hall as she walked in the front door. He drew her into the first room, the little sitting room.

'Forbes has gone completely off his rocker. He's locked himself in his bedroom and won't come out and won't let anybody in.'

'Let me talk to him.'

'He won't even talk to his father.'

'Is this because of Smith?'

'I don't know what it's because of. I would have shot the wretched dog for him if I'd known this was going to happen. He's absolutely completely mad. We'll have to have him put away.'

Bobbie walked slowly up the stairs. The hall was deserted. She banged on the door and called, 'Forbes, it's me, Bobbie. Let me in.'

There was no response.

'Forbes? Forbes?'

She waited but nothing happened and after saying his name several times she began to fear for what he could be doing and she ran downstairs and outside. There Terence was busy.

'What happened with Major Stillman and the dog? Did you see?'

Terence stood on his spade and considered.

'The Major, he pretended to the old dog they were going after rabbits and then shot him. I had the hole dug ready but he didn't come back. I heard the shot, I hung on and then I went up the wood and there he was, standing over the animal's body. He didn't say owt and when I talked to him he looked all funny at me. I carried the dog's body away and filled up the hole after it and the Major was still standing there. I couldn't talk to him. He wouldn't come into the house so I went to get Mr Stillman and your dad and they talked to him for ever so long but he wouldn't come in, he just stood there and then all of a sudden he went upstairs and into his bedroom and locked the door.'

'Can you break it down? I'm afraid as to what he might do.'

'Those doors are solid,' Terence said.

'Then get an axe.'

It took a long time for Terence to hack sufficient of the door away so that it gave, but when it did she realized she had been overly imaginative. Forbes had not done himself harm. He was standing by the fire and looked at her in surprise when she reached him, as though he had no idea she was there.

'Are you all right?'

'What?'

'You locked the door. I shouted and shouted,' Bobbie said. 'Didn't you hear me?'

He didn't answer, he just looked at her.

'I ought never to have let you do it,' Bobbie said.

Her father and his father came in and persuaded him downstairs. The evening progressed as though everything was normal but it was not, Bobbie knew. Forbes ate nothing at dinner, nor did he speak unless spoken to and even then it seemed an effort.

When he excused himself early and went to his room his father said to her father, 'He might have to go back to Dundee if he doesn't get better.'

'It could be just a temporary lapse,' John said.

'It doesn't look like a temporary lapse to me.'

Forbes would not sleep in her room though she urged him to, since his had a broken door, but in the middle of the night she thought she heard him moving next door and when she went through he was standing by the window with the curtains opened and was staring out into the garden. Moonlight flooded the room.

'I wish you would tell me what's wrong,' she said.

He turned slightly but said nothing and went back to contemplating the night. Bobbie went to him.

'Are you sad about the dog because he belonged to Charles?' she said.

'I can't believe he's dead and it's all over. It's all gone.'

Bobbie took his face in her hands and kissed him. Forbes moved away.

'Do you want me to stay with you?' Bobbie said.

'Stay with me?'

'Yes.'

'No.'

After that, although she went back to her room, because he didn't seem to want company, Bobbie didn't sleep and she knew, even though she wasn't in the same room with him, that he didn't sleep either. He was uncommunicative that day and the next. Bobbie could not understand, though seeing him without the dog was strange.

On the Friday, in the middle of the morning, Forbes came to her office. He rarely did such a thing and she was the more surprised that he should turn up now when he had been silent and withdrawn all week. She gave him tea but was so taken aback that she almost dropped her cup and saucer when Forbes announced, 'You seem to be doing all the work. I'm sure I could be of help.'

'Help?'

'Yes. You're . . . you're having a baby and . . .'

Bobbie looked into the clear brown eyes. She could not tell him that she thought he wasn't capable of it.

'It's been a difficult week,' she said. 'I know you were upset over the dog—'

Forbes interrupted her. It was the first time he had done so that she could think of since he had come home, or was it just the first time he did it abruptly?

'Men are dying in their thousands in France. I think we can forget the dog, don't you?'

Bobbie didn't know what to say.

'Look,' Forbes said, 'I'm planning to open up my father's office across town and the house—'

'The house?'

'You don't really want to go on living with those two old men, do you? I thought you might . . . prefer to live with me.'

His look was so direct that Bobbie stared.

'What will your father say?'

'I've already told him.' Forbes laughed. 'He said he had always known I should be put away. Have you time to come and look at the house?'

Bobbie was too astonished to tell him that she hadn't. Forbes ushered her out of the building and down to the car. He drove her across the town and within minutes they were going down the drive of his home. Bobbie had forgotten how large and imposing it was, stone, with pillars at the entrance, a big garden all around. Weeping willows swept the drive as the land fell away towards the river. Forbes unlocked the front door and Bobbie stepped inside. He followed. Their voices echoed in the hall. The staircase swept away to the upper reaches of the house.

She became excited at the idea of having a house of her own and it had no personality stamped upon it as theirs had, no pictures of dead people, no reminders of better days. A pale afternoon sun filtered through the floor-to-ceiling windows and as she stood in the drawing room she could see where the gardens went right down to the towpath and from upstairs she could see the cathedral across the river.

The furniture was draped with holland covers but as he went through the rooms Forbes pushed aside many of these and the rooms became places where his family had lived. In a way Bobbie wanted to move from Hector and her father but she was not sure she wanted to live alone with Forbes, especially when he was behaving so strangely, but she had no choice. She could not suggest to him anything which would have been acceptable. She wished that she could stop wanting to run away to Dryden Cameron. The man she had thought he was did not exist. She must learn to keep this in mind.

'I was hoping we might move next week,' he said.

'So quickly?'

'Why not?'

'And the business?'

'I'm going there now.'

She suggested she should go with him but Forbes said he didn't know what was needed and when he did he would ask her to come over and they would transfer back the work from her premises and the people he thought fit to help. She went to the factory but that was the first time she had gone home in the evening and he was not there. He was still at his new office across town.

They moved as he had promised and she didn't mind but she found that her days were constantly interrupted. He had not asked her to help with the business other than by sending the necessary files and paperwork and the people who were involved but he seemed to think she wanted to help in the day-to-day putting together of the house, things like hiring staff, seeing to the running of it, such as organizing shopping, cooking, meals, bedlinen, new curtains, cleaning.

'Forbes, I don't have time for any of this,' she told him when they had been in their house a fortnight and she was exhausted with detail.

They were sitting having dinner in their new dining room and she was beginning to think the move had been a bad idea. Forbes came home every night at half past seven and seemed to think everything should just happen.

'What do you mean, you don't have time for it?'

'I have a factory to run.'

Forbes looked down into his wine glass and then at her.

'You don't have my father's business to look after any more, at least you won't have, I'm going to take it all on over the next few weeks.'

This was true. To her surprise she had resented it and she thought other people resented it too. They had come to her with their concerns and complaints during the last fortnight and they were many. She told them it was just that Forbes was not used to business any more and it would take time. She did not dare to suggest he could not do it and she was unsure whether he could not or whether it was just that she had liked running it for herself.

'I have the factory.'

'You won't have for much longer.'

'What?'

'I have a very capable man in mind to take over the factory.'

Bobbie didn't think she heard much of what he said after that, she was so very angry with him. He didn't hear her anger or didn't choose to.

'He was invalided out of the war, lost a leg, but he has a fine mind on him, I always thought so, and you will be the better for knowing that somebody capable is taking over.'

'I don't want anybody to take it over. It's mine.'

'You have just told me that the house and the factory is too much for you,' Forbes said. 'How will you cope with the house, the factory and a baby?'

'I won't be coping with the house or the baby. We will have a housekeeper and a nanny and I will go back to the office.'

He looked at her.

'I don't think you will,' he said.

'What do you mean?'

'I mean I don't think you'll want to. You'll have enough to do.'

'It isn't a question of what there is to do, Forbes, it's a question of what I shall want to do and that factory is mine. I shall always want it and I don't think you should interfere and I certainly don't think you should put somebody else in my place. Only weeks ago you could scarcely manage to get up in the mornings and now you're trying to tell me what to do and everything has altered.'

'Everything has altered, you're right. I feel like somebody who has woken up from a nightmare. You won't need to worry about anything ever again. You can stay at home—'

'I don't want to stay at home—'

'But you will. I know that you will.'

'You have no right to try and make me do that.'

'You've got it wrong. I'm not trying to make you do anything.'

'It's my factory.'

'It's your father's factory. At least it is at the moment.'

Every sense shrieked at Bobbie.

'What do you mean?'

'He's having everything made over to me.'

'To you and not to me?'

'It's the same thing, surely. I'm hardly likely to run off and leave you destitute, am I? Don't you like the house? You don't seem very pleased.'

'I just . . . I just . . . I don't want you taking everything from me.'

'I'm trying to make things better.'

The pained look on his face reduced her to bitter amusement for a few moments.

'I didn't think we'd come to this,' she said.

Seventeen

B obbie had not felt threatened by anything in her life as she felt threatened by this coming child. It took all of her body, her energy and her imagination. She hated to admit to herself that Forbes had been right, she had very little to give to anything during the last two months of her pregnancy. She cursed Dryden Cameron a thousand times and most of all she wished he was there, that they were married. Sometimes she even wished she was waiting in a horrid little house in a pit row for him to come home to her.

She was terrified that the child would be brown-skinned and of how she would ever explain away such a result. She lay in bed alone night after night. Her body made her feel like an elephant or a whale and she was so uncomfortable that she was glad Forbes did not offer to join her – and she worried.

Bobbie had for some months played a game with herself that this child was Forbes's, that Dryden Cameron was nothing but a nasty dream and she did not want to talk about him or think what her life with him had been like. Everything had gone wrong and was out of control. She decided that if she had to she would send his child away. And then she thought of how his other child had died and it seemed a particularly cruel thing to do. Perhaps she could send it to him but then how would he explain it? Besides, she had told him she was not having his child and it seemed best that she should stick with her story.

In her weaker moments she prayed that the child would be light-skinned, that she would have no reason to send it away. If she was obliged to do something like that she knew she would never again have an easy moment.

During the last few weeks she became so tired that she could not work but it galled her to see the man Forbes had chosen to take her place at the factory. When she was introduced to Albert Martin she wished she could like him. He was calm, in spite of the limp, the stick and the artificial leg. He had been involved in such a factory before the war he told her and was glad to be going back into management. He smiled and told her that he would take care not to do anything which she would not like. Bobbie hated his smile.

During the final month she could hardly move for bulk and fatigue and her father joked and said was she sure it wasn't twins. Bobbie hoped fervently it was nothing of the kind but the doctor assured her that as far as he could tell it was one child and she had nothing to worry about, everything was normal. Bobbie thought he must tell every pregnant woman that, if only to reassure her.

She wanted to go to Dryden even more than usual and on several occasions almost set out to see him but each time she succeeded in stopping herself and she was glad because the day came when the pain began and after that she did nothing but curse him. She had not wanted this child, it had already caused her a great many problems and when she was in agony hour after hour she thought she was somehow being paid out for the sin of having gone to such a man in the first place. The labour went on for two days and it was the longest two days of Bobbie's life. She thought the sweat and effort and the being pregnant would never be over, that the child would never be born, and when it finally was and the doctor pronounced that the baby would be fine and so would she and the midwife showed the baby to her she was relieved to see that although it had a shock of dark hair her own bright blue eyes stared back at her and the baby had pale skin. She was rather disappointed to learn that it was a boy. She did not imagine that the man Forbes had become would let another man's child be his heir.

The baby, as far as she could judge, looked nothing like Dryden. None of its features resembled him in any way. When she was able she lay down and went to sleep, happy in the knowledge that he could make no claim to it and that it would no longer matter that she had married Forbes in such haste. Later he came to see her and to her astonishment he seemed delighted about the baby and kissed her on the cheek and wanted to pick the child out of its cot.

'What shall we call him? I think you should choose, you did all the hard work.'

'I don't know. Will your father expect the child to have his name?'

'You could bear to call him Hector?' and they both laughed. Their fathers were highly delighted the baby was a boy and they both wanted him to have their names but Hector had a better idea.

'My other name is Iain and since that's the Gaelic for John it would give him both our names,' he said.

For a moment she was inclined to tell them the truth, that the baby could not be the heir because he was nothing to do with the Stillmans at all, and she glanced at Forbes but he was not looking at her, nor did he say anything.

They had hired a nanny and a nursery nurse and she knew that she was lucky not having to deal with the baby all the time and for the first few weeks it was very pleasant being able to sleep and sit about recovering her strength but within a month she was ready to go back to work, tired of houses and babies and the trivia of domesticity.

She tried to talk to Forbes about it but he was never at home. He was always at the various department stores or in Yorkshire, visiting the mills, or seeing to a hundred different problems so that she envied him his work. He left early, was very often gone for two or three days at a time and came back late and, since he had no interest in the house or the child and these were at the time her only concern, they had nothing to talk about even when he did come home. It was early March, cold and windy, and she was restless.

'I want to go back to work,' she said after about six weeks – for at least the tenth time.

'There's no rush.'

'That's what you said last week and the week before. Have you given Mr Martin his notice?'

'I don't intend doing anything of the sort. He's a very good man.'

'I know he's a good man, Forbes, but he's in the way. That's my factory.'

'Ours.'

'Ours then.'

'He runs it very well.'

'I ran it very well and will again. Get rid of him.'

'I can't. He has a wife and family and he needs to be there.'

'I need to be there.' She got up from the supper table, unable to bear this any longer, but she only went as far as the fire.

'No, you don't,' Forbes said. 'You need to be here.'

'There's nothing to do here.'

'There's plenty to do. I don't like arguing with you and we've been through this several times. We are married, you've had a child, we have a huge house and it would be very nice if I could come home and be comfortable in it.'

'You are comfortable.'

'No, I'm not. You're chafing at the bit to get back to the factory and everything is suffering. Those lamb chops tonight tasted like leather.'

'There is a war on, Forbes.'

'I had noticed. A lot of men returning injured have no jobs. Do you think women should take the ones there are?'

'This is slightly different, surely.'

'Is it? It doesn't look different to me. Forgive me, but Albert Martin runs the factory better than you did and if you can't see it then you should.'

Bobbie was so enraged she could hardly speak.

'In what way does he do that?' she said.

'He's less sentimental, he makes people do as they're told, do their jobs. It's going very well. We're turning out more work than we've ever done. I don't want to be disparaging about what you did but this is efficiency at work.'

'Really?' Bobbie said.

'Don't be cross. He is the right man for the job.'

'You must get rid of him. I want to go back to work next week.'

'I'm afraid I can't do that.'

'Then I shall go to my father.'

'That won't do you any good.'

He was right. Bobbie went home. She wanted to weep. She could look back now and see how pleasant her life had been when Forbes was a different sort of a man. It had been so much easier. Her father was of very little help and said that there was nothing he could do.

'The business belongs to you and Forbes and you are married. You must sort it out between you. I can't get involved. His father is very pleased with his progress. He's almost back to his old self.'

This was true, Bobbie thought. It was especially true that evening when he came to her room. She was sitting at her dressing table, not doing anything, just fuming over his stubbornness and the injustice of it all and he walked in. He hadn't done that since before Iain was born and she did not welcome him now.

'I gather you went to see your father,' he said.

'I'm surprised you noticed. You don't seem to have time for anything these days.'

Forbes came up behind her, she could see him in the mirror, and he put his hands on to her shoulders and then he leaned over and kissed her on the neck. Bobbie jumped up and moved away. She reached the side of the bed and sat down. Then she looked up into Forbes's brown eyes.

'Wherever did you go?' she said. 'You used to be kind.'

'I can be kind now.'

'No, you're not. You're just like you used to be.'

'I shall never be like I used to be, more's the pity,' he said and sat down beside her and then lay down. He did nothing more. It unnerved Bobbie. She didn't move for a long time nor look at him and nobody said anything. She felt as though his eyes were boring holes in her back but the second she tried to get up he pulled her down and that was the first time she had been afraid of him. She turned away as best she could, considering he was watching her.

'I'm sorry you don't like me. Look at me.'

Bobbie did, though she could not see him for tears.

'You didn't care about Smith,' she said.

He looked patiently at her for a few moments and then he said, 'Bobbie, I don't remember Smith, not as an old dog.' He let go of her and moved away slightly. Bobbie sat up.

'What do you mean, you don't remember him?'

Forbes didn't answer for a few seconds and then he said, 'All I remember was the shot. I didn't know we were married, I didn't know I was living here. All I remember is the war and then the shot.'

Bobbie stared at him.

'Why didn't you tell me?'

'You didn't like me. I couldn't remember what I had been like but whatever I had been like you preferred it. And then I discover we're married.'

Bobbie went on staring and then she said, 'Oh God.'

'Well, say something else,' he insisted. 'Say it's funny or . . . say something,' and when she didn't he got up. 'It is funny, isn't it? You and me married.' He didn't laugh and neither did Bobbie. 'It's difficult when you don't like me.'

'And do you like me?'

He hesitated but it was only manners she thought and his honesty overcame that.

'No, not much,' he said, 'but there's the baby.'

And then it dawned on Bobbie. He thought the child was his. She was tempted to explain everything but somehow she couldn't. She couldn't do any more than sit there, trying to take in the situation.

'You told me you had fallen in love with me when I was eighteen. Do you remember that?'

'I remember you at eighteen but that was nothing special. Everybody was in love with you and it's a long time ago. I always thought of you like a . . . like a sister,' Forbes said and winced. 'I haven't always thought so, apparently.'

'Or now,' she said. 'Coming into my room like that.'

'What would you like me to do? We are married. I don't have much choice. I feel as if I haven't . . . touched anybody in forever. I couldn't believe it, those two dreadful old men and that awful house of yours with those naked marble statues everywhere and pictures of your mother and . . . I couldn't bear it, and the way they'd left you to struggle on with a mountain of work. Miserable old buggers. At least I'm getting the work right.' He glanced at her. 'You look awfully tired. I'm sorry, I didn't mean to frighten you or to tell you any of this but you keep looking at me like I'm Attila the Hun and I get so confused. I don't really want to go to bed with you. I just want to go to bed with somebody,' and Forbes walked out and slammed the door after him.

Sleep never came near. She tried to work out what to tell him but she couldn't decide and the following day she had a visitor and that made things worse. She was lying half asleep by the fire, having not slept the night before, and Freya came in softly, touching her on the arm and saying, 'I've got a gentleman outside. Mr Cameron.'

Bobbie's first instinct was to say that she wouldn't see him, to run upstairs and get Freya to tell Dryden she was not there. It wouldn't do, he was in the hall and she had nothing to be afraid of, so when Freya ushered him into the drawing room she was surprised and apprehensive to find that he was not the person she had kept in her mind. Somehow she had built up a picture of a person who was between the devil and her husband but the moment Dryden stepped into the room she remembered how much she had loved him, why she had fallen in love with him. It made her want to behave stupidly and cry. How could she have given this man up? How could any woman give him up? He stood there with his hat in his hands in the middle of her drawing-room floor and said in his sweet soft voice, 'I went to the factory. I thought you might have gone back to work.'

Bobbie was half inclined to tell him what had happened but she couldn't.

'I know I shouldn't have come,' Dryden said, 'but I heard

nothing about the baby or you and I was worried and I heard a rumour that you had had a little boy—'

'He's not yours,' she heard herself say. Who was this awful deceitful woman? She saw his eyes and almost wished she hadn't said it.

'Can I see him?'

'He's asleep.'

'Please.'

How did a man know when a child was his, Bobbie wondered, other than ordinary distinguishing traits? How did he know? And if she went on saying that the child was Forbes's son and she was married to Forbes and he acknowledged it, there was nothing this man could do, or would his unreliable sixth sense do the rest? She led him upstairs to the nursery and then it was like magic. The moment Dryden leaned over the cot the child opened his eyes and without asking, as though he had done it a hundred times, Dryden picked the baby up out of the bedclothes and into his arms and he held the baby away from him so that they looked into one another's eyes and the child reached out his arms. Bobbie told herself that the baby was too little to distinguish anyone, recognize anything, and it was just reflexes, but it did seem to her that the child saw him, knew him. Dryden drew the child near and kissed him on the forehead and smiled at him and said comforting words and for the first time Bobbie thought what it would really have been like had they been married. She had taken this man's child from him when he had no one. All Dryden said when he put the baby back down was, 'You're right, he doesn't look anything like me. What do you call him?'

'Iain.'

'It's a good Scottish name.'

He lingered there as though he were loath to go, as though he might imprint upon his memory the long lashes over the pink cheeks, the dark hair, the perfect mouth, the tiny fingers, and then he said, 'I must go. I have to get back to work.'

They walked slowly down the stairs and he complimented her

on the house and when they reached the hall he said, 'When are you going back to the factory?'

'I don't know. Forbes has put a manager in.'

'People say Major Stillman is a lot better.'

'He's certainly recovered,' she said.

'I'm so pleased. Thank you for letting me see Iain. I hope things go well for you,' Dryden said and he left.

Eighteen

In the days that followed Dryden's visit Bobbie couldn't rest. She had nothing to say to Forbes but she imagined he did not notice since he came home only to sleep and then she went to bed early and locked her door. He did not mention it and she was glad of that. Within the week she went to the factory for the first time in almost five months and was appalled at the difference.

There was no sound other than the sewing machines on the main floor. The girls and women had their heads down and nobody spoke as she walked across the front of the room and into the offices. Phyllis was not in the outer office. Inside she could see Albert Martin. He too was hard at work. He got up with difficulty when she walked in, apologizing for his clumsiness.

'Where's Phyllis?' Bobbie asked him.

'Mrs Machin doesn't work here any more. We had a disagreement, not the kind of person we need in a place like this.'

Phyllis had worked there from the beginning, had been kind and taught Bobbie almost everything she knew. Bobbie could remember the quick smile, the eagerness and Phyllis's wedding. She tried not to think about that.

'Mr Stillman is pleased with the progress we are making,' Mr Martin said.

'It's very quiet in there.'

'People work better when they concentrate.'

'And when they are cold and wet?'

'What?'

'The roof appears to be leaking in the main entrance and the stove has gone out. In this weather these things appear to me of vital importance.'

'It will be fixed.'

'I'm sure it will and I shall come back to make certain it is.'

Bobbie left without speaking to any of the girls. She was ashamed. She drove to Deerness Law, trying not to think how things had been, how young and in charge and unencumbered she had been. Phyllis lived in the end house of Prince Row. Bobbie banged on the door and soon Phyllis answered and was so overcome that she cried. Bobbie hugged her and went in. It was lovely in there, the fire burning in the kitchen, the range shining, and Phyllis had just made scones so they sat over the kitchen fire and ate them, thick with butter, and drank three cups of tea each.

'You should have come to me,' she told Phyllis.

'What was the point? I couldn't work with that man.'

'And you haven't found another job?'

'I'm going to apply to the munitions factory. The thing is . . . we just lost a bairn so I'm taking it easy for a few days.'

Bobbie hugged her and said how sorry she was but she thought it showed how far apart they had grown that Phyllis had gone through such an important loss and she hadn't even known about it. Phyllis asked about her own baby.

'Thriving but you know me, I'm desperate to get back to work.'

'It's not the place it was and that Mr Martin, he's like something out of Dickens, shouting at people and ordering them about. If it wasn't war work I think a lot of them would have left. Mind you, it's got to be better than the munitions factory, but we all have to do our bit, don't we? Do you think it'll ever be over, Miss Bobbie?'

Bobbie was still there when Tan came home at tea time, she hadn't realized it was so late. He scowled at her. Bobbie wasn't sure whether the scowl was for the loss of Phyllis's job or just because he was tired and hungry. Bobbie tried to leave but Phyllis ushered her into the front room while she made the tea. Tan, clean and changed, came in there and it was obvious that his wife had made him be polite. He fairly glowered.

'How's the pit?' Bobbie asked him.

'Unlike the factory we have a good manager.'

'I know.'

'Do you? Mr Martin said things to my Phyllis that a man shouldn't say to a woman, nasty disrespectful things. Do you know what I think? I think he's the kind of person who likes to put his hands up women's frocks.'

Bobbie went on looking into Tan's honest set face, but with difficulty.

'He what?'

'Oh aye, he does. If he'd laid a finger on my Phyllis I would have knocked his brains out but other lasses they put up with it.'

'Phyllis didn't tell me that.'

'She wouldn't, would she? There's nowt you can do about it, being married to the major and all that. Pitmen are like muck, eh?'

'What?'

Tan flushed, realizing, she thought, that he had said too much and been rude.

'Nowt.'

'I'd rather hear what you think.'

'I don't think you would and it's not my place.'

'No, please.'

Tan's blue eyes were almost fiery.

'I've lived a few doors away from Mr Cameron for almost as long as I can remember. This was my dad's house. His wife's been dead fifteen years or more and in all that time I never saw him court a lass. He never led any woman to believe that he would do her down or gave her to think that he might want her when he didn't.'

'There was a good reason for that.'

'Was there? Sleeping on your own is a cold sort of thing. I know, I did it for years before I married Phyllis.'

'I couldn't marry him.'

'Him being a gyppo and all that? He saved Mr Forster's life, you know, years ago down the Prince, and every time there's an accident or somebody not well he's always first there.'

'But his wife—'

'Oh aye, I know. She was a stunner, I mean really, but the coldest bitch on earth. She never cared about him. She wanted Mr Forster. She got Mr Cameron to wed her on account of a bairn and then she treated him like muck.'

Bobbie was angry and on her feet.

'You would say that.'

'And Mrs Forster, she was no better than you. You—'

'Tan Machin, shut up!' his wife declared from the door as she came in bearing a tea tray. 'Don't you speak to Mrs Stillman like that. I could hear you from the kitchen. Don't you have any manners?'

Tan went bright red and then there was silence.

'I won't stay, thank you, Phyllis,' Bobbie said.

'Now look what you've done,' Phyllis said to him. 'We never have visitors and it's no wonder, you going on at them like a schoolteacher.'

Even in his confusion Tan said, 'It isn't right. He's got nowt,' and then he walked out.

Bobbie listened to the clash of the back door.

'Eh, I'm ever so sorry,' Phyllis said.

Bobbie stayed just long enough to down a cup of tea because Phyllis had made it and insisted. By the time she got outside it was dark and she could see the light burning in Dryden's house. She was going to get into her car and go straight home but she didn't. She crept up the yard and tried the back door and it was not locked, it was never locked.

He didn't hear her. He was in the kitchen, had just come in from work, and she could see him through the yard window, standing in front of the range, boiling the kettle. She didn't even say his name but he sensed she was there and turned around. All he said was, 'Why, Bobbie . . .' and pleasure suffused his face.

'I was . . . I came to see Phyllis.'

'Would you like some tea?'

'I've had about six cups since I got here and then I had a row with Tan.'

'A row?'

'He's very defensive of you.'

'He would be. He thinks I'm just lower than Jesus.'

That made her laugh.

'You are,' she said. 'You save people.'

'Hell!' Dryden said and then he made the tea and she watched him and she could understand how the small ceremonies of life got people through. 'Sit down.' He pulled out a chair at the table for her and Bobbie sat. And then in spite of the fact that she didn't want any he poured tea into white cups. They had pink roses on them.

'These are very pretty,' she said.

'Esther Margaret's best china. We never used them. I'm always breaking stuff, so we're down to that.'

'Dryden . . .'

'No, don't say it. Tan is . . . he's like that and none of it matters. You were right about me, I'm not . . .' and then he stopped and looked down at his tea as though somebody had put salt in it.

Bobbie never knew afterwards how she sat still. That was when she knew with a kind of hard, grinding realization that Tan Machin was right but the truth was the same. She could never have married this man. She would have lost everything and learned to hate him. She did not want to come here and be his wife in this dirty insular little village. There was no room here for somebody like her and he could not have led her life, nobody would have accepted him.

'I don't believe you were untrue to me,' he said. 'I know why you say it, I understand that, but I don't think you would do such a thing. I don't think you would do it to Major Stillman either . . .'

'He's changed,' she said, 'he's just like he used to be.'

'None of us is like we used to be,' Dryden said.

'Maybe not but he's . . .' She didn't say any more. It wasn't fair to talk ill of the man she had chosen in front of the man she had given up and he didn't look as if he wanted to hear it.

'The baby is lovely,' he said and smiled almost to himself.

'I could bring him to see you sometimes.'

'Could you? I would like that.'

'I must go. Thank you for the tea.'

Dryden told her that it was a pleasure and Bobbie could not resist touching his mouth with her lips when she got to the door and then she walked rapidly down the yard in the fading dusk and out into the back lane.

Nineteen

V inia tried not to think about Joe's absence from the house but she became aware that quite often he was not there at night. She made the mistake one May night of walking into his room and finding him fully dressed.

'Something the matter?' Joe said.

'No. No, it's just . . . it's late. I wondered if you had gone to bed.'

Joe didn't answer that, like he was waiting for her to leave, and Vinia let loose in her head a thought she had not dared to allow before this.

'Are you . . . is there somebody else?'

He didn't answer that either.

'Are you having an affair?'

She waited for him to deny it, to offer some kind of reasonable explanation so that she wouldn't need to worry.

'Joe?' she said finally and then she went nearer. 'You are, aren't you?'

'I don't have anybody else, at least not like that.'

'Not like what?'

'That I care about.'

'Then what are you doing?'

She was very close now and panicking.

'Talk to me, Joe, tell me.'

'Why?' Joe turned to her. 'You've hardly spoken in months and as for coming near me . . .'

He made for the door and she thought she was right, he had been waiting for her to go to bed. She followed him down the stairs.

'Where are you going? Joe.'

She ran outside after him. It was foggy and raining.

'Don't leave me here, please.'

Joe stopped. It was wet fog with icy fingers. He stood patiently until she stopped pleading with him and then he said, 'I'm going to somebody who puts up with me, that's all. It's not important.'

'Somebody who puts up with you?' She gazed into his green eyes. 'I don't understand.'

Joe avoided looking at her.

'Sadie Haversham,' he said.

Vinia thought she had gone mad and was hearing things. Either that or Joe had gone mad. Her husband, her clever fastidious husband, went to a whore?

'But . . .' She wanted to claim him for hers, tell him he couldn't do such things. 'You pay Sadie Haversham to go to bed with you?'

Joe was looking at her now. She wasn't sure she didn't prefer it when he looked the other way.

'I do, yes.'

Vinia ached to cry but somehow she couldn't.

'Much?' she said brightly.

'Yes. She's very expensive.'

Expensive. And Vinia thought, yes, she would be, young and pretty, able to pick and choose, but Joe was a pit owner, he could afford to bed a whore like that and why shouldn't he? His wife didn't want him. Was that what their marriage meant to him? He couldn't have her and fidelity and loyalty didn't matter, all that mattered to him was his body's urges?

'How could you do such a thing?' she said.

'Oh, it was easy,' he said. 'She was burning wood on her fires. Can you imagine that? But she doesn't any more. She has good Black Prince coal.'

Vinia hit him. It was the closest she could get to hitting herself, which was what she wanted to do. Joe didn't move. She was the one who cried. He stood there as though nothing had happened, and all around them the fog created strange shadows in the darkness.

'Please don't go,' she said.

'There's no point in pretending, Vinia,' he said. 'You've spent years and years putting up with me—'

'I never did!'

'You always did. I don't understand why you haven't left me, especially after everything that's happened. If you want to go, now I've given you the perfect excuse. We could be divorced. It is adultery. I'll take the blame. It's my fault.'

Vinia waited for him to be the person he used to be and offer comfort but he didn't. He stood while she cried and by the time she had stopped he was gone.

Sadie was the perfect person for him, Joe thought. She didn't care about him, so there was nothing to be lost. She seemed to like having him there though he couldn't be sure of that since he felt she would be like that with every man she let into her house. It was a very warm house these days. He had lied to Vinia. Sadie was cheap to him because he paid her in coal. It came straight out the pit so it didn't cost him much, being his to start with, but if she had had to buy it conventionally it would have cost a lot more. No money exchanged hands so there was no awkwardness. The only rule was that he could be there on Wednesdays and Sundays, no other time. Joe didn't mind that. He had no wish to encounter other men on Sadie's doorstep.

There was no evidence of anyone else and while you were there you could imagine there was only you but Joe was aware it was not so. Sadie lived well within the walls of her house, she wore expensive clothes, ate good food and kept the kind of whisky he liked though he still didn't drink much. Sometimes they drank tea together like they were an old married couple and he and Vinia did nothing together.

He wasn't really surprised when she found out, he wanted her to, so that she would know how far things had gone, how much they had lost, but he also resented her knowing because he had no intention of stopping going to Sadie's. It was the one area of his life that he enjoyed. His work was too hurried and fraught these days, the war cast its darkness over everything, and he was overworked and his friendship with Dryden had ceased and the food shortages were getting to everybody.

By now so many families had lost somebody and yet the war showed no signs of being over, it went on and on like a nightmare you couldn't wake up from. Sadie was the only relief. Joe went there gladly, casting off the problems of his life in Sadie's arms. Now however it was a problem itself. He could not shake off the image of Vinia standing in the fog outside their house. He worried about whether she was crying, about how upset she had been. How had he thought she might not be?

When it got light he went home. She was sitting in the kitchen with a cup of tea, over the stove, her eyes red from crying and not sleeping. As Joe came into the kitchen she looked up.

'I'm going to leave you,' she said.

'Leave me?'

'Yes. It's obviously what you want and I don't want to stay here where I'm not wanted.'

It had not occurred to Joe that his wife might walk out.

'I never wanted you to leave,' he said.

Vinia got up.

'The flat above the shop is empty. I'll go and live there.'

'You would hate it.'

'And you think I don't hate this?'

Joe couldn't think what to say or do and before he got any further Vinia went upstairs. He didn't follow her. He didn't want to watch her packing. He couldn't think of a single thing that would help.

Twenty

B obbie told Forbes that she wanted Albert Martin removing. She told him one May night over supper. She had tried to be civil and he ignored what she said. Their evening meal had got later and later because Forbes was too busy to come home. He seemed to think she was being funny when she told him.

'I went there,' Bobbie said. 'He's dismissed Phyllis – you didn't tell me about that . . .'

'I didn't know . . .'

'You should have known . . .'

'I can't know everything. I don't think I would recognize the woman,' Forbes said, throwing down his napkin as though he had anticipated this and was about to get up and walk out.

'The women are miserable. There's no heating, no light. They aren't allowed to talk. It's like Bleak House.'

Forbes looked at her.

'They're turning out more and better work than they've ever done—'

'I want you to get rid of him. How many times do I have to say it?'

She was glaring down the table. Forbes regarded her steadily and then he said, 'No.'

'Then I will.'

'You can't. You don't have the authority. He has a contract. The only person who can get rid of him is me and I don't want to.'

Bobbie was so frustrated that she threw the gravy boat at him. She realized the second she had done it that it was a completely stupid mindless thing to do. The gravy flew every-where, including all over the tablecloth. The gravy narrowly missed Forbes, the gravy boat missed him by yards but he got out of his chair and came to her and pulled her up out of her seat in a way that made her heart pound. He put her against the wall and it was just this side of violence. Bobbie thought she had never been so frightened. He didn't do anything else. For a moment he looked like the man she had known and then he ran.

She stood, breathing carefully for a few moments, and she laughed at the idea of the gravy boat and a tear ran down her cheek and then she went after him, out of the door and down the garden towards the river. Thomas Maugham's words came back to her and she was afraid that Forbes might do something to himself.

It was almost summer. The night was mild and not dark. He had left the front door ajar. She ran down the garden path, which led to the towpath, amidst trees and lawns. There the lights from other people's houses threw yellow baubles upon the water and the old buildings were comfortingly the same as she remembered them. He was not there. She went out of the gate at the bottom on to the towpath and walked along a little way and then she jumped, as he said from behind her, 'Don't worry, I haven't thrown myself in, or do you wish I would?'

She turned around and there he was in the shadows.

'I thought you were a good swimmer,' was all she could think of.

'I am. I'd have to weight my pockets with stones and—'

'Don't. It isn't funny.'

'No? I was amazed when I found myself back here, married to you, being treated like an idiot, and worst of all I have the feeling that you quite liked me out of my mind.'

'You weren't out of your mind.'

'I was completely lost,' he said. 'You have no idea how you look at me across the table, like I was . . . I hate it here. I hate everything in this bloody horrible world. I wish I was dead!'

'No . . .'

'All my friends are dead. Porky . . .'

161

'Porky? When?'

'I found out today. They're all dead and I'm . . . making uniforms for them, making uniforms for people to die in.'

Bobbie went nearer and tried to touch him and he swung away. Thomas Maugham was dead. He and Lottie had not been married. Perhaps they should have been. People should be together. And then something occurred to her.

'There's been somebody else, hasn't there?'

'What?'

'You are or have been in love with somebody else.'

'No.' Forbes shook his head.

'Forbes, you have.'

He stood for a few moments, and she could hear the sound of the river and nothing more, and then he said, 'There was a girl in France. Her husband came home. She thought he was dead. Funny, isn't it, all those people . . . but he came home and she – she couldn't leave him, not after that. I had forgotten all about her.'

'And then you were married to me.'

'I couldn't think of us . . . but we must have, mustn't we? I thought when I had a child I would know.'

Bobbie never knew afterwards why she did not tell him. She opened her mouth to do so but the sound would not come out, she was too worried, too suspicious. What might Dryden do then and she would lose her home and the factory and . . . it was not as if Forbes had anybody any more but she felt guilty and deceitful and low.

'I'm going to the factory tomorrow,' she said. 'I'm going to take it back for mine and you must do what you please,' and she turned and walked back to the house.

'Mr Stillman is going to find you something else to do.'

Bobbie was sitting in what she always thought of as her office but Albert Martin was still behind the desk, looking at her not as she had thought he would but with fear.

'I have a wife and three children, Mrs Stillman, and one leg. I can't afford to lose my job.'

'You're not losing your job,' Bobbie said. 'You're a very competent manager.' She didn't think he was a competent manager at all but she had to say this to him because she knew that if the company got rid of him he would have difficulty in finding anything else. She didn't know what job Forbes would give him, it would have to be a desk job, the man couldn't walk very far.

'Major Stillman told me I was making a good job of this, that he was pleased with me.'

'You aren't losing anything,' she said. 'We'll work together for a few days and then Mr Stillman will find you something better suited to your capabilities.'

She had the roof fixed. The weather was good so she did not have to worry about the heating but she had that seen to and she went about, chatting to the girls. She thought the atmosphere of the place lifted immediately.

She went to Deerness Law and saw Phyllis, who was pleased and promised to start that week. It was the middle of the day and Dryden would not be at home. There was no sign of life coming from his house and she made herself not go to the pit, though she very much wanted to see him.

When she got home halfway through the evening, pleased with her day's work, Forbes was waiting for her in the sitting room.

'I've had Albert Martin to see me. You can't dismiss him just like that, you had no right to do it.'

'I had every right,' Bobbie said. 'It was obvious you weren't going to do anything and since you won't listen to me I had no alternative. If you can't find him anything else then pay him off and be done.'

'Is that how you think it is?' Forbes said, glaring at her across the room. 'That man risked his life and gave up his chance of ever being able to work properly again and that's all you have to say because you aren't happy doing what other women do?'

'I've never been able to do what other women do.'

'Now's your chance.'

'I don't want it.'

Her words echoed around the room.

'You never listen,' she said. 'Find him an office job some-where else.'

'And put another man out of work?'

'What are you going to do, Forbes, save the whole world?'

There was silence again and a very strange expression came into his eyes and he said, 'Isn't that what men do in war, they try to save the world? It's an old military tradition, dying for your country, at least giving your legs for it and then coming home and having somebody tell you that it was all very well you offering to die for your country but you aren't entitled to live decently in it when you're one of the lucky ones and come back?'

'That's not fair!'

'Well done!' he said. 'How mature. I am not going to move Albert Martin. If you must then work alongside him . . .'

'I don't want him near the women.'

'What?'

'He touches them.'

A bitter smile reached Forbes's face.

'I don't think you need to worry. The nature of Albert Martin's injury means he is of very little use to a woman, rather like the rest of us really.'

He had gone so pale she thought he was going to faint.

'It isn't my child, is it?' he said.

Taken aback by this Bobbie stared at him, cursed herself, tried to think.

'It isn't, is it?' he said again.

'No.'

'We've . . . never been to bed together, have we?'

'No.'

Bobbie found the floor fascinating.

'You knew,' she said. 'I didn't try and hide anything from you.'

'I was prepared to house another man's child?'

'Yes.'

'How very benevolent of me. It's one thing giving a man a job when he comes back from the war, it's quite another to extend apparent paternity to his child. I'm supposed to make this boy my heir when he's nothing to do with me?'

'We didn't know it would be a boy.'

'But you knew I didn't remember any of these . . . details? And it's obvious that my father doesn't know and that your father doesn't know. Can you imagine if they did? Why didn't you marry its father?'

'The baby isn't an "it",' Bobbie said, almost in tears. 'I'm sorry. I was trying to protect him.'

'From what?'

'From you rejecting him. You knew all about the baby. It was your idea we should get married.'

'My God, I must have been the perfect person. I didn't bother you in the bedroom, I gave my name to your bastard, I was like a little lap dog, wasn't I?'

'You were a very nice man, not like you are now!' Bobbie declared and would have walked out except that he got hold of her and turned her to him.

'You will stay here and be a good mother and Albert Martin will run the factory. If you don't I will tell your father about the child. I will denounce it as somebody else's and after that I daresay we will find a good home for it. As for the man who got so very close to you when other people have tried, he can be dealt with. It all rests in your hands, you see. Now we will go in to dinner in civilized fashion, since I think I just heard the gong. I'm very hungry, aren't you? You must be after such a hard day's work,' and he grasped her by the arm and propelled her across the hall and into the dining room.

Twenty-One

V inia moved into the flat above the shop. The place had been a shoe shop before she rented it and when the owner had died she had bought the premises so it was no difficulty except that it was tiny, she wanted to cry when she realized what she had done. Worst of all Joe did not try to stop her, beyond talking to her. She could not understand how she had got to this dreary little place from the big house on the fell where she was the pit-owner's wife. Here she was a small shopkeeper, an entirely different level of society, and although Joe never made anything of who he was and did not especially court the local businessmen and landowners she was acutely aware of what she had done. He didn't stop her from taking anything either but there was the old man's furniture left upstairs and, uncomfortable though it was, she stubbornly took nothing beyond her own clothes, her books and one or two ornaments which had been her mother's.

People looked askance at her when she ventured out. She was in no doubt it was all over the village that she had left Joe. Women in pit villages didn't do such things but that was mainly because they had not the means, she had no doubt many of them had cause through drunkenness, brutality or unfaithfulness. In vain did he assure her that he was not in love, that she was all he cared about.

She could not prevent herself from feeling low that first night when she looked around, most of her belongings still packed and the unfamiliar sounds of the street startling her. She had not thought how quiet their house was. Some young men were yelling beyond her kitchen window. She tried to be construc-

tive. She made some tea which went cold. She couldn't eat.
Halfway through the evening there was a banging on the door
and she ventured down the stairs and there stood Dryden on the
doorstep.

'What in the hell are you doing here?' he said.

Vinia could have told him to go away but somehow they were
halfway upstairs before she drew breath. He looked around at
the two small rooms and then at her.

'What is going on?' he said.

'I've left Joe.' Vinia tried to maintain her composure. 'Who
told you?'

'Vinny,' his look was all patience and concern. 'Everybody
knows. You're here, you've moved in.'

'Did Joe tell you?'

'We don't speak, not unless it's about a pit matter. We
haven't had a proper conversation in months. We aren't friends
any more. I saw Em.'

Em Little had tried to talk her into going back.

'You can't leave him there on his own, Vinny, you just can't.'

This had not been the comfort she was expecting.

'He doesn't want me any more.'

'That's impossible. He's always loved you.'

'He has somebody else.'

Vinia had assured herself that those words would never pass
her lips, her pride would not allow it but his reaction was
everything it should have been. His dark eyes widened in
disbelief and the look of surprise and horror on his face set
as though it were frozen.

'What?'

'He goes to bed with Sadie Haversham.'

'Sadie Haversham?'

'You know her, surely.'

'Joe's sleeping with her? How could you let things get this
far?'

'I don't know. I don't know what happened,' Vinia said and
turned away to hide the tears. 'Plenty of men do it, I know they
do, and their wives . . . their wives put up with it but . . . I can't.

He leaves me alone at night in that house and goes to her. I can't stay there in circumstances like that and he won't give her up. Even though he knew that I knew what he was doing he still went to her.'

Dryden didn't say anything to that. He wandered about the tiny sitting room, like a dog at a fair as her father would have said, and from below she could hear the boys shouting in the street. Would she ever get used to it after the silence of the fell?

'Would you like me to talk to Joe?'

'Won't that make it worse?'

'Could it be worse?'

There was nobody at home when Dryden reached the house on the fell late that evening and he didn't feel he could go to Sadie's house. Joe sent a message with Addy the next day to Dryden's office saying that he wasn't well, but Addy stood in the offices, lips thin and said, 'Told me to go and not come back, he did, just like he was his dad. That's the first time he's spoken to me like that, Mr Cameron, in all the time I've worked for him.'

Dryden tried to say the right things to her and when he had time, late that morning, he went again to Joe's house but there was no reply. After that he went to Sadie's. It was the middle of the day by then and Sadie was standing outside her house on the grass, pegging out washing. It was a lovely day, Dryden thought, the heat mist above the valley. There was something about this house, Dryden thought, that reminded him of his time at the farm, or what he thought his time there had been. Some of the smells from the garden, roses, vegetables and clean clothes on the line, were so much the same that it made him feel uncomfortable.

'Is he here?'

Sadie turned, peg in hand, and did not choose to misunderstand him.

'And what would he be doing here at this hour?' she said.

'He is though, isn't he?'

Sadie looked at him again. Dryden met her eyes.

'Do you still go to my grandmother's house?' she said.

How did Sadie know he had been there?

They went inside and it was even more alike in here, with the scent of fresh bread, the homemade wine bubbling, clean rooms, bare and white. Sadie made as if to stop him going further and then didn't. All the doors and windows were open to the heat. Dryden made his way up the stairs, pushed open the bedroom door and there was Joe, lying asleep on a big white double bed, wearing shirt and trousers. Dryden felt a rush of sympathy, it reminded him so much of the day when Vinia had come to him and he was like this and had given up.

Joe's fair hair was like a yellow storm against the white pillow. He awoke and turned over, gazing at Dryden as though he didn't quite know him, his green eyes almost black they were so dark.

'You drunk?' Dryden offered.

Joe considered, eyes narrowed, mouth pursed up. He nodded.

'I would say . . . yes, pretty much.'

'You idiot.'

Joe went on regarding him steadily and then turned on to his back and looked at the ceiling.

'What does it matter?' he said. 'My wife's left me.'

'I saw her.'

'Of course you did. She ran to you.'

'No, she didn't,' Dryden said, irritated. 'She left you because you were bedding Sadie, you complete and utter fool. She's living above the shop. How can you let her?'

'It was her decision,' Joe said, sitting up and looking around and then finally locating what he wanted on the dressing table and getting up and going over to it, a decanter of what looked to Dryden like brandy, and a glass beside it. Joe poured until the glass was almost full and swallowed a good half of it before regarding the view from the window with satisfaction.

'Your father used to go on like this,' Dryden said, not knowing what would make any difference.

'I'm beginning to understand him. They say it takes you most

169

of your life to know your parents. Well, I've finally turned into my father.'

'You have not turned into him,' Dryden said, venturing nearer as Joe poured more brandy. He took the decanter away from him. 'He didn't care about the pit or the men and their families and you've looked after Vinia all these years.'

'Do you know why he didn't look after my mother?' Joe said.

'I don't know anything about it.'

'Well, I'll tell you. It was because he thought I wasn't his.'

'He what?'

'My mother would go with anybody, they were never sure who fathered me and that's why he put her out and that's why he didn't like me.'

'That's ridiculous, Joe. I never heard anything like that before and I don't believe it and neither does anybody else.'

'It's true,' Joe said.

'Rubbish.'

Joe looked at Dryden.

'Shouldn't you be at the pit? Who's looking after things? I pay you to be there.'

'I'm here with you, aren't I, you stupid idiot? It's your pit. You should be there. Howay man, you can't stop here all day.' He poured water into a dish from a jug and gave Joe the soap and towel which were nearby. 'You get washed and I'll go and ask Sadie to make some coffee.'

He went off downstairs. Sadie was in the kitchen and when she looked up from where she was pouring hot water on to coffee grounds Dryden thought she looked so much like the way he had seen her grandmother that he couldn't think of anything to say and then suddenly he realized something, he didn't know why, just that he knew it absolutely, like you sometimes instantly knew the clues to a puzzle.

'You don't have men come here any more.'

'Yes, I do.'

'No, you don't.'

'How would you know?' Sadie said.

'So why did you let Joe?'

170

She didn't answer. She put out cups and saucers and a big plate with a cake on it.

'His hair was dark with rain,' she said.

'So you pretend to him that there are other people?'

Sadie looked squarely at him.

'I don't need nobody's money. My dad died and left me plenty.'

'You pretend to Joe.'

'I don't want him to think I fancy him,' Sadie said.

'And do you?'

'Of course I don't. He's who he is. He's Joe Forster. He's the pit owner.'

'You should never have let him over the doorstep.'

'This place reminds you of my grandmother's, doesn't it?' Sadie said.

'No.'

'Yes, it does. I saw you looking.'

'How did you know I went to your grandmother's?'

'Joe told me.'

'I don't think he did.'

Sadie poured out coffee and cut cake.

'My grandmother knew you,' she said.

'How could she do that?'

Sadie put down the knife she was using to cut cake and beckoned him into the sitting room and there, above the fireplace, was a painting. It was a picture of the Haversham farm, as it had been in the days when he was a child and as he had come to know it when he was grief-stricken over Tommy. The house stood against the hillside on a summer day, its garden in full bloom, and there, lying in the meadow as he had been on the morning he met Rowan Haversham, was a dark-haired, brown-skinned man, wearing a black suit, at the front of the picture.

'That's . . . that can't be me,' Dryden said.

'It is you. Who on earth else could it be around here? Do you think the place is teeming with gypsies? My grandmother painted it.'

171

'Your grandmother has been dead for years and the – the man in the painting is the same sort of age that I am now,' Dryden said.

'Do you want coffee?' Sadie said and she went back into the kitchen.

Joe came slowly down the stairs like someone who wished he had not drunk so much but that was all the evidence he gave as to his state of mind or body. He took the cup of coffee from Sadie without a word, drank it, thanked her and followed Dryden to the outside door. They walked back through the village.

'Aren't you going to the shop?' Dryden said.

'I'm going to work.'

'She's very upset about this, Joe.'

'She's upset?' Joe stopped. 'How the hell do you think I feel? She hasn't – we haven't . . .' Joe said and then stopped. 'It's finished. It's over.'

'It can't be.'

'Why can't it be? Because you say so?'

'Not because I say so.' Dryden tried to keep his patience but it wasn't easy. 'You can't just give up on it.'

'I thought you'd be pleased.'

'Don't come that. It isn't like that any more and you know it isn't . . .'

'I don't know anything of the kind,' Joe said. 'You've always wanted her. Go on then, go ahead, take her.'

'She loves you, Joe.'

'No.' Joe looked beyond him at the row of houses in front. 'Nobody who loved me could treat me like this, like I'm . . . disgusting scum and not fit to touch her. Shall I tell you something? Shall I?' Joe looked so sharply at him that Dryden looked away. 'She hasn't let me anywhere near her since the day we found out that Tommy died. You know how long that is, you know to the very day and the hour. I couldn't go on living like that any longer, the grief never ended. It just never did. You got over it though, didn't you? You bedded Miss Bloody Grant.

My wife grieves over your child as though it were hers and you
. . . you go about bedding young women like nothing mattered.'

'She's married,' Dryden said.

'That doesn't stop you. It didn't stop you wanting my wife all
those years. Well, this is your big chance. Go on, have her. She
spent night after night lying awake wanting you, wishing she
could stop the hurt. I don't care any more, do you hear? I don't
care.'

Joe tried to leave but Dryden stopped him. It wasn't difficult.
He was so drunk he could hardly stand up.

'I tried to make love to her,' Dryden said, 'when things were
at their worst. She came to the house and I got her down on to
the bed and she wouldn't let me. When I touch her, when I kiss
her, I'm our Tom to her, and I'm not you. I'm not a gentleman,
I'm not a pit owner. I'm nobody, and the kind of women I like
they don't want me because I don't have a fine house and status
and background. Vinny is too proud to give herself to me but
even if she wasn't I taste like our Tom to her.'

'You bastard!' Joe said.

'That's right. That's exactly it, Joe, so you see there's nothing
to worry about and in time it will be all right.'

Joe tried to hit him but he was too drunk and Dryden moved
out of the way easily.

'You love her,' Dryden said. 'If you hadn't you would have
had an affair but you didn't, you went to Sadie, thinking it
didn't matter. You can't just give up. It's not as though you can
have some kind of relationship with Sadie. She's a whore.'

'You're so delicate,' Joe said.

'You haven't fallen for her?'

'I go to bed with her. Do you think that doesn't create
something between us?'

'Aye, you give her what for twice a week and she gets coal.'

'That's not like it is.'

'That is like it is and that's all it is. She goes to bed with you
because you pay her. To think any other way is plain daft. Sadie
doesn't want you. She doesn't want anybody and the truth of

the matter is that you don't want anybody either because instead of having an affair you went to a whore.'

'I couldn't have done that . . .' Joe said, swaying.

'Yes, you could have. You're the pit owner. You're Joe Forster, you're somebody in the area. Plenty of women would have you if you asked. You don't want to get involved. You love your wife.'

Joe didn't deny it this time. He didn't say anything. They set off walking again, into the village, down past the school and the cemetery and the little terraced houses. The village was basking in the summer sunshine.

'Will you go and see Vinia?' Dryden asked when they reached the pit.

'No, I won't,' Joe said and went into his office and closed the door.

That night Dryden dreamt he was back at the farm, lying in the field with the mist rising from the valley below but it was Sadie and not her grandmother who was standing in front of him as he lay on his back in the field. He could smell newly cut grass and roses and the heady scent of sweet peas which grew against the wall and then it was not him, it was the gypsy he had met when Tommy had gone to the camp on the fell and the old gypsy with a red jewel in his ear had come forward to claim Tommy as one of them. Yet Dryden knew that in Sadie's picture there was no jewel and it looked exactly like him. Everything was as it had been that day. He did not understand it.

Twenty-Two

B obbie spent more and more time at her father's house that autumn until her father turned troubled eyes on her and suggested that there was something wrong and Hector was talking about going back to live with them beside the river because they were both so concerned.

'There's nothing to be concerned about,' she assured him, smiling the kind of smile she had used a lot lately. She smiled like that across the dinner table at Forbes and across the breakfast table and at weekends across the lunch table and if the weather was wet, across the drawing-room fire. She did not thankfully have to smile like that at him across the pillows. It was the only saving grace. She had had to go back to Deerness Law and tell Phyllis that she could not have her job back because Major Stillman wanted Mr Martin to go on running the factory.

'Why?' Phyllis had said, white-faced.

Bobbie shook her head.

'He's put me into a – an impossible situation. I'm sorry.'

She had wanted to run to Dryden but she couldn't, it wasn't right. She couldn't run to anybody. Forbes was polite and she was quiet and she did not know where it would ever end. Her father and his father were undeceived. They knew that she was miserable and they tried to involve her in what they were doing and she went often to the house because she had nothing else to do.

And then one November day she met her father in the hall and his face was lit.

'They've found Charles. They've found him. They're sending

him home. He was hurt and lost his memory but he's coming back. You must tell Forbes and we must have a big party. You must go and tell him now and we'll make all the arrangements. Charles is coming home, after all this time. Can you believe how lucky we are?'

Forbes was at the factory that day, one of the rare days he went there, but for once she did not care that they were fighting to such an extent that they barely spoke. She didn't even care about Albert Martin or that when she got there the workers were silent. She rushed through into the office and burst in. She didn't see anybody but Forbes, even though several men were gathered there.

'They've found him!' she declared.

Forbes looked at her.

'What?'

'They've . . . they've found Charles.'

The other men shuffled from the office and for the first time ever she wanted to take him into her arms and kiss him. It seemed to her that nothing mattered and he would be glad as she was glad.

'Isn't it a wonderful day? They've found Charles alive. He'd lost his memory but he's in hospital in France and they're going to ship him back and we've got him. He'll come home and everything will be all right.'

At some point in her hurried speech and her enthusiasm she realized that Forbes was not joining in with her joy but she was like a tap turned on and could not stop. When she did the office was full of silence like a church at a funeral, heavy.

'Forbes . . . I know things have been difficult and I haven't been good to you and I'm sorry but everything will be all right now. You'll see.'

He didn't answer. He didn't look at her. She went around to where he was sitting at the back of the big desk and took his face in her hands.

'I know our marriage isn't what we wanted and I wish I had behaved differently. I did it for the best, really I did, I wouldn't hurt you, I wouldn't hurt anybody but especially not you when you were so generous to me, so kind. Please, be glad. Aren't you glad? He was your best friend ever in the whole world.'

'No, he wasn't,' Forbes said and got up.

She didn't understand it. She watched him walk around to the other side of the office and pause several times.

'Well, if he wasn't he was one of the best, wasn't he?' She tried to smile brilliantly at him. The smile faded by the time he looked at her.

'It's a mistake, Bobbie.'

'How can it be a mistake? You don't know. It's made you cynical, all this awful time, but it will be better now. You and me and Charles, just like when we were children. Do you remember that?'

'Yes, I remember it.' His voice was soft, almost faded. 'Charles had other . . . better friends than I was to him.'

'What do you mean?' She didn't understand why he was not ecstatic. 'Forbes . . . he's coming home.'

Forbes looked straight at her.

'No,' he said.

'Why do you say that? They've found him. He was . . . he was missing. He had lost his memory. Now he's coming back.'

'Bobbie, Charles is never coming back. He's dead.'

She lost patience.

'You are mad,' she said, 'completely. I'm going home now. I'm going to wait for Charles and be glad for him and for me and most of all for my father.'

'It isn't him, Bobbie. Don't get yourself worked up about it.'

'You don't know that,' she said, shouting at him for possibly the first time. 'You think you are so important and know everything but my father is about to get his son back and not like yours did, not somebody horrible and flawed like you. My father's son is coming home to him and if you can't be glad you're even worse than the person I thought you were!'

She left the office and neither of them said any more and she went back to her father and was glad that he was glad. She rather wished he hadn't planned a party, she thought that Charles would be disorientated at best, confused, tired and wanting peace and his family but her father had waited for so long and he had known in his heart that God would not allow Charles to die and he wanted to celebrate his son's triumphant return and it would be wonderful.

Also it would shift the balance of things, she thought, and Charles would be able to talk to Forbes as she did not seem able to. Charles had always been between them and somehow she imagined how useful that would be now. She could see them both, in her mind's eye, sitting in front of the fire, and her marriage would be improved by Charles's presence. She longed to see him.

The first night after they had found out he was alive and coming home she stood by the open window in her bedroom and looked out across the river. It was a perfect sunset and the river was so completely calm she could not hear the running water nor any noise in the little city and she thought that when Charles came back she would learn to love it all again. He would play his beloved piano, the old tunes would ring out and it would be like it had been before he went away, they would be happy again. She kept bringing to mind her father's face, how it had been lit that day as it had not been since Charles went to war and he began worrying.

What would Charles do? Would he still want to pursue his music or would he take on the business? That would give Forbes something to think about, Charles helping to run the business, Charles on her side. He would not let Forbes treat her like this . . .

She heard a soft knocking on her door but ignored it and after a little while the door opened and Forbes stood there.

'May I come in?' he said.

'Why bother asking? You don't ask about anything else.'

Forbes came in, hesitating, and closed the door. It seemed to take him ages to do it and then he stood by the door as though somebody else was coming or he was not sure he should be there.

'Everything will be different when Charles comes back,' Bobbie said. 'He is entitled to half my father's business, you

know, morally entitled, even though I'm sure you could produce lawyers in abundance to keep the whole thing for yourself.'

'Bobbie . . .'

'My father hasn't looked so well in years. Maybe he'll want
to go back to work too. You could have a very interesting
situation on your hands with the whole of the Grant family
wanting a slice of the business and when Charles finds out how
you've treated me—'

'He's not coming back.' Forbes's voice was so loud, so
violent, that she looked at him.

'You can't bear it, can you?' she said. 'He was always so
much nicer than you, all those friends who died, they were all
better men than you. Do you think there's something in that,
that God wants particular people? If he does you're going to
live to be very old, you are such a complete—'

'He's not coming back,' Forbes said again. 'There's been a
mistake.'

'He was missing. How do you know there's been a mistake?
Can you not have a little bit of faith? Can you not think even in
the depths of your mind that there is at least a possibility or
have you turned into such a dreadful person that you don't
want to share the business with anybody, even Charles? Is that
it? You want everything for yours?'

Forbes didn't answer any of her accusations. He looked as if
he didn't want to be there, turned back to the door and then
stopped.

'I'm sorry I lost my temper about the factory. I thought the
child was mine and then you didn't even bother to tell me that it
wasn't, even though you must have been aware that I no longer
knew . . .'

'How am I supposed to keep up with your states of mind?'
Bobbie said and then realized how cruel that sounded.

'I will move Martin,' Forbes said.

'I'm sure you will, now that Charles is coming home. How
would you face him otherwise? And perhaps you think I'm
going to invite you in here? I'm not.'

'Don't worry,' he said. 'I don't want to be in here,' and as if to prove it he went out and shut the door behind him.

Bobbie managed to avoid Forbes during the next two days but it didn't take much doing, he stayed out of the way. He was never there for breakfast and in the evenings she could not guarantee he would come back to eat before she went to bed. That suited her. Her mind was so full of Charles and her father and their reconciliation that she did not give him a thought. It was such a pleasure to go to her father's house and there was a big change. The place seemed lighter, happier, and Hector confided to her when they had coffee that her father had cleared away her mother's things, given them to friends or to the servants and no longer wanted to keep up the illusion that she was alive. His son's return would heal him, Hector said.

The music room was open to the light of the hall and the windows in there were open to the sweet summer air and when her father saw her he came to her and kissed her and he was like a different person, his face clear and full of pleasure for the first time that she could remember.

He had the house decorated with flowers and the three of them had lunch in the garden, chicken and champagne and strawberries, as though Charles were already there, and her father talked gaily of what wonderful times they would have and of the party which he planned for the end of the month. He had thought about it and they must give Charles a week or two to get used to being at home. The place would be full of music again and Charles would be able to help Forbes with the business. At the sound of his son's name Hector's face filled with dismay.

'I asked him to make time to come for lunch. Does he ever think about anything but business these days? He's not even civil when I see him.'

Bobbie couldn't tell them what Forbes had said about Charles, she could not bear to think about his behaviour. She spent her days with the two older men and waited.

Two days went by and nothing happened and then a third

and her father's face began to lose its joy as frustration set in. He could not wait any longer for Charles to come back. What was causing the delay? Hector spoke to the authorities and they did not seem to know what was going on but Charles did not arrive. At the end of the fourth day she was glad to go home mid-evening and kiss her child and try to cling on to the idea that her brother was still alive. Forbes came home. She expected him to make discouraging remarks but he said nothing, staying in the study all that evening.

She was surprised therefore to discover, when she went to kiss the baby goodnight, that Forbes was up there in the nursery. She had thought he would take no more interest in the baby, having discovered it was not his, instead of which he had the child in his arms and was standing by the window.

'He's supposed to be asleep,' she said and he turned with the baby.

'He is,' he said and put the child down into the cot with more deftness than she had given him credit for, like he was used to it.

'I spent the day at my father's,' she said. 'Everything is ready for Charles. My father is so happy, I've never seen such a change in him. Everybody is so excited.'

Forbes looked down at the sleeping child.

'Except you of course,' she said.

Charles did not come back the following day or the one after that. Her father was bright, cheerful. The weather changed. It began to rain. The windows of the music room were closed and the preparations for the party did not go forward. Hector began to absent himself from lunch and she and her father sat in the dining room and watched the summer rain pour down on to the lawns and there was silence between forced talk. Bobbie began to go home early in the afternoons and by the beginning of the second week she could hardly bear to go to the house for fear there should be bad news or she should cry.

She thought that if there had been a mistake surely somebody would let them know so she took comfort in the silence but it went on and on. Each day she thought her father's face was less assured, less happy. Hector would meet her in the hall when she went over and kiss her cheek and say, 'My dear, there's no news. Whatever are we to do?' He began to say things like 'They shouldn't have built up our hopes' and 'What if they were wrong?' and 'What if Charles doesn't come home?' and her father had begun to take up a vigil, sitting in the hall where he could see the drive, as though Charles might arrive by motor any minute. She did not dare to suggest to him that it was not going to happen. She did not think he could stand another blow.

That night she went home and cried for the first time, privately and alone in her room, but when she paused for breath over the tears Forbes was there.

'Have you heard something?'

'No.' She wiped ineffectually at the tears. 'My father believes Charles will come back, he has always believed it. How can they raise your hopes and then dash them in such a manner?' She looked up. She was sitting in a big velvet chair by the window. Forbes stood near. 'You never believed he would come back. Was that just cynicism?'

Forbes stared out of the window as though something was happening but the view was just the same as it had always been.

'Was it?' she prompted him.

'It was just an educated guess, that's all,' he said. 'I didn't want you to get your hopes up when there was no chance.'

'Isn't there always a chance?'

'No, I don't think there is, not after all this time.'

'It does happen,' she said. 'He could have been like you and not known who he was or what was going on. He could have been lost. He could have been badly wounded and . . . and left somewhere. Anything can happen.' He didn't reply and she needed reassurance. 'Can't it?'

'I suppose,' he allowed.

'You're a great help, Forbes, a great comfort.' Into the silence she said, 'You used to call me "old thing". You never say things like that any more. You were so . . . you talked differently, like you were someone else. What will I say to my father if Charles doesn't come home?' she said and her voice broke.

Forbes got down beside the chair and because there was nowhere else to go and because he offered she put her face in against his shoulder but only for a few seconds before brushing him aside.

'I must believe that Charles will come back. He has to.'

'It's not going to happen,' Forbes said.

'How can you be sure?' She glared at him through her tears. 'Don't you think the power of prayer and certainty can win?'

'No.'

'Please go away,' she said. 'I can't think when you're near.'

The following day Hector came to her before she had a chance to go to him and she could see by his face that it was not good news.

'They made a mistake,' he said.

She had thought nothing could be worse than not knowing. Knowing was. She wanted it to be the second before he came in, she wanted it to be the second before Charles left the station. She thought she would have given anything to see his smile, to hear his voice, to have him play one single note on the piano. She wanted to go back to the day when they had found out he was alive and would come home, to hold her father's happiness, to see her father's new-found energy, his strength, so that he could accept her mother's death and live on for the fact that his son was alive. She wished it were any moment but this one.

'What did they say?' she asked when she could speak.

'That he is dead for certain, that there was some kind of mix-up with another man and that he was never missing in the first place.'

'My father has been told all this?'

'Yes.'

She wanted to lie down on the floor and wail as she had heard women in other cultures were allowed. She wanted to be anything but British so that she did not have to stand there and accept this.

'I think you should be with him,' Hector said.

She wanted to run so far away that she could not be brought

back, to dash out of the door with her son in her arms and cash in her hand and never return and instead of that she had to smile and say the right things and go with Hector to her father's house.

At least he drove but when she got there the curtains were closed, the music room was locked and her father was in bed as though he could not summon the energy to go on any further. She would have offered him comfort if he would have accepted it. He turned his face to the wall. She wished that she could go home and hold her child in her arms and forget about all this. She said everything she could say but none of it made any difference and she had not thought it would. Hector was grey-faced with distress but when she suggested he might like to go back to his own house he shook his head.

'I can't leave John like this. To lose your son is the hardest thing on earth. For it to happen twice is unbelievable.'

She even wished Forbes was there, though what use he would have been was hard to imagine with his having thought from the beginning that Charles would not come home. And then it occurred to her that he had been adamant, sure.

In the early evening she went back to her house and waited for him and when he came home she called him into the sitting room and there she said to him, 'You knew Charles wouldn't come home.'

Forbes looked tired, thinner than he had been and he had not been very fat to start with. His eyes were careful.

'You knew,' she said.

'I didn't know.'

'You're a liar. Were you there when he died? You were, weren't you? You knew he was dead all this time. When there was all that stuff about him missing you didn't believe it because you knew he was dead. Why didn't you tell me?' His gaze was everywhere but on her.

'There was nothing to know,' Forbes said and tried to get out of the room.

Bobbie stood against the door.

184

'Tell me.'

He avoided her gaze still.

'I want you to tell me. Why didn't you tell me before?'

'I didn't know.'

'You had forgotten that your best friend had died?'

'He wasn't my best friend.'

'You keep on saying that.' Bobbie was exasperated, hurt. 'I don't understand. But you know now, don't you? You remembered. Anything you have to say might help my father.'

'It won't,' Forbes said and tried to move her. Bobbie resisted. He stood back.

'Why won't it? How are you so sure? You did see him die. You did, didn't you?'

'Yes.'

'You were certain?'

'Positive.'

'Then why was he missing and not just dead? Why the mystery? Why did they pretend?'

'It was very complicated and I didn't remember anything after that.'

'Complicated? We have a right to know. He was my father's only son and he's dead and you knew he was dead. You could have spared us all and given my father a chance to get over it and then he wouldn't have had to go through all this. He's lying with his face to the wall in his bed. He may never recover from this.'

Forbes didn't answer. He got hold of her and moved her away from the door and opened it. She grabbed at his arm but he pushed her off. Bobbie ran after him into the hall and across it into the dining room, where the maid, Annie, was putting the dinner on the table and he evidently thought she would say nothing. He went over to the sideboard and poured whisky from the decanter into a small glass.

Bobbie picked up one of the tureens on the table and threw it at him. It missed, it was heavy, broke against the wall and there was crockery and potatoes all over the wooden floor.

Annie stared at her and without a sound she went out and closed the door.

185

'I want you to tell me or I shall go to my father and yours and tell them that you cared so little about any of us that you knew Charles was dead but you didn't bother to inform us all this time.'

Forbes drank the whisky and then he said, 'I had the papers falsified, pretended that it wasn't him. Another man had gone missing. I had it all switched round.'

'Why would you do such a thing?'

'To save his reputation, so that your father and you and those people who loved him didn't find out.'

'Are you saying that my brother did something dishonourable and you tried to protect him?'

'No.'

'Then what? If you weren't trying to protect him . . . Was he a coward? Did he get men killed? Did he try to save himself instead of other men? I don't believe he would have done any of those things.'

'You're right, he didn't do any of them.'

'Then why should you need to protect him?'

Forbes looked regretfully into the empty glass as though he would have liked more but was trying not to.

'He died in another man's arms.'

Bobbie stared and the room, which had been quite still up to a moment ago, began to revolve alarmingly.

'Another man's arms?'

'Yes.'

'His best friend?' she guessed.

'Yes, that's right. Julian.'

The room was going faster but her anger outdid it for speed.

'You are telling me that my brother liked other men?'

'They were lovers, yes.'

'You goddamned bloody liar! Charles was not like that, he could never ever have been like that. How can you say such things? My father . . . my father . . .' She choked on her feelings. 'You are the person who has no honour, no decency, to say such things about a man who is dead and cannot defend himself.' She stopped there.

186

The room wasn't going round any more. Forbes was very pale and he went to the decanter and tried to pour the whisky and it came out of the neck of the decanter and all over the place because his hands shook so much. He didn't stop pouring, as though he had no control over his actions, he went on pouring the golden liquid everywhere but in the glass, all over the sideboard until it began to run on to the floor and even then he kept pouring.

Bobbie didn't stop him or assist, she just watched until the decanter was empty and then it was as though he had to pull the object from his fingers with the other hand and he couldn't and he dropped it and it smashed, dully because it was such heavy glass. It made so much noise and he looked down at it as though he were surprised.

And then he looked at her as though he had forgotten she was there and he said, 'There are lots of ways to die far worse than that.'

'If you think so why did you keep it secret?'

'Because I knew what people would think and say and how hurt you and your father would be and because I cared about him. When people are dead we like to think of them as we knew them.'

'You didn't like not being his best friend?' she said. 'Perhaps you cared about him like that too? Perhaps it's you that's like that and that's why you don't come into my bedroom? You prefer men to women. You're saying these things for your own benefit. Charles wasn't like that. He wasn't. I was his twin. I would have known.'

Later she remembered what she had said and was sorry. It didn't matter to her that Charles loved another man better than anyone else. It was just that her father's expectations of him had been so high. If Charles had been here now he would have been expected to marry and produce an heir. Dear God, she thought, between us we can't give him the child he would have wanted, nothing but a gypsy's bastard.

She was worried about Forbes too. He had carried that

187

burden knowingly. Later she went into the study and he was working. How could he work when they were all so upset, or was it the only thing left? At least he had that, he had not allowed it to her.

He didn't look up. The big desk was like a wall between them. He went on writing as though he couldn't stop and she thought of him pouring the whisky all over the floor and all over his hands.

'I'm sorry,' she said. 'I didn't mean to go on at you like that. I know very well that you would never have let Charles down. It was just that I wanted it to be different. Please don't be angry.'

Forbes put down his pen.

'I'm not angry,' he said.

'I wish you had been able to tell me and we had been close enough so that I would have believed you and been able to live with it. How could you go on, knowing?'

'I've seen a lot worse. I've seen horses drown in mud and men blown to pieces. Charles died with the person he loved the most. What more can anybody ask? Lots of people die alone.'

'You couldn't even let Smith die alone,' she said, going to him.

'I killed him.'

'What else could you do?' She didn't want to touch him although she thought she should but when she tried he backed away from her hands and then she wished he had let her hold him, touch him. He was almost insubstantial, it was worrying. Not threatening, not difficult and powerful, almost like he had been before, the man she had been grateful to marry. And then he changed. He got up and said, 'Your father doesn't have to know any of this.'

'I wouldn't tell him. He's suffering enough.'

Forbes didn't say anything to that.

'You think he hasn't?' she said.

'He doesn't understand. He's of the generation that thinks war glorious. My father's the same. You know, the thin red line and all that, the sort of men who believe in heaven.'

'Don't you believe in it?' she said.

188

'I believe in hell, I've seen it a thousand times. God isn't looking after any of us, he really isn't. Your father still has you.'

'And what am I? I'm your wife.'

'I didn't mean to do that to you,' Forbes said. 'I was hurt that Iain isn't mine. I wanted a child, at least I thought I did. Now it seems to me that each time a man fathers a son he's war fodder. I couldn't bear it and I didn't want your father and my father to have to bear it either.'

He walked out and left her there and all Bobbie wanted was to go to Dryden. She knew that she didn't have the right but she was lost, lonely. She ran downstairs without thinking and got into her car without stopping. She drove to Deerness Law and the sun set and the fell dissolved into a kind of pale golden mauve with the little farms in the valley like dolls' houses and a grouse flying up before her. She had never thought of the fell as a holy place but she did now. There was something about that much silence, that much space, all the air and the sky and land and there was nothing to stop it, there was no up and down like other land had. God would have been pleased with it, she thought. He could dwell there, so near the sky that on a good summer's night when the stars were low you could touch anything and yet there was nothing to touch. Men were dying in their thousands. Who could explain it?

She reached Dryden's house and parked the car and ran up the back yard without thinking and he was there as she had known he would be, turning to her as she stepped down from the pantry into the kitchen.

'I just couldn't manage any more,' she said.

She did not stop thinking about Forbes, that was the difficult part. He couldn't manage any more either but because he was not the man she had expected him to be she had left him.

Dryden took her into his arms and she remembered who he was and how he felt and tasted and smelled and it was better than before because it had been such a long time.

'I want to be here with you.'

'You can't.'

'I want to.'

He was holding her at an almost polite distance.

'Is this revenge?' Bobbie asked.

'You have to try and make things work . . . without me.'

'I can't do it.' She said this from his shoulder, from his shirt.

'Yes, you can. Think about Iain.'

'Dryden . . .'

'No.'

He kissed her. He kissed her all over her face, sweet kisses, and he was so close, as she had dreamed on innumerable nights that he would be. Why were they not together? It had been her fault.

'It was all my fault.'

'Oh no, nothing is ever anybody's fault, not all. The timing was all wrong. The days were all wrong. It was all wrong. Another time, another day and everything will be fine. I wasn't the right person, or in the right place, and you have nothing to reproach yourself with. I loved you.'

She moved back and tried to look objectively at him.

'Does that mean you don't any more?'

'I will always love you.'

'Oh God!' she said. 'Why didn't I marry you?'

'Because, unlike me, you knew it wouldn't work. You were sensible. I was stupid. But you have Iain and I am so glad and I have him too in a sense and I have learned to be pleased with that. You should go back now.'

When she had gone he cursed himself and whatever better nature he had. What was the matter with him, did he no longer see the opportunity when it presented itself? He could have had her, he could have taken her to him. It was unnatural, he told himself, and then laughed. He had a son and as much as she might deny it the child was his, he knew it with an unerring instinct. Many a night now he would go to bed and think about the child, his perfect limbs and his sweet smell and his tiny fists and Dryden thought, yes, his child lived. There was nothing more to accomplish. He would go to bed and sleep, thinking that a child of his might grow up and live and be there and be his life's inheritance and he was happier than he would have thought possible. He could think back to the day they had met and afterwards and he thought that if it had been left to him none of it would have happened, he was too hurt, too pathetic, too finished, too old. But in spite of that she had had his son and there was no more you could ask of a woman than that. God had been there in his purest sense and with luck his son would live. She and her husband would look after the child.

Dryden went to see Sadie Haversham that September. He hadn't meant to go or maybe he had, maybe he was waiting for the right time or opportunity though he couldn't understand why suddenly it was the right thing to do. All he knew was that Joe was still seeing her twice a week, at least as far as he could judge, and Vinia was still living above the shop. She had lost weight, she was skinny and for the first time ever he could see what she would look like when she was old. He felt that she wanted to go back to Joe but she couldn't. Her pride wouldn't let her. Joe hadn't asked her but he knew that, having a big house and all the luxuries that went with it, two rooms above a shop, once her temper had righted itself, was a mean way to live and she must have longed to leave there and go back to the house where she had lived for so many years. And she must miss Joe, Dryden knew she must, but he kept away. He didn't want her compromising her principles because she was lonely or worse still wanting him so that she could never go back.

Staying away from her was difficult but he had to do it. As for Joe, Dryden knew he wouldn't listen so he didn't bother wasting his breath talking to him. Instead, that Saturday afternoon in September he went to Sadie's house, knowing that Joe would be there later, maybe she would listen, maybe she would talk to Joe. Maybe she wouldn't.

The clothes were out on the line. Did Sadie wash every day? Had her grandmother done so? It was breezy up there above the dale and a perfect clear day when you could see every building, every small hill. Sadie was not outside but she was at home. She opened the door to him.

'Dryden Cameron,' she said. 'What on earth do you want?' and she raised her eyes.

Dryden followed her through her spotless house into the kitchen where the range was so clean it almost dazzled.

'What if I said tonight?'

'Don't be silly,' she said.

'You told me it wasn't the money but what on earth could you gain from Joe's prestige in the village?'

'What do you think I do it for, fun?'

'Maybe. Is he fun?'

'Not much.'

'So.' Dryden walked about the kitchen until he came to the window and there he looked out across the garden and tried not to think about her grandmother and the farm and how confused he felt about it all. 'It isn't the money and Joe's not a lot of fun and you can't go anywhere with him. The truth of the matter is, Sadie, that you're in love with him.'

'Don't be daft,' Sadie said. 'He's too old.'

'Is he? Less than forty. Is that old?'

'Well, it wouldn't be to you, would it, because you're old too.'

'You told me that you don't need his money. You haven't taken anybody else in for years. You said.'

Sadie didn't reply immediately. She fussed with the fire and the kettle and then she turned around and said, 'He's nice. He's a gentleman. I don't mean all that stuff about money and land and being able to impress people. He's a real gentleman. He's kind and he understands how you feel and . . . he likes women. Not the way other men do, I mean really likes them. I never met anybody like that.'

Dryden sighed.

'She does want him.'

'No, she doesn't.' Sadie looked defensive. 'She left him. She didn't look after him, she didn't kiss him . . .'

'Sadie . . .'

'What? You can't have somebody like that and not want him. Fancy giving that up? She must be out of her mind.'

That had been part of the trouble, he thought, she had been out of her mind, maybe they all had. Part of her love for him had been her love for Tommy. Nobody had ever loved anybody else's child more than Joe and Vinia loved his boy. To have nowhere for that love to go, somehow it defeated all the kinds of love you knew or thought were yours. It made you bitter and angry, closed you in against other people's regard for you. He and Joe and Vinia had been like islands. Tommy's death had shattered everything they knew and now it was affecting other people. Sadie loved Joe, he could see by the sparkle in her eyes that she did, so she would be hurt too. Was there never to be any end to it?

She knew. She looked down and then she looked at him and she said, 'You think I should give him up, don't you?'

Dryden couldn't think what to say. He didn't want to be the cause of distressing anybody, he had done enough, he and his son. He felt responsible for all of it and Sadie was looking at him with appeal in her face.

'You are in love?' he said.

Sadie raised her eyes again.

'No. Yes. Yes. I thought I couldn't like anybody. I never like anybody and I've turned them down in droves, you have no idea and then he comes to the door and he just stands there, dripping with rain and his eyes are the most beautiful thing I have ever seen and . . . he's . . . he's just the best. I would give the rest of my life just to spend a week with him, to be married and be . . . belong to him. She doesn't know how lucky she is, the silly bitch.'

'It's not so simple.'

'No. You're in the road.'

Dryden couldn't take the frank look but he stood it.

'I can't think what she wants you for,' Sadie said, so matter of fact that it made him laugh.

'She doesn't really.'

'You are strange though.'

'Why am I strange?'

'You just are. I've never seen you close up before you came here. I can see what they mean now.'

'What?'

'You know things other people don't.'

'No, I don't,' Dryden protested.

'Yes, you do. Let's face it, you knew my grandmother.'

'No, I didn't.'

Sadie looked sceptically at him.

'And in any case,' Dryden said, 'how the hell would you know that? I didn't tell Joe so don't come it. How did you know?'

Sadie didn't say anything but she closed the distance between them.

'My grandmother told me about you.'

'It wasn't me! And your grandmother's been dead for years.'

'Oh yes, it was. You're unmistakable.'

'There are other gypsies.'

'But not like you, not brought up here so that you know pits and book learning and also . . . you have that hint of here, you look like the people here for all you're dark and tall. You have a look of your mother on you, a kind of. . . something that binds you to this place. Other gypsies don't do that, they don't live somewhere all the time like you do. Even your son didn't, did he? They hanker to be away, but you . . . you stay here. This is your place. You'll die here and it's a better place for you being among it.' Dryden thought it was probably the nicest thing anybody had ever said to him. 'That's why my grandmother thought so much of you and tried to aid you, because you're of the same soil and she cared a lot about the soil, like you care about the pit. It will be all right.'

Sadie kissed him. It wasn't like anybody else's kiss, it wasn't to do with either of them, it was from another time, to do with the loneliness he had felt after Tommy died, a shield against such things. She drew back and looked at him.

'I will send Joe home,' she said.

Twenty-Three

That evening Joe didn't go to see Sadie. He had intended to but something told him it was not the best thing to do. He liked being there but more and more he was aware of not being with Vinia and he missed her increasingly. He kept reminding himself what their life together had been like, how it had degenerated into a joyless existence. He had better than that with Sadie. She wanted him there. Vinia did not but more and more Joe remembered what his life had been like before Tommy had died and he wanted some of that back. Most of all he wanted his wife back. He had not thought he could learn to hate his home. He had hated it when his father was alive and he could hate it now because he was even more alone there than his father had been. At least his father had had him. He had no one.

Just after the shop closed Joe stood in the doorway of the hardware store across the road and watched Em Little leave and then he walked slowly across the street and went into the shop. There was a moment or two before Vinia came out from the back, saying, 'We're closed,' and then she stopped in the doorway.

She was a shock to Joe. He was used to Sadie, who was young. His wife was no longer young but his overwhelming feeling was one of love. He could he ever have let her go? Had she no idea how bored he was without her? How much time they had wasted and why? He couldn't see it now. He couldn't see why their marriage had fallen apart. He loved her so much that just to see her after so long was wonderful. He found himself smiling.

'Vinny,' he said.

'Why, Joe. What are you doing here?'

I want you to come home. Why couldn't he say it? It was the age old tale of man, he thought, bitterly amused at himself. Fear of rejection. She had already rejected him so many times. He wanted to go to Sadie. Sadie did not reject him. She would be waiting for him. She would have made a meal. Her house would be warm and welcoming and there would be the smell of beef casserole with dumplings. She very often made that on a Saturday night.

'I just . . . wondered how you were,' was as far as he got.

'I'm fine.' She didn't look it, he thought.

She was very smartly dressed but then it was part of her business. If she didn't look good women would not have their clothes made there. Her eyes were unhappy. She did not move forward into the front of the shop, as though she were waiting for him to leave. She didn't look like a woman waiting to be asked to go home. He had committed the ultimate sin. He had gone to another woman and by the look of Vinia he was not forgiven.

'How is the shop doing?'

She stepped into the room.

'Very well, thank you. How is your work?'

'Fine,' Joe said and that completed the enquiries. He thought how they used to spend hours sitting over the fire on long dark winter nights, talking about the customers, the problems, the pitmen and their families, making plans, discussing what they might do. What hope was there for either of them if they couldn't think of anything to say?

'The shop looks . . . it looks good.'

She gazed squarely at him.

'There was no need for you to come here.'

'I'm . . . I'm not going to see Sadie any more.' Joe had a struggle getting the words out.

'Oh, and why is that?' Her voice was not encouraging. Neither were her eyes, which were sharp and unforgiving.

'Because I . . . because I . . .'

'You needn't do it for me, Joe. You needn't think it will make any difference because it won't. Do you seriously think I want you back after you've been with her? You broke your marriage vows. You didn't think about me. You . . .'

She stopped there. She needn't have, Joe thought, the damage had been done with the first sentence. All he wanted was to get out. He didn't care how cold and lonely his house was, he didn't mind that he did not love Sadie. Anything was better than this.

He went home. He was surprised to find how uncomfortable it was. How strange that he had not noticed before. Addy had been gone for weeks. It had not seemed to matter during the dry sunshiny summer days. He had learned to ignore the layer of dust through the sunshine on the furniture. There were no lights to greet him, no smell of food cooking, nothing but empty grates, cool rooms.

He went into the study and tried in vain to light the fire there, laughed at himself and then it was not funny that he could not manage the paper, sticks and coal. The house was damp, the paper too, and a wind had got up on the fell, what they called 'a lazy wind', too idle to go round things it tried to cut straight through, howling down the hall and under the study door, which had never fitted properly.

It would not have mattered if Vinia had been there. This room, like all the rooms, was just as she had left it. He had altered nothing. Why? Because he had been waiting for her to come back. You fool, he told himself, reaching for the whisky bottle. He had committed the ultimate sin, knowingly, and she would never forgive him for it. He thought longingly of Sadie's warm house, of her body and her bed, food, comfort and how agreeable she was and then, without thinking about it, he turned around and swept the papers, the inkwell, the lamp and everything else on to the floor, everything which had lain untouched on the desk for so long because they had both worked in here at one time and he had not done so since she left. He did the same with the ornaments in the sitting room, the vase where the flowers had almost disintegrated and the water was rank, slimy and when the surfaces were empty and the floor littered he went to bed, congratulating himself that he did not need another drink, that he was not Randolph, that he could handle what was happening to him.

He made his way up the dark shadowy stairs and into his father's room and when he opened the door the air was so cold it knocked the breath out of his lungs. The window had come off the latch and was banging back and forward in the freezing autumn night. Joe stumbled across the room and tried to catch it as it flew back against the wall but even when he managed to hold it it would not stay shut. The catch was broken.

He decided he could not stay in here so he went across the landing and into the room that he and Vinia had shared. He stood in the middle of the room. It was not much warmer in here but at least the windows were closed. He thought he could smell the very faint scent of his wife's perfume. It was not quite flowers. It was almost lavender. It reminded him of how she had left him, of the garden she had neglected, the house which only here was anything to do with her. How could she have gone?

Joe breathed in the sweet smell. It was getting fainter every second. He opened the wardrobe. A great many of her clothes were still there and the smell of perfume though faint was mixed with the woody closed-in wardrobe aroma. Joe leaned nearer and buried his face in her clothes. He had had other loves in his life. When he had been not much more than a boy he had wanted Esther Margaret, who had been seventeen and blondely beautiful, and after that he had loved Luisa Morgan, the daughter of the foundry owner, Thaddeus Morgan, but they were old memories to him now. His wife was the true love of his existence – you only have one, Joe thought – and she was more important to him than anything on earth.

The trouble was that she did not and never had loved him in that way. Dryden had been the most important person in Vinia's life and because of it so had his son. Joe knew very well he could not compete with that. He felt as though he was stuck in the middle of something with no way forward and none back.

He went to bed and thought back to the nights when they had lain there by firelight and made love and talked. He tried to make himself believe that it would never happen again.

Twenty-Four

O n the first day that Joe did not turn in for work Dryden carried on as usual. By the second day he was so busy that he did not have time to think. One of the miners had been slightly hurt underground and Dryden had to take him to hospital. While he was away several matters occurred which needed dealing with so it was very late and he was tired by the time he got home but on the third day when Joe's office was empty he left the mountain of work which had accumulated – and was just about to go to Joe's house during the middle of the morning when Joe arrived, bright and smiling, apologetic. He went into his office.

Dryden was relieved. He popped in an hour later to find Joe staring out of the window. An hour after that he was in the same position. Dryden hovered in the doorway.

'You all right?'

Joe said nothing.

'Did you look through the papers on production levels?'

Still nothing.

'Joe . . .'

'Just . . . let me be.'

The first word held emphasis. The rest was barely audible. Dryden went into the office.

'Have you seen Vinny?'

'Yes.'

Dryden didn't like to enquire any more closely. Whatever had happened it had evidently not been a success.

Joe seemed to grow bored with the window and turned away.

'You know what women are like,' he said. 'I went to someone

else and no man has ever been forgiven for that. It's what she did, of course.'

'What do you mean, "it's what she did"?' Dryden said, letting go of the door.

'You and Tommy always came first.'

Dryden said nothing to that. It was true, at least of Tommy.

'It could be mended, surely.'

'No, it can't be mended.' Joe rounded on him as Dryden felt sure he had not done before. 'You're always bloody well there! What chance has anybody got?'

Dryden was astonished. Joe had not said such a thing to him before. He didn't reply. Joe sighed.

'I just wanted one person to put me first and she never did.'

'Joe . . .'

'I think you should leave.'

At first Dryden thought Joe was telling him to get out of the office.

'Leave?'

'Yes.' Joe looked down. 'I don't want you here any more.'

Dryden stared at him for a few seconds and then panicked. All he had left was his work and the little house where he had been happy after his child was born. He wanted to protest, to say that it was not his fault, except that it was, his and Tommy's. How sweet it was to include his child's name in anything. It had been two years and sometimes Dryden thought that Tommy's life had been his own dream. There was no evidence of his existence, not even a picture that his son had drawn. He had Tommy's letter saying that he would be coming home. He kept that letter in the inside pocket of his jacket always. His son's life and nothing more substantial to show for it than a piece of paper which somebody else had written.

'What will you do for a pit manager?'

'I'm sure I'll think of something,' Joe said.

Dryden's composure suffered under the sarcasm.

'Now.'

'Right this minute.'

Dryden said nothing more. He went out of Joe's office and

into his own and there he left the desk neat and collected his jacket and he walked out into the darkening autumn afternoon and the rain.

Joe regretted his actions straight away but he was too angry to do anything about it. He went home and it was only when he crawled between what had once been white sheets that the guilt hit him. To blame Dryden for everything that had happened was one thing. To make him pay so dearly was another. He resolved to go to Dryden's house in the morning and then persuaded himself that Dryden would not take any notice of him anyway.

He finally slept and only awoke a few minutes before he was due to leave the house. His hopes were in vain. Dryden did not appear and although Joe had a great deal of work to do he broke off at lunch time and walked the very small distance between the pit and the row.

The back door was closed but not locked. He banged his fist against it and when nobody answered ventured inside, saying Dryden's name softly. To his relief it was just as it had always been, everything in place. He had forgotten what a clean house looked like and it was immaculate, the only thing about it which he wasn't keen on was that the fire had not been banked down for the day. It was clean, the grate swept and empty, and the house gave off a strange, cool echoing.

But Dryden could not have left, Joe reasoned, because everything was in order, and then he noticed the bookcase in the corner and it was usually full to overflowing. It was almost full now but there were spaces, as though someone had deliberately chosen and removed favourite authors. Joe stared for a moment and then he ran up the steep stairs and into the bedroom and there he opened the wardrobe. It was empty and so were the drawers and so were the surfaces. Dryden had gone.

Joe was stung by jealousy. Dryden had gone to Vinia, it was the only place he could go. How could he do that and how could she let him after all the problems? The thing that Joe had dreaded all his life had finally happened. He strode up the main street, burst into the shop. Vinia, who was talking to a customer, looked around at the noise. Joe ignored the other woman.

'Where is he?' he said.

Vinia went on talking but while Joe hovered she kept glancing at him.

Joe went through into the back room. In there Em Little was busy at the sewing machine. She wished Joe good afternoon and carried on with what she was doing. Vinia followed him in there after the customer left.

'What on earth are you doing here?' she said.

'Is he upstairs?'

Vinia frowned and then she said, 'I don't know who or what you are referring to.'

Joe went on looking at her and then he turned and dashed up the stairs that led to the flat.

'Joe!'

He went in, expecting every second to discover Dryden but he didn't. Somehow, as he looked, Joe's inadequacy and stupidity hit him in the face like a sledgehammer. He thought of his home and all the time that they had been happy together there and all the space, the half dozen bedrooms, the kitchen, dining room, study, sitting room and garden and he wanted to hit himself over the head with something large enough to fell him.

His wife had followed him upstairs. His wife. He wanted to weep for how she was not his wife any more.

'What are you doing?' she said.

Joe stood in the middle of the bedroom and he was undeceived. Dryden was not here, nor had he been, and whatever was he doing here himself and what had he imagined?

'Joe?' she said again and he turned and she was the woman he had married, the woman he adored, who had never loved him. It was a hopeless situation. She came nearer softly.

'He's gone.'

'What on earth are you talking about?' she said.

He had missed her up till now. He had longed for her up till now but before now he had kept at bay the things he loved so much about her, her common sense – how unromantic – her way of making him see things just as they were. When he didn't answer her she said, and in a way that made him want to weep and run out because he couldn't have her, 'Oh, Joe, whatever is the matter?'

And there was nothing else to say.

'Dryden has left.'

She did not understand, and why should she, what he had done. There was no way out of this.

'Why?'

'I was so tired of him.'

'I don't see.' She was right, she looked disconcerted, ready to be reassured that he had not done this. Joe stood in the middle of the room.

'I was tired of Tommy being dead and Dryden living without him and all of us . . .'

'He won't have gone far,' she said.

'I went to his house and . . . he's not there.'

'He wouldn't just go.'

She meant he wouldn't go without telling her, without seeing her.

Joe was not aware of how long the silence which followed went on, just that it was long enough for him to say, 'I didn't want him here any longer.'

And she stumbled and faltered and said, 'But why?'

'Because he means so much to you and I'm so jealous.'

'Oh Joe,' she said. 'He doesn't mean as much to me as you do.'

Joe left the shop and went to the station. He didn't know why. There was no train. There was no one standing on the platform and if Dryden had left there was no reason why he shouldn't have done it the night before. Joe walked up and down the platform until the stationmaster, who knew him well, came to him.

'Something the matter, Mr Forster?'

'Did . . . did Dryden Cameron board a train today?'

'Nay, Mr Forster, yesterday afternoon.'

'Was he carrying a suitcase?'

'Two,' the stationmaster said helpfully.

'Do you know where he was going?' Joe had no pride left by now even though the stationmaster's eyes widened with surprise that he should not know that his pit manager had left and why.

'Could be anywhere after Bishop Auckland, couldn't it?' he said and ambled away.

Dryden thought that he might go further than Bishop Auckland even though he had no idea of the jobs that might exist south of there. In the end, having nothing else to do, he got off the train in Bishop Auckland and tried to find somewhere to stay.

At the first bed and breakfast they said 'no coloureds'. At the second the woman retreated with a blush and at the third they said they had no vacancies. He was about to give in when he thought he might put up at a hotel so he went to the best hotel in the area and said, 'I would like a room for a couple of nights.'

'Let me get you some help with your luggage,' said the woman.

Dryden was astounded. It was a wonderful hotel, it had views across the valley and up the other side where the road went off towards Spennymoor and Durham. He looked back at the room. It was large and well furnished with a big double bed, a wardrobe, a chest of drawers, a writing table, a chair by the window and an easy chair by the fire. The fire burned big and comfortingly. He didn't know what to do now. He sat by the fire and tried to read but he couldn't concentrate. He didn't want to stay here but he didn't have any reason for going any further. There were lots of pits here and all over Durham. Surely he could get a job at one of them. It didn't have to be a manager's job, at least he didn't think so, anything would do as long as it was something he was capable of. He had contacts. He knew pit managers and pit owners all over the county from meeting them at the Black Prince and with Joe at various functions and get-togethers.

There was a pit owner who lived locally whom he knew well. He could go and see him either early tomorrow evening – it was too late to interrupt anyone now – or at his offices tomorrow. He would go there in the morning and make an appointment. Feeling that he had achieved something, Dryden went down to dinner.

He found eating difficult. He could not put to the back of his mind the things Joe had said to him. He could not believe that he had lost his whole way of life, the house which had been his home for so many years, the job that he had thought was his for good. He missed the men and their conversation. He missed Joe and even though he rarely saw her he missed Vinia.

He couldn't sleep. He got up long before breakfast and walked the short distance up the street, into the marketplace and to the Bishop's Park. Beyond the gates the palace was set back and in front of it were the gardens and woodland which belonged to it. He made himself go back for breakfast even though he wasn't hungry and after that he walked the other way up the main street to where Newbottle and Company had their main offices. Fred Newbottle owned several small pits in the area and was a kind man. He would help if he could, Dryden knew.

He walked into the gloom of the office and asked if he could make an appointment to see Mr Newbottle, preferably today if he could, but if not then as soon as Mr Newbottle was available.

A door opened and Fred Newbottle appeared. He was a short, stocky man with a red face and a large smile.

'I thought I recognized that voice. How long is it since we met?' and he came across, hand outstretched and guided Dryden through into his office, enquiring after Joe.

'We've had a disagreement,' Dryden said, not sure whether to tell anybody but deciding that he must be truthful or he wouldn't get anywhere. 'That's what I'm doing here. I need a job. I thought you might know of something.'

'A disagreement? Sit down. Sit down. You and Joe? I thought you were practically boys together.'

'We were. Things haven't gone too well since Tommy died.'

Nobody knew better than Fred, Dryden thought. He had lost his only son in the war too. He nodded.

'It's like everything suffers in the wake of something like that. I don't think I'm sane any more. You just get up in the mornings and find something to do. Iris and me, we get to the tea table and then we congratulate ourselves over what we've achieved that day. I'm sorry things are so bad for you.'

They drank coffee while Fred tried to think of anyone who needed a pit manager and he told Dryden he would make enquiries. He offered to take Dryden home for dinner at mid-day and, although Dryden attempted to refuse, Fred wouldn't have that and said Iris would be upset to think he had turned one of her dinners down. She was a friendly, generous person so Dryden agreed.

They lived not far from the hotel in a semi-detached Victor-ian villa with gardens which sloped down the valley to the front and the side. Dryden thought Iris Newbottle was going to cry over him because they had both lost their sons but she didn't. Neither did she reminisce or ask difficult questions.

They ate minced beef and dumplings with potatoes and carrots and then had apple crumble and after that they sat over the fire for a while and then he would have left. He knew that Fred had to go back to work.

'Why don't you come to the Mary with me this afternoon?' Fred offered. 'Ray Hobson is managing her. I know he'd be glad to see you.'

Dryden went, almost happy, full of Iris's dinner and Fred's kindness. He didn't understand how they went on like they did but at least they had each other. Fred dragged him back to tea, even though Dryden protested more than he had at dinner time and when Iris was happy about how much he had eaten she told him he was to get his things from the hotel and stay with them.

'I've put on you sufficiently,' Dryden said.

'We have six bedrooms. Do you think I would let you go back there when I have all these empty rooms? Now you do as you're told and let's hear no more about it. We'd be glad to have you stay.'

She insisted on Fred's going with him and when they got outside into the cold night air Fred said to him, 'We need the company, you see. We miss our Laurie something terrible.'

'But you have work to do.'

'You can always help. I'm glad of another opinion. Our Laurie was going to do that too, he was going to be the son of Newbottle and Son. You know what it's like when you have to run a business by yourself. Oh, I talk to Iris and she's very good but to talk to somebody who knows exactly what the problems are that's another matter. Let's have a drink at the hotel after we get your things. I could do with a stiff whisky.'

Dryden was happy to agree. It was only then that he realized he was tired of his own company and although the hotel had been comfortable and the food good it would be much better to be at Fred and Iris's house. He paid his bill and collected his belongings and then they went through into the hotel lounge. The first person Dryden saw was Bobbie, sitting by the fire, drinking tea, and he could see even from across the room that something was wrong. She was white-faced and held the cup and saucer almost clenched and she did not notice him or anybody. Fred had just seen a business acquaintance at the bar and hailed him so Dryden excused himself and went over.

She heard or saw him and looked up and when he reached her Dryden thought he had never loved her more. He wanted to pick her up in both arms and carry her away. She looked surprised, pleased, taken aback.

'Why, Dryden,' she said, 'what are you doing here?'

Twenty-Five

I t seemed to Bobbie that Forbes became less efficient by the day. He was at home more and more and he was quieter than he had been. She did not notice much for the first few weeks but then she was very often at her father's and had managed to persuade him out of bed and downstairs for at least a small part of each day. It took all her energy and imagination so that she scarcely saw Iain for any length of time.

And then it seemed that she came home several days running to find Forbes in the nursery and when she spoke to him he was vague. She was so tired that she slept deeply each night so when the night came that she awoke in blackness with the fire out and the room cool she could not think what had disturbed her.

There was silence. It could not be that Forbes had awoken shouting because he never did any more. She got out of bed and ventured into the night nursery, where a light burned low, and there her child lay, sleeping peacefully in his cot. She almost went back to bed but hesitated outside Forbes's room on the landing. What if it was like that time when she had gone in and he was crouched in the corner? She told herself not to be foolish but the idea took hold of her and she couldn't rest. She went back to her room and listened. She had never been in his bedroom here. Strange to think that before they were married she was always in there but since he had become the awful person he was she had avoided getting close.

She went back to bed and strove to sleep but it was no good. She turned over and over. In the end the day began to break and she was glad of it when the shadows greyed in the room. She pulled back the curtains to see the first streaks of red in the sky and as she did so she caught sight of a figure in the garden. Shocked, she drew back but she could soon see clearly Forbes's tall thin form, almost like a ghost. He was standing quite still beside a tree as though he were an extension of it and he too was waiting for the dawn.

Her first instinct was to go outside because something about his demeanour made her think he had been there for a long time, possibly hours. All night? Was that what she had heard, him leaving the house, going down the stairs and out of the door. What on earth was he doing? He was better. At least she had thought so but sane people did not stand outside on freezing December nights like that.

She stayed, waiting for him to move, as the day announced itself in red and then as the time went on and the light grew and he stayed where he was, without making any decision, she put on some warm clothes and stepped outside. There she hesitated. She did not want to shock him with her presence and she did not know what to say. She was half-inclined to go back inside and then she stepped on a twig and it cracked in the cold silence and he heard her and turned around. It took several seconds before he focussed on her.

'Bobbie?' he said as though she could have been anybody else.

'I saw you from the window. Have you been there long?'

'I'm not sure. Yes. A long time.'

'Why?'

He didn't reply. He went back to watching whatever it was that he had been watching and, since the river flowed, slow and newly menacing below them, she was disconcerted, worried, her instinct was to drag him back inside.

'Why, Forbes?' She went closer. He glanced at her.

'I don't know.'

It was not the truth, she discerned, but it was all he could say.

'Come back inside. You must be frozen.'

'I'm fine.'

'No, you're not. Come in and I'll have some tea made for you. The servants are up and about and Iain will be awake soon.'

'You can't think how much I wish he were mine,' Forbes said and she didn't like the finality of it somehow.

'We'll have a baby for us, don't worry,' she said rashly.

'Will we? How?' His eyes were so frank. 'You don't want me and . . . it's all so complicated.'

'What is?'

'Everything.' He turned back to viewing the river. 'I find I don't care about anything any more, like there isn't a place for me here.'

'That's not true. You have your work and your father and me.'

'I keep thinking about the silence.'

'What silence?'

He didn't answer her.

'What silence, Forbes? Why don't you come back to the house?'

She persuaded him up the path, inside and then into the morning room and there it was so normal and ordinary, with toast and marmalade and tea. He sat down in civilized fashion and ate and drank.

'What are you doing today?' she said.

He looked blankly at her.

'I'm going to the Stockton shop,' he said. 'I'm having the whole place reorganized.'

They talked about it for half an hour or so and she was reassured. He was enthusiastic about the shop, had good ideas, seemed keen to implement them. There was nothing wrong with him that work would not mend, she thought. Shortly afterwards she left. She finished her tea and toast in haste, kissed him goodbye – something she hadn't done before – went up to the nursery and saw Iain briefly and then hurried off because the morning was going on without her and she needed to keep up with it.

She reached her car, was about to get into it and then stopped. She never knew why. There was no reason for her to go back to the house. She stood for several seconds and then she ran, bursting into the hall, skidding on the floor, opened the dining-room door. All she could see was the remains of break-fast. She went back across the hall and opened the library door and there he was with a gun in his hand and she screamed and ran at him and the gun went off and the noise that it made rang round the library and then she was on the floor and he was there with her. They were this big heap of each other and Freya was there and all she could think was that he was dead and that she would have to tell his father and she was sobbing.

In amongst the crying she realized that he was not dead, he was not even injured. The bullet had missed both of them and hit the bookcase. He opened his eyes to her and she was on her knees on the floor, crying, and there was the smell of the gun and its report resounded. Freya hovered over them.

'Go out and shut the door,' Bobbie said through stiff lips.

'But Miss Bobbie . . .'

'It's all right. Just leave us, please.'

She waited and when the door was closed she pulled him up into her arms. He didn't resist but neither did he help and she shook him.

'What did you do that for?' she said.

Forbes looked past her as though something fascinating was happening behind her.

'What did you do it for? You stupid, stupid person! Look at me. What did you do it for? What?' She thought she would go on asking him the same question for years, as though those words were all she had left to hang on to.

'There were no stones by the river,' he said.

'Oh God,' Bobbie said.

His father and her father arrived and they brought Dr Hazlitt with them, his slimy smile filled the house. Bobbie thought she would find out who had betrayed her and dismiss them but she had not the energy. She came downstairs, smiling, ready to pretend, but they knew, she could see. Her father tried to talk to her and so did Hector.

'We must have him put away.'

Who had said it?

Forbes had made no protests, no claims, but when she went back to him he said, 'I'm not going back there.'

'You aren't,' she said.

'I'm not going back to Dundee. I want to die here.'

'You're not going to die, here or anywhere.'

He looked at her in amusement.

'Oh, Bobbie, Bobbie,' he said, 'think how peaceful it would be, how quiet. This is a world I don't know, run by people I don't understand. I don't want to be part of it any more. Let me go. The child isn't mine and you have plenty of money. It isn't as though you ever loved me. It doesn't matter. Why don't you marry the man who gave you your child? I know you love him. Let me go, please.'

For answer she kissed him. His lips were dry like old rose petals, sweet with a hint of what had been, before he turned his face away.

She didn't dare to leave him even for a second. She was terrified that he would find another gun, though she thought she had confiscated them all and locked them up. She had visions of him going to the river. She wished they did not live so close. She thought of all the awful stories she had heard of men hanging themselves, throwing themselves from windows. His father and her father and Dr Hazlitt wanted to talk to her without him there so she sent Freya to sit in a seat by the window in his bedroom. The one thing she had been able to do was persuade him to go to bed. He did not even ask her to stay with him. He seemed to want nothing.

She went wearily downstairs to the study, where her father and his father and Dr Hazlitt and another doctor were ensconced, and the minute she walked in they started up about him going back to hospital and how irresponsible it was of her not to let him be put away and how if anything happened to him it would be her fault.

She didn't listen. All she could think was that he had been fine until the nonsense about Charles coming home. That was what had done it. He had been himself before then – obnoxious, capable, almost brilliant. Now he was again the man that she had married, insane, kind, hopeless. She could see it in his eyes. And he did not want to be that person. He was not meant to be that person. He was meant to be irritating and clever and trying to manoeuvre her to suit him. She did not love him then. She only loved the hopeless man who could not kill a dog to save his suffering but he had done it somehow and at his own expense. He would not survive long like this.

She would have to leave him and sooner or later he would find a way to rid the world of himself. What did they call it? The realms of the dead. Like it was nothing more than a different kind of railway carriage, she thought stupidly, another world, another life.

'He isn't going anywhere,' she announced.

'He will die,' her father said, 'and you will have done it.'

Better here than some hospital bed. Better here where he might remember the brief spell of happiness when he had walked the old spaniel and she had been kind to him sometimes and he had smoked her Turkish cigarettes. His own father had said nothing and she knew that he wished she had let Forbes shoot himself. He thought it was the honourable thing to do. He would have been proud Forbes took that way out. It would have been the conclusion of the problem. She had only pro-longed it.

'He's staying here,' she said again and the doctors shook their heads and her father protested.

She got rid of them and went back upstairs. Forbes was out of bed, wearing an extravagantly patterned silk dressing gown. Freya looked worried, then relieved as Bobbie appeared in the doorway. When Freya had gone he looked at her.

'You've had a bad day, old thing,' he said.

Bobbie made herself not cry.

'Why on earth did you do it?' she said.

She went and sat on the window seat beside him.

'It's not such a big thing, you know. Millions of people have died in the war and of disease. What is it to you anyhow?'

'We're married.' It was a ridiculous thing to say so it was no surprise to her that he laughed.

'That was just to give Dryden's baby a name,' he said. 'Let's go and see the baby.'

They went. He took the baby – who was awake – and held him up to the fading daylight and then he sat down with the baby in his arms.

'Isn't he beautiful? Aren't you proud of him?'

'Forbes . . .' She got down beside his chair. 'Promise me you won't do it again.'

'I won't.'

'You're not looking at me.'

'Are you calling me a liar?'

'Yes.'

That made him laugh too.

She did not let him out of her sight after that. When they went to bed she followed him into his room and he said if he had only known that was what it took to get her in there he would have done it sooner. She turned away from him in bed but since he didn't protest she turned back and he was looking at her.

'I will have to go back to work tomorrow.'

'You will do nothing of the sort.'

'I will. You can't do it all yourself.'

'Is that what you thought when you tried to shoot yourself?'

'You'll be able to sell it.'

'I will not do anything of the kind.'

'I do love you.'

'It isn't fair to try and kill yourself and then tell me that you love me. And you don't, not when you're in your right mind, you don't love me one little bit.'

'Ah, but I'm not in my right mind, am I? And you like me now.'

'I do not like you.'

'Yes, you do. You see, I remember these things. I can't do much about them but I remember them. Are you going to stay here with me?'

'I am, yes.'

'Oh, that's nice,' he said and then he went to sleep. He was easy to sleep with. He slept very deeply for hours and hours and seemed tired all day.

She had one important meeting that week so she recruited Freya to watch him.

'You are not to leave him alone even for a second. I will hold you responsible,' she said.

The meeting was at a hotel in Bishop Auckland. Bobbie did not know how she was going to learn to control everything but she realized that Forbes had – Albert Martin apart – chosen people well, because when she called the shop managers and business people to the hotel to say that he would be away from work for a little while, though she did not explain the circumstances, they reacted well and seemed capable of managing their various parts of the business without him. She could not help but think he had done that on purpose, so when he was not there she would not have to go on alone.

By the end of the day Bobbie was exhausted but she wanted to have tea before she drove back to Durham to face whatever the evening might bring, so she went into the hotel lounge and ordered tea. She sat by the window and watched the street. She did not notice the two men who came in and she heard the unmistakable sound of Dryden Cameron's warm, soft voice. A thousand memories filled her mind and she looked across the room and there he was and she feasted her eyes on his tall, lean, elegant figure, dark-suited and half turned away. He had a glass in his hand and was chatting. She could not hear the conversation, just his voice like a sweet song, and then her tea came and when she spoke to the waitress Dryden must have recognized her voice also and she wondered what memories it evoked for him. He looked over, excused himself to the other man and then he came to her and as usual her main desire was to break down all over him.

'I lost my job.' It was all he said but even though the words were steady she was not deceived.

'Oh, Dryden, I'm sorry.'

'I'll get something else,' he said. 'How's Mr Stillman?'

Bobbie tried to say that Forbes was fine. She even smiled. She got the words past her lips like chunks of ice.

'He tried to kill himself,' she said and then the words tumbled past one another and it was so much easier, it hurt so much less when she had told Dryden. The pain and the burden dropped from her like a landslide.

It did not matter that they were in a public place. It did not matter how soft her words were because she knew he heard every one.

They went outside into the shadows to the side of the hotel. A thousand stars shone. He took her into his arms and kissed her.

Twenty-Six

After Joe had left, Vinia did not know what to do. As far as she was aware Dryden had no friends beyond business acquaintances so he had nowhere to go. She tried to think where he could have gone but by the end of the afternoon she was no closer to a solution and she went very reluctantly to Stanley House. She didn't want to go to the pit so she unlocked the door and walked in.

A blast of freezing air hit her and it was dark but when she had lit lamps the scene was no better. In fact it was worse. She could not believe this cold dark dusty house had been hers. It had about it the cheerlessness of a place where nobody had been happy in a long time. She went from room to room. Dead ash filled the grates. Dust covered the surfaces. The kitchen smelled of mice.

Vinia couldn't bear it. She found old newspaper and some sticks and plenty of coal and she lit the kitchen stove and the fire in the sitting room and then she set to work. She boiled the kettle and scrubbed the table and the kitchen floor. She took crockery from the cupboards and washed it all and she threw out the food which was mouldy.

She put polish and duster to the sitting room and then she thought she heard the door and when she looked up Joe stood there and she saw for the first time how dishevelled and uncared-for he was.

'This house is a disgrace,' she said.

'What does it matter to you? You left,' Joe pointed out. 'What are you doing here anyway?'

And that was when she realized that this was nothing to do

with her. She had no right to walk into his house and start cleaning.

'You're only here now because you're worried about Dryden, though what the hell makes you think he's here I can't imagine.'

'Don't you have a clean shirt?' was all she could say.

'No, no, I don't. I don't have a clean shirt. I don't have anything. My wife walked out and left me for some bastard gypsy!' Joe said and he walked out.

She found him by the kitchen stove.

'Has it made you any happier that he's gone?' she said.

Joe didn't reply immediately and then he said, 'He was the best friend I ever had. He saved my life once and my sanity dozens of times. Now look what I've done.'

'You could undo it.'

'How?'

'Why don't you go and see Mrs Stillman?'

Joe turned.

'You think he could contact her?'

'I don't know. He might, but don't go tonight. It's late and dark and it's beginning to snow. I have to get back.'

Joe insisted on driving her. Nobody spoke on the way. She thanked him and said goodnight but when she got back she hated the flat. She had forgotten how small and poor it was and how large and luxurious Stanley House had been. She wanted to be there so much she thought about walking home in the snow except that it was too hard and too deep and she could get lost on the fell.

She resented that Joe no longer thought of it as her house though what else he could have thought was doubtful. Up till now she had found a kind of peace in the rooms above the shop but that had all gone. She went to bed and lay there, thinking about how she would have scrubbed the floors and beaten the carpets and washed the bed covers and had everything there as it used to be. She thought of Joe's grubby clothes and his no doubt grubby bed and she couldn't stand it.

She wanted to run back to her husband and her house and

her life but she didn't. She heard her father's voice in her head, saying, 'You've made your bed and now you have to lie on it.'

Joe was not even sure where the Stillmans lived. He knew that her father had a house outside the town but that they did not live there any more. He went into the centre of the city and asked and was soon directed up the bank beyond the marketplace to Claypath and along the cobbled lane, halfway up, to the gates, which were closed. Nobody questioned him when he opened them and took his car down the drive to the house.

There were lights on. Joe rang the bell. After a short interval a maid in uniform came to the door. Joe explained himself but she said, 'Nobody is at home, sir. I'm sorry.'

Just then a car came down the drive and a beautiful, dark-haired woman got out. Joe recognized her. She had visited the pit offices more than once. It was Roberta Stillman.

'I'm very busy, Mr Forster,' she said.

'All I need is a moment of your time. Please,' Joe said.

She led him into a sitting room, where to her evident surprise her husband was sitting by the fire. A maid got up and went out as they walked in. Mrs Stillman seemed agitated, distracted, but Mr Stillman was friendly. He poured a drink for Joe and one for himself, asking Joe about the Black Prince pit. Mrs Stillman refused a drink and stood over the fire, smoking a cigarette and saying nothing.

After a short while Mr Stillman got up and said he rather thought he might go up and see the baby and when his wife politely objected for some reason, he smiled and said that there was nothing to worry about, he wouldn't be long.

Joe waited only until the door had closed and then he said to her, 'You've seen Dryden?'

'He told me that you had got rid of him.'

'It was a mistake. I lost my temper. Could you tell me how to get in touch with him? I want him to come back.'

She hesitated.

'Please.'

'I saw him at the Ivy Tree Hotel in Bishop Auckland less than an hour ago.'

'He was staying there?'

'He was with another man, having a drink. I don't know who it was or where he went after I left.'

She kept glancing towards the door, agitated, and it was not just that she wanted him to leave, Joe thought. There was something the matter. Whether it was something to do with Dryden he didn't know. He thought Forbes Stillman's quiet smile had somehow upset her. Whatever, she was not concerned with him.

Joe drove straight to Bishop Auckland. Mid-evening was giving way to night but he was pleased with his work so far. If Dryden was staying at the hotel it should be easy to talk to him, though beyond 'I'm sorry' and 'Would you come back?' Joe could not imagine what he would say.

He parked to the side in the car park and went into the thickly carpeted foyer, where a young woman stood behind the reception desk.

'My name is Joe Forster. I believe you have a friend of mine staying here, Mr Cameron.'

She consulted a book in front of her and then shook her head.

'I'm sorry, Mr Forster. Mr Cameron left today.'

'Have you any idea where he went?'

'No.'

'Or the name of the man he was with?'

'It was Mr Newbottle.'

'Fred Newbottle, the pit owner?'

'That's him.'

'Thank you,' Joe said. He walked the short distance to Fred Newbottle's house and banged on the door. A short stout woman answered it. Joe had met Iris Newbottle several times at various functions and she recognized him. She was polite but not effusive.

'Mr Forster,' she said.

'Good evening, Mrs Newbottle. I'm looking for Dryden Cameron. Is he here?'

'You'd better come in,' Mrs Newbottle said.

Joe stepped into the hall. The floor was black and white tiles. There was a big piece of hall furniture, like a sideboard, and various doors on the left. On the right was a big dog-leg staircase, halfway up it a stained-glass window, and Joe's attention was caught because Dryden was walking down the stairs. He paused and regarded Joe levelly.

'Perhaps you would like to come into the sitting room,' Mrs Newbottle offered.

Joe followed her in. It was a big room with floor-to-ceiling bay windows, a big fire, wood panelling, and there before the fire sat Fred Newbottle with a brandy glass in one hand and a cigar in the other. He got up.

'Why, Joe,' he said, 'how very nice to see you.'

He didn't sound pleased. He wouldn't. Dryden had told these people what had happened, Joe thought.

'Take a seat. Can I give you a drink, a cigar?'

'No, thank you,' Joe said, as the door opened and Dryden came in.

Fred Newbottle took his cigar but not his drink and left the room.

Joe couldn't think of a single word to say. He couldn't even look at Dryden. Worse still Dryden chose that moment to smile. Joe wished he wouldn't do that, there was no need for it, no reason. It was not a superior smile, more an acknowledgement that Joe had chosen to find him.

'How did you know I was here?' Dryden said.

'I went to see Mrs Stillman.'

'That was astute.'

'I thought so. Dryden, I didn't intend any of this. I'm sorry. I should never have treated you like that. I needed somebody to blame.'

'I know.'

'Do you?' Joe scrutinized him but he couldn't see any more. He never could with Dryden. 'But you left anyway?'

'Things have been getting worse for so long. What's the point?'

'The point is you're my friend and my pit manager and I want you to come back.'

'That's very kind of you, Joe.'

Joe waited for him to go on and when he didn't Joe said, 'You won't though?'

'No, I don't think I will. Thanks.'

'Has Fred offered you a job?'

'No.'

'But you think he will?'

'I think he might.'

'And if he doesn't?'

Dryden looked at him almost in apology.

'My money is all put away safely. I've had nobody and nothing to spend it on all these years.'

'So you don't need to work?'

'Not without a good reason.'

Joe realized then that he had not believed Dryden would turn him down. He thought he would be able to apologize and that Dryden would come back and everything would be all right. What had made him think that, when things had been so wrong for years and years?

'What shall I tell Vinia?'

Dryden didn't answer for a few moments and then all he said was, 'You think she's going to come running after me?'

'Of course I don't.'

'Well then, tell her anything you like,' Dryden said and he walked out.

Mrs Newbottle came in before Joe had the chance to go after him and demand explanations. Demand? For the first time he could do nothing.

'I think you should go, Mr Forster,' she said.

Bobbie wished with all her heart that you could hold people's kisses, that you could bottle or package them and remember the taste and the feel. If she closed her eyes she could bring back to mind the various street noises, the odd car, the voices echoing from across the street, the smell of stale beer which hung around every hotel and pub, but there he was in her mind, shielding her from the threat of another man's suicide, from the work problems, from the night. He was the only person who had ever done that, she thought, no wonder she loved him. His kisses were wonderful. She didn't know how she could go on any further without him.

When Joe had left she trudged upstairs to the night nursery and paused in the hall. Forbes was singing a lullaby to the baby, it was a song she could remember from her childhood and his voice was sweet and on tone. She went in. He had the child in his arms, asleep. He put him down into the cot but the child didn't stir. He didn't ask about Joe, he didn't ask about the meeting. She knew that the person he had become had no outer life. He could not go on like this, sooner or later when she slept or left him he would try to kill himself again, she felt sure.

'We should get another dog,' he said. 'Don't you think Iain would like that?'

'He's a few months old. Why should he want a dog?'

'We could get a pair of spaniels. We could call them Smith Two and Jones One.'

'Very funny,' she said.

'I'd like to have dogs again.'

'Do you miss him?'

'Isn't it funny, a dog never says a word to you but you feel closer to him than you do to most other people? Can we get a dog? Just one?'

'We aren't here.'

'I'm here.'

'You won't be. You're coming to work with me on Monday. I'm not leaving you here by yourself.'

'To work?'

She took him to the factory with her, all dressed up in a grey suit and looking the part. He went out and chatted to all the girls. Everywhere he went they laughed and he stopped them being useful. He sat in the office with her, drank gallons of tea and spoiled her concentration, flicking rubber bands across the desk at her, dropping papers all over the floor, staring from the window at the day as though he longed to be outside and then sitting down on her desk and saying to her, 'Can we go home now?'

'It's half past three.'

'I'm bored, Bobbie. Let's go home and have tea. Let's.' When she didn't answer, trying to read the papers in her hand, he leaned over and kissed her on the mouth. To her surprise it was as good and sweet a kiss as any of Dryden's. When she protested he did it again, taking her face in his hands as though he were practised at such things and then turning his brown eyes full on her and saying, 'I love you very much. Let's go home.'

'I wish that you would do something useful,' Bobbie said, exasperated. 'I've given you half a dozen things to do today and you haven't managed any of them.'

'Freya is making jam tarts.'

'How do you know that?'

'She told me this morning.'

'You asked her?'

'How else would I know? They'll still be warm if we go now. Let's go home, Bob. We could bring Iain downstairs and sit by the fire . . .'

'All right, all right. We'll go.'

He was right, she thought. The minute she opened the front door the smell of hot jam hit her sweetly. Warm pastry, cake, toast. Her childhood returned to her in an instant. Forbes ran upstairs for the baby, Freya brought in the tea on a tray and they sat by the fire. Later, Forbes lay down on the sofa with the baby on top of him and they both slept and she went away to the study and tried to work. Rain was falling into the river, she thought, going to the window. She turned at the sound of the door. It was Forbes.

'Where's the baby?'

'Nanny has him. Where else would he be?'

'You're always working,' he said.

'Somebody has to.'

'Why? Why can't we just buy a boat and sail away, you and me and Iain? Or we could go and live in Spain where it's always warm and have a vineyard.'

'We are in the middle of a world war.'

'It's nothing to do with us any more.'

'Isn't it?'

He faltered.

'It's taken almost everything. Why can't we keep the little we have left and leave?'

She didn't answer that.

'Don't you want to leave Dryden?'

'I don't have Dryden.'

'Wasn't that where you were the other day, when Mr Forster came?'

How on earth had he known that, she thought, gazing at him in astonishment.

'He'd kissed away all your lipstick and you hadn't put any more on.'

'It's nothing to do with you,' she said. 'Go away and leave me alone.'

He did. She stood for a minute or two and then she ran after him. He was in the sitting room.

'I would like a dog,' he said. 'I would like something to hold.'

'You can hold me,' Bobbie said and she went to him.

For a few minutes he was content with that and then he wanted to kiss her and touch her. Bobbie pulled away. The memory of Dryden's embraces was fading fast enough. She didn't want competition for them. Forbes didn't protest.

They changed, they had dinner. He sat on the sofa and pretended to read a book. Bobbie went back to the study to work. A short time later she thought she heard a faint click. She charged into the sitting room but he was gone. She did a quick check of the downstairs rooms, calling for Freya and Nanny but he was not in the house. She did not even pause to put on her coat. She ran all the way down the gardens, skidding as she went because it was icy, until she reached the gate at the bottom. She wished then as she had wished a thousand times that they had not come to live here, that they had stayed at her home, where if he was going to do something awful at least she would not have to face it alone. She even wished in those few minutes that she had let them take him away, she could not go on for the rest of her life like this.

He was not on the towpath. She wondered whether he had deliberately deceived her and gone somewhere else, found a gun, was even now halfway up the drive in the freezing darkness putting an end to it all, and then a calm voice from the garden said, 'What are you doing out there?'

She spun round and he was standing at some distance behind her, wearing a thick coat, another over his arm and his hands in his pockets. Bobbie wanted to laugh, cry, shout at him, anything, the relief she felt was so great.

'I was looking for you.'

'Were you? I brought your coat,' he said, coming to her. 'It's too cold to be without. You'll get your death.'

Bobbie began to laugh but his face was so puzzled that she made herself stop.

'Where were you?' she said.

'I was in the cellar. I thought you might like some wine later.'

Bobbie felt weak, light-headed.

'I would like some now,' she said.

'Would you really? It's a good thing I thought then, isn't it?' he said and they trudged back up the garden together towards the house.

Twenty-Seven

D ryden was homesick. He stayed with Fred and Iris and they were kind and he knew that he filled the gap in their lives where their son, Laurie, would have been. They were a lot older than he was, they had married late and had one child when they were forty so, although he was much older than Laurie would have been now, he provided the illusion and it was enough.

Dryden liked being there. Fred treated him with respect and courtesy at work, as though Dryden were above the pit managers, next to him in line of seniority, and Dryden knew he was giving Fred invaluable help so he did not feel guilty or as though he was taking advantage in any way and he was irritated at himself for wanting to go home. He had nothing there. He lived alone. He hardly ever saw Vinia. Joe didn't like him any more or want him at the pit. And yet he missed it. He missed the clean wind across the fell, the people he had known in the village. Bishop Auckland was not a big town but it was big compared to Deerness Law, where everybody knew everybody's business.

Dryden could not understand why, living with lovely people in a big house with every luxury Fred and Iris could contrive in wartime, being involved in running six pits, all he wanted was his own little office and the pit where he had worked all his life, where he knew each man by name, had worked with fathers, sons and now in some cases had taken on the grandsons. He helped them with their problems. He had comforted wives and mothers, given them extra money, even threatened men before now, that if they raised their fists to their wives again he would put them underground for good. He could stop a fight with a word, knew a man's problem by observing him and each night he could go back to his little house and be safe there as the wind moaned low through the gorse beyond the pit.

However, he had refused Joe's offer and could not go home so he stayed where he was, working so hard that Fred laughed and said he could not keep up. Fred introduced him to the other influential men in the district and Iris had lots of friends and gave small dinner parties. She asked single women to these. Dryden was certain they were all charming and delightful. Unfortunately the only woman he wanted was married to a man whom the war had driven insane. It did not make for the kind of thing Dryden felt comfortable competing with. Nightly he tried to remember the taste and feel of her but as the weeks went by their last meeting and the kisses by the Ivy Tree Hotel faded until they were a memory. He wished he could have seen her just to find out how she was but he could not do that.

The bad weather began to retreat and Dryden longed to see the fells, so one Saturday afternoon in April he borrowed Fred's car and drove out of Bishop Auckland. It was a fine clear spring day and the little fields were deep green. He could see higher over as the road turned into a steep bank towards Deerness Law, the moors and high lands of Weardale.

He did not like to go to Joe's house or to the pit, although he longed to see it, but in the end he could not resist. He drove past his house, to the end of the row, and halted the car outside and within moments of him doing so, it seemed, Joe came out of the office, smiling broadly and saying, 'Why, Dryden, what are you doing here?'

'I just . . . I just wondered how you were getting on.'

'Come in,' Joe urged him and although his steps lagged because he told himself he shouldn't Dryden found himself within the office building. The other people weren't there, it was empty, as it would be on a Saturday afternoon. He would not have been there had he thought Joe was still around. He had imagined Joe at home but then, like himself, Joe had nothing to go home to or for. It was so very reminiscent of his own life and he could pity Joe as he could pity himself the loneliness. The hardest time of all was half past four. Later there was the fire and a drink and some dinner and on the few warm days the sun dazzled you with its brilliance long into the evening, but when you had struggled through the afternoon, half past four was almost impossible.

It was nearly that now and Joe had learned to stave off the time with tea. Dryden admired it. They sat in Joe's office and observed the ritual with solemnity and then Dryden was unwise enough to ask after Vinia, as he felt he must, and Joe faltered. He didn't do it visibly. Anybody who hadn't known him well wouldn't have noticed but Dryden had known him too long. He knew how Joe breathed.

'I thought when you weren't there . . .' Joe said and stopped. 'That sounds awful.'

'No, it doesn't.'

'I thought it might be better. With you out of the way . . .' Joe's green eyes almost pierced him. 'The trouble is that when you're not there you're more in the way than when you are and if that sounds ridiculous I'm sorry. The way that she feels about you is . . . it's somehow containable, but without you she goes away to nothing, she doesn't want anybody and if you don't come back I will never live with her again and I don't know whether I can stand that. I miss her so much and she misses you like part of her has been torn off and if I'm honest nothing is right here without you. There now, I've said it. Are you happy with Fred and Iris? Is this just a visit?'

'I want to come home,' Dryden said.

Joe's eyes would have made emeralds look dull.

'Do you really?' he said.

Dryden went alone to see Vinia, at least Joe sat in the car while he went in.

'Aren't you coming in with me?' he had said, pausing.

'No, not yet.'

'You sure?'

'Yes.'

'All right.' Dryden took a couple of deep breaths before he got out of the car. It was strange how nervous he felt. There was nobody in the front of the shop. Perhaps she and Em were in the back, talking, or Em had gone home, since it was nearly six o'clock.

There she was alone, sitting at the little desk where she did her accounts, in the peace, the place tidied for the weekend, but then he realized she too had nothing else but her work. She had no reason to hurry anywhere. He said, 'Vinny,' very softly and she stopped writing and listened to his voice and then she got up and turned.

She gave a little scream – it was a good thing the shop was empty – and threw herself into his arms. Holding her like that for the first time in so long he remembered how much he loved her, how much he would always love her, and he was just pleased nobody else saw it. She started to cry and then to pretend she was not crying and then to draw back so that she could look at him but she put her fingers into his hair so that Dryden couldn't help getting hold of her again. By the time Joe thought fit to get out of the car and come into the shop he had stopped holding her to him like they were riveted. And when Joe came in she said his name half a dozen times at least as though she needed to hear it in the air and she said as she had said to Dryden, 'I missed you so much.'

It would always be difficult to watch them, Dryden thought, but he had done it so many times that in a way it felt right and though he minded, he didn't want them to be apart and unhappy and his heart was elsewhere and although that was not easy either it made things easier here.

Dryden was aware that Fred and Iris were expecting him back to dinner so he didn't stay much longer but he knew that he would be back, probably very soon.

'Your house is just as it was,' Joe said and Vinia promised to have Meg clean and have everything ready for him and Joe said he would like him to come in to work on Monday if that was all right with him and Dryden thought that suddenly everything with regard to his home and the pit and them was all right.

He went back to Bishop Auckland and over dinner he told Fred and Iris he would be leaving.

'I didn't think you would stay,' Fred said and Iris kissed him and when he apologized they would have none of it.

'You must go home,' Iris said. 'It's the best thing there is.'

Joe watched Fred's car out of sight and then he turned to Vinia. He knew things would not easily be repaired. He wanted to ask her to come back now but he knew that she wouldn't, that it would take time and energy and perseverance, so he smiled and said that he must get back and she let him and he went home.

He had asked Addy to come in and clean and cook several weeks since, he couldn't stand the mess any longer and so it was a much better house than it had been as far as comfort was concerned. There was pleasure in dinner and wine and a clean bed and warm fires, but somehow he missed his wife the more because she was not sharing it, although despite everything he could not go to her. He had done that once and she had turned him down. If he lived there another hundred years alone he could not go and beg her to come back.

He was pleased about Dryden, more than he had been about anything in a very long time. His guilt eased, the horrible negative feelings which had been there for so long died. Joe fell asleep by his sitting-room fire, almost happy.

Vinia told herself that she could be happy living in the flat above the shop, even after Dryden and Joe left, but the moment they had gone and she went upstairs she saw it for what it was for the first time, shabby, unfriendly, though she had tried to make it home. The quietness echoed. The street noises were no longer something she wanted to hear. She was desperate to run home to Joe. She told herself that it would be dark soon and might not be safe on the streets, it was Saturday evening, the drunks were out early, but she could not rest. She wanted to go back to him so much that every minute was like an hour. How had she stood it here for so long, in these two small rooms without comfort or companionship? She did not know. All she knew was that she could not bear it a moment longer. She put on her coat, ran down the stairs and out of the back door and up the lane and then on to the front street.

It was not dark yet but it would be soon. The buildings and sky were blurred in half-light and the pubs were lit and the smell of beer came from them and she could hear men's talk and laughter. It was the biggest night of the week. They could get drunk because they did not have to get up for work.

That was one thing. She knew where Joe was. He would not be in some pub. She hoped and prayed he would not have gone to Sadie. She did not quite trust him not to have done that, if he was sufficiently fed up with everything. It was the one thing she might never forgive him but then she had not let him near her and men were hopeless at things like that, she knew.

She hurried past the Black Prince pit and Dryden's house, which was in darkness, and then on to the fell, a trifle nervously because by then it was dark and it was cold and there was a wind sweeping across the fell and she was never quite sure about it. It was one thing to live in a great big house there and be safe and be the pit owner's wife, it was another to be outside on a cold spring night, not quite sure of her reception.

She saw the lights before she reached it and she stopped and stood there. Joe had not pulled the curtains along the windows to keep out the draught. Perhaps he did not like the feeling of being closed inside on his own. She often felt like that, how much more lonely it was in a house by yourself with the world shut out, like you were dead maybe, completely alone in a strange insulated way. She had often that winter, though the windows were iced, left the curtains open in the flat above the shop just because she could see lights from there and know other people existed. She only drew them when she went to bed and even then she was half-hearted about it because she hated the nights alone in her cold bed. She was nothing more than a small shopkeeper who nobody cared for.

She stood for a few moments longer and then walked quickly up the drive towards the lights. She banged on the front door like a visitor but Joe would hear her because he was in the sitting room at the front. She waited. Nothing happened. Perhaps she had been wrong and he didn't want her there. Why did he not answer the door? He must be able to hear her. She banged again and after a little longer a light came on in the hall and the bolts shot back and Joe stood there, hesitating as though he wasn't quite sure who she was and then he said, 'Vinny, you shouldn't have come over the fell on your own.'

'It isn't far.'

'Come inside. It's cold.' Vinia thought it was the sweetest thing she had ever heard.

The house looked so big and grand, the huge hall, the sitting room with its enormous fireplace and the hearth so clean that the flames glinted on it. Addy had been hard at work, Vinia thought, looking around her with pleasure and contentment at how much better it was than the last time she had been here. She was embarrassed, she didn't know what to say. Suddenly she felt like an intruder.

'I hope you don't mind,' she said.

'Mind?' Joe looked astonished. 'I love you, Vinny. I love you more than anything on earth.'

He had never, she thought, held back. Whatever Joe did he did it honestly and completely. He was still hers, Sadie had never really had Joe, he had been hers all along.

'I've had Addy sort the house out. Do you want to look round?'

She laughed.

'No.'

'I've got some champagne in the cellar.'

'Something told me you had. I don't want to go back to the flat.'

'You can stay here under any terms you choose.'

She went close.

'I don't want to make terms, Joe, I just want you,' she said.

Twenty-Eight

Bobbie and Forbes went back up the garden and into the house. They drank some wine and went to bed. Bobbie was all too aware of his gaze following her across the room as she undressed and brushed her hair and after enduring long minutes of him sitting on the bed fully dressed she stopped and said, 'Aren't you going to bed?'

He said, 'Bobbie . . .' and went no further.

'Do you want to go and sleep in your own room?'

'No, I want to stay here with you.'

'It isn't going to be like that,' she said.

He said nothing. She had expected an entreaty but nothing happened.

'I just . . . I . . .' Bobbie said.

'You love him,' Forbes said helpfully.

'I do, yes.'

He got up and went into the other room and closed the door. Bobbie went to bed and lay awake in the darkness, listening to him walk the floor. There was a particular floorboard which creaked. Sometimes she thought he had given up and gone to bed and then the noise would start up again.

Bobbie stood almost two hours of it and then she threw back the covers, got out of bed and went in to him. He had paused by the window and was standing with his hands in his pockets.

'You'll be exhausted in the morning,' she said.

'There are spiders round the bed.'

'What?'

'Great big ones with long legs. When I lie down I can see them.'

'There are no spiders,' Bobbie said.

'Sometimes there are lions. They sleep just at the end.' He nodded towards the bottom of the bed.

'There are no lions.'

'They're not there now,' Forbes said.

'Go to bed.'

Bobbie went back to her own room.

She took him to work with her every day after that. He did nothing. No matter what she gave him to do, no matter how simple the task, he could not complete it. He didn't go out and talk to the girls any more. He didn't make conversation. He didn't even ask to go home. He just sat or stood by the window in her office and stared out, smoking cigarette after cigarette, waiting for the day to get past.

She took him with her to the mills and the shops but he didn't seem to notice where he was, and when people addressed him he merely stared. In the evenings at home he sat over the fire, not reading or saying anything. He didn't eat and she knew very well by then that he didn't sleep.

Her father and his father visited at the weekends or she and Forbes went there.

'He's getting a lot worse,' her father said, some three weeks later when Forbes had wandered off into the library after Sunday dinner.

She didn't need to be told Forbes was getting worse. Each day he deteriorated further. She was exhausted. She gave in and let him sleep in her bed. He hadn't asked but it was easier than worrying about what he might be doing. He didn't offer to touch her, he didn't speak to her. He lay there hour after hour in the darkness and very often got up and wandered the house. He did not acknowledge Iain's presence, go to see him or talk about him.

One Sunday afternoon she determined to jolt him out of his silence.

'Would you like to go for a walk?' she asked, following him through into the library.

'What?' He looked at her as though he barely recognized her.

'The woods will be pretty today. Come on.'

They put on their outdoor coats and she put her hand through his arm and walked him away from the house and down past the garden to the pond, where she stopped.

'Do you remember this?'

'What?'

'This is where Terence buried Smith. Do you remember it?'

Forbes looked the other way.

'Do you remember the dog, the spaniel? Forbes, look at me. Look at me.'

Her voice was insistent. He glanced at her.

'You loved the dog. He followed you around the house and then he got old, didn't he? And he was in so much pain and you pretended to him that you were going for a walk and you brought him up here and then you shot him, didn't you?'

Forbes didn't respond.

'You shot him,' she said, 'because it was kinder than letting him go on.'

'No.' Forbes dragged his arm away from her and although she called his name he walked very fast back to the house.

'I didn't do it,' he called at her as he went inside.

He wouldn't have any tea. He wouldn't come out of the library. He stood there against the door until the early evening, when she told him they were going home and then he came out and she drove back.

Forbes went straight up to his room and when she went after him he had closed the door and she could hear his body slide down the door until he reached the carpet. Bobbie stood there for a few seconds and then she said, 'Maybe we could get another dog. You would like that. You wanted to get a pair of spaniels, didn't you? Springers. Black and white springers. Wasn't that what you wanted?'

She sensed rather than heard him move away from the door. She went in slowly, carefully. He was standing by the fire.

'Don't you want another dog?'

'No.'

'Because you had to shoot the old one?'

'I don't want to talk about it.' He turned away.

'Why don't you want to talk about it?' she said. 'It was the right thing to do. It was a brave thing to do and kind. The old dog adored you. He loved you and you were good to him because he had been Charles's dog.'

'No.'

'Yes. When we used to take you to the station we had to lock him up or he would try to run after Charles and for days and days after you had gone he would cry.'

'No.'

Forbes moved back from the fire and into the shadows of the room as though her voice would not reach him there.

Bobbie went over and got down beside him.

'Tell me about it,' she said.

'There's nothing to tell.'

'Did he sense what you were going to do, is that it? Were you afraid to cause him more pain? Tell me.'

She waited. She waited a long time while he didn't move. Silence filled the room, the whole house. Even the fire was silent. Bobbie couldn't think of anything else to say. He didn't move so she didn't move either but after a long while her position became intolerably cramped and she longed to ease it, to get up.

'It was dark.'

Bobbie waited. She wondered whether to prompt him but she didn't dare. It hadn't been dark, was all she could think.

'The darkness fell late and there was no moon. Low stars. Stars like you could own them. But the day . . . the day had gone on and on. Some got back. Some had died.'

Bobbie no longer wanted to stay there. She wanted to get up and run out of the room, anywhere she didn't have to listen to this but she couldn't. It was as if her whole body had gone into cramp.

'And lots of them were hurt. I could hear his voice. Even though other men shouted for their mothers or for help. I could hear him saying my name, just like he did when we were little and he got into things he couldn't get out of. There was nothing to be done. We couldn't get near while there was light. I couldn't risk the other men. We had to wait but it was summer, as though the light was never going to fade. I lay there and listened to his pain. When it was dark we went out and tried to find him and other wounded men were taken back to safety. There were so many. By the time I reached him Julian was dead and Charles was . . . holding Julian in his arms and Julian's body was . . . so close. He had been holding Charles near. Charles was . . . he was in so much pain, so very badly hurt.'

Every instinct screamed at Bobbie to shut him up because she knew, she thought now she had always known what came next and she did not want to unburden him and burden herself and that was why over all these months she had left him alone in that place with this knowledge, arguing with herself that he was a man, that he was supposed to be able to bear all this, but there were some things which nobody should have to bear alone. Charles had been a part of her like no one else had been or would be. She would have done almost anything to keep up the pretence as her father did that Charles was still alive. There was a tiny hope within her which believed it still and it was about to be destroyed forever.

'He begged me to finish him off, so I did,' Forbes said.

Bobbie let go of her breath in a sob. Forbes moved very slightly.

'I shot him. I killed him,' he said.

Bobbie had no idea how long they sat there. She thought she would never move again. Forbes kept his hands over his face and after a while they began to shake. She wanted to question him, to know more, to be reassured of . . . she wasn't sure what. Yes, she was, that he had done the right thing, that he was certain Charles would die, and then she dismissed these thoughts as foolish. She wanted to know and did not want to know what Charles's injuries had been, that they did not kill him immediately but made him want to die. She could not imagine, did not want to imagine what it was like to die like that and yet she did because he had been a part of her and she would have done anything to have taken the pain away. She knew now that loss was total, that was what she had learned from this. She would never see her twin again ever.

More importantly if she left Forbes because of her feelings, if she did not show him affection and understanding, if he thought for a second that she did not condone what he had done she was quite certain that he would die, so when she could, when enough time had passed and she could move and the shaking of his hands got worse and worse, she went forward and took him into her arms and held him there.

'It wasn't your fault,' she said. 'None of it was your fault.'

Forbes gave a sigh and then he put his arms around her. Eventually she said, 'Come to my bed. Come and sleep.'

It took time to get up off the floor after being there for so long. She had pins and needles in her feet but they went into her room and took off most of their clothes and then she put him into bed and got in beside him and took him into her arms again and after a short while he went to sleep. She thought that she would never sleep but the quiet sounds from the street way over across the river and an owl hooting in the garden were somehow reassuring and she felt herself drift away and she was so thankful, so thankful and so bitterly sorry that she could sleep when Charles had had such a hard death and she had loved him so much. How resilient people are, was her last thought.

Twenty-Nine

T he war ended that summer and, in a way, that was when
Forbes came home.

They slept together that first night without touching and in
the morning nobody said anything. They got up and bathed
and dressed and went down to breakfast and, over the table,
just as though they went on like that every morning he said, 'I
would like to come to the factory with you. I won't get in the
way.'

'You're never in the way,' she said.

He smiled at her and they went off together to the factory. He
didn't do much that day. She thought he looked so tired and she
was worried that he would turn back into the awful person he
had proved himself to be after he had shot the dog. The person
his father so admired. He sat in her office and read various
papers and smoked and drank coffee. When she offered him
lunch he shook his head. They didn't talk much but in the
evening they went home and ate a huge dinner and drank a
bottle of wine and halfway through the evening he looked
apologetically at her and said, 'You don't mind if I go to bed,
do you?'

'I don't mind at all.'

He got halfway to the door and then stopped.

'Thanks,' he said.

'For what?'

'For not asking questions and for getting me to here,' and
then he went out and shut the door.

Bobbie worked for a couple of hours and then went to bed.
He had gone to his own bed. She was not sure whether or not

she was pleased about that. There was still time for him to become the unbearable young man she had been so impatient with.

The following morning at breakfast he said he thought he might go and look around the mills.

'Why don't I come with you?' Bobbie heard herself say.

'I can manage.'

'I'm sure you can. I could drive.' As though I had nothing else to do, she thought, but then he needed her there.

They packed a suitcase each because the mills were in Yorkshire and although they could have driven all the way back they wouldn't have been able to get round more than one in a day and they owned three. They called in at the factory first and she issued instructions and he didn't interrupt as he would have done at one time, or give her advice, he sat in the car and waited and she was pleased and surprised at the sensitivity of it. When she got back in all he said was, 'Everything all right?'

'Everything's fine,' she said.

It was a bright day, clear and the drive down was easy. Halfway there he said, 'We could go to the coast.'

'We could, yes, except it's the wrong way.'

'Let's anyway.'

'I thought this was business.'

She thought about Dryden and the trip to Scarborough and how disastrous that had been but this was not. The North Yorkshire coast consisted of what had been tiny little fishing or smuggling villages and each one was a jewel. She couldn't decide where they should stop for lunch but it was decided for them. She drove the car over the hill at Loftus and there was Staithes, laid out before them. She drove down the hill, Boulby Cliffs falling away heavily on one side and fields on the other, and then turned left into the village and along a little way and then, plunging down into the heart of the tiny town, she thought it was everything anybody could ever have hoped for in a seaside village.

The tiny houses clung to the hillside, one on top of another almost, and it had a natural harbour with cliffs to either side and seagulls perched or soaring above and on the front a small beach and in the water fishing boats and too close to the water to be safe was a pub. They left the car and went inside and sat by the windows, which looked out over the bay, and they had fish and chips and beer.

The beach wasn't big enough to be walked on so after they had eaten they moved on, not very far, to Runswick Bay, and there was a beach that you could run along for an hour, with the village to one side and the tide halfway down and then what appeared to be an endless golden stretch of sand, with caves halfway along and cliffs rising above.

They spent the afternoon there and then as they got back into the car he said, 'Shall we find a hotel somewhere close?'

'We should go.'

'Oh, come on. Just for tonight.'

They set off away from the coast across the moors and there was a big hotel, only a few miles away. They asked for two rooms and Bobbie thought the proprietor looked strangely at them. She found that she had packed a very smart black dress and wore that to dinner and he complimented her and she found that she was pleased to be there. They lingered over dinner, drinking brandy when it was late, wishing one another goodnight in the narrow hall and then she was reluctant to leave him.

'I've had too much to drink,' she said, standing outside her door.

'Do you want me to see you in?'

'No!'

'You've done it with me.'

'That was different.'

'How was it?' he said, coming closer.

'It just was.'

He kissed her. Bobbie tried to pretend to herself that it was a surprise but it wasn't, it had been almost there all day and it was a very nice kiss and she liked it and she had to tell herself that this was not the man she loved. It was the man she was married to. That was quite enough justification for a woman who had

243

had too much to drink. She kissed him and then she opened the door to her bedroom and they went in, still kissing, and after that, oh dear. She didn't remember Dryden, she didn't remember anything. She was perfectly happy on the rug with him and in bed and she knew that she would be sorry in the morning but she didn't care.

Somebody once remarked, Bobbie thought when she came to in the sunlight, that you could either have good evenings or good mornings but not both, and it was certainly true of this morning. She did not want to get out of bed, only too aware of the man sleeping beside her. However, when she took her face out of the pillow and stopped inwardly calling herself names she found that he was awake and was looking at her in amusement.

'I'm glad you think it's funny,' she said.

'It wasn't funny,' he said, 'it was nice.'

'Forbes . . .'

'All right, all right, so I'm not Dryden Cameron.'

'I wasn't going to say that to you.'

'Of course you weren't. How very tactless that would have been. We are married however. We are allowed to do that if we want to and you did want to or are you going to disclaim responsibility and go for drunkenness? It was only one night, you're unlikely to be pregnant, so what difference does it make?'

'It does though, doesn't it?' Bobbie sat up in her determination to make herself clear and pulled up the bedclothes around her in sudden self-consciousness.

'Does it?'

'Well yes, it's like a . . . a boundary.'

'Didn't feel much like a boundary. Felt a lot better than that,' Forbes said. 'You think I'm going to pounce on you every night, do you?'

'No . . .'

'Don't flatter yourself,' Forbes said and he got out of bed.

'I didn't mean to upset you.'

'I'm not upset. I'm . . . I'm grateful. God, what a horrible word, I'm grateful that I'm still here and that I want to do that, even if you don't give a shit about me.'

'I do care about you.'

'Not like that,' Forbes said, putting on his clothes as he found them from where they had been carelessly dropped on to the floor. 'You love a man you can't have. Maybe that's why. It's all to do with not being able to possess him. Maybe you're just the sort of person who never wants what they can have,' and, half dressed, he picked up the rest of his clothes and his shoes and slammed out of the room.

'Oh bugger!' Bobbie said.

She didn't pretend to herself that he would come back inside and apologize so she dressed and went after him. He was standing outside, looking out across a sea of moor. She stopped some way behind him and she thought he was so much nicer than the person he had been. That was the one redeeming feature of people who went through too much. If they survived they were better, the steel through the fire and all that sort of stuff. Forbes was now the kind of man any woman would have been proud to be married to. She could be the envy of the entire district within months.

She walked up behind him and to her surprise he said, 'I don't love you.'

'What?'

'I don't love you. Last night was just . . . it was just because you were there and because I was there and . . .'

He went back inside. Later that day, after breakfast, she drove across country and they spent the next three days going around the various mills and he was like somebody else, somebody incredibly competent without the nastiness which she had hated. He didn't really need her there and they slept in a hotel but separately and they spoke only when necessary and after that they went back to Durham. She went to the factory and he went to the shops.

* * *

245

It was late summer when the French girl came to the house. She came there without warning, without a letter. She turned up one Sunday morning when they were sitting in the garden, drinking coffee and talking about work. Freya came out of the house and across the lawn and Bobbie looked up from her chair. Freya said, 'There's a lady to see Mr Stillman,' and Forbes got up with a glad cry and he hugged to him the slight dark figure in the cheap frock, saying her name over and over.

Bobbie didn't move. She waited as they talked rapidly in French until he remembered her and then he turned and said, 'Bobbie this is Mariette. Mariette, my wife.'

The girl's face fell, her eyes darkened.

'You are married,' she said in English. 'I am so sorry. I did not mean to come here.'

'Do sit down,' Bobbie said. 'Would you like some tea or some coffee?'

'No, no.' She would have left but Forbes sat her down. 'I must go.'

'Haven't you come a very long way to see Forbes? You can't go now.'

The girl was too thin to be pretty, Bobbie thought. Perhaps, like many other people, she had seen too much. Her figure was as slender as a boy's. They had tea on the lawn and Bobbie could see how very much in love with Forbes she was. She kept looking at him as though he might disappear and she might be left thinking she had conjured him from the air.

Mid-evening when they had eaten she said that she must leave and Forbes drove her into the city to find a hotel. It was only when he returned that Bobbie realized something. She was jealous. How could that be? She was in love with Dryden, she had always been in love with him. Forbes might be her husband but he had no hold on her, he had her affection and nothing else. She did not want him, not really. Why then did she not want anybody else to have him?

She had been upstairs. She came halfway down as he reached the hall.

'You're late.' What had they been doing? Had he made love

to Mariette? Had they gone into a hotel room together and . . .
Bobbie couldn't bear to think of it.

'She didn't want to be there alone and she wanted to talk.'

'What about?' Bobbie came the rest of the way down the
stairs.

'Oh, her husband, her life . . .'

'Has she left him?'

'Yes,' Forbes said. He didn't say the word easily, he said it as
though his announcing it would make it real and as though it
was his fault somehow that she had come here in search of him.

He went into the sitting room. Bobbie followed him inside.

'Would you like a drink?' he offered.

'Yes, thank you. I would.'

The light had not gone from the day and it had been hot. It
had been the perfect day, at least it would have been if the
French girl had not turned up. She wanted to wind the day back
and for it to be that morning when things had been less
complicated and they had been talking about the factory. It
was her favourite way to spend Sunday mornings and she had
got used to Sundays, having a meal together, taking Iain for a
walk by the river in the afternoon. She had not realized how
much it had mattered to her.

He poured whisky for them both and she waited for the usual
Sunday evening peace to descend but it didn't. Everything was
spoiled. She could hear the river below and the silence of the
sleeping child above and suddenly she could see how everything
wouldn't work all over again. She had thought she did not want
him here. Now she wasn't sure. No, she was. She didn't want
the French girl here or anywhere that would interrupt things.
She could not bear any more change. She just wanted to go on
day after day working and coming home to this house and her
child and . . . and to him. Perhaps it was too late for that.

'Is she staying long?'

'I don't know.'

Bobbie sat down in a big leather chair.

'She did come for you though?'

'Yes.'

'Did you . . . when you were in France did you promise to marry her?'

'She was married. How could I do that?'

'But you were in love with her?'

'Yes.'

Bobbie downed the whisky in her glass and needed more but she didn't like to say so. He seemed to divine her need and came over with the decanter and poured so much into her glass that it was heavy to hold. He did the same for his own glass and subsided into the chair across the french windows, which were open. It was a beautiful night, clear, warm, cloudless. She tried to imagine what her father would say when Forbes wanted to divorce her, what his father would say. How she would never be accepted into society as a divorced woman and how long and silent the evenings would be when she was all alone. The hours would stretch into eternity. Would she have to tell her father that Forbes was nothing to do with her child, that he had never loved her nor she him, that it had been a sham, a convenient pretence? Her father would feel duped, silly, perhaps even worse. And it was no longer true, that was the ridiculous part, at least for her.

They had spent one night together. Only one. It was enough, that and the days, that and the way that he was so good to her child, that and the way that he ran the business so well, that and how they sat over breakfast and read the papers and chatted, that and how they came home to one another at night and there was all the rest. There was how much he had loved Smith and although she did not like to think of it, how very much he had loved Charles. He had put his very sanity and thereby his life at risk for her brother's sake. If he loved this French girl now, she must not try to hold him because of legalities and tradition. She owed him that.

'Did you tell her that if she left him you would marry her?' she asked.

'Hardly.'

'What then?'

He looked at her.

'I was young and it was war and . . . she's very pretty.'

'What are you going to say to her?'

'I don't know. She can't go back to him.'

'Do you want her to?'

'No.' He answered her quickly.

'We could be divorced.'

'What?'

'We could.'

'Why should we do that?'

'You don't love me. You told me when we stayed near Staithes. You can't have forgotten.'

Forbes didn't say anything for what seemed to her like hours and was probably only a few minutes.

'It was a defence mechanism,' he said.

'A what?'

Forbes turned sharp eyes on her.

'You are in love with your bloody gypsy. How many times have you told me? I can't be him. I can't be Iain's father. I can't be anything you want me to be.'

'I don't want you to be anything different,' Bobbie managed. 'I like you very well as you are.'

'What about him?'

That was too difficult to explain, she thought. She knew that Dryden had gone home though she had not seen him, Phyllis kept her informed of all the goings on at Deerness Law. Dryden was back, Phyllis had said some time ago, in his house and at his pit. Bobbie knew that was where he was meant to be, as she was meant to be here.

'I don't see him any more,' she said.

Forbes took a quick slug at his whisky before he said, 'I thought I loved her. It was an illusion. I don't want her. I told her . . .' He wasn't looking at Bobbie. 'I told her we were married and that I couldn't leave you.'

'I should think not. Whatever would your father say? Whatever would my father say?' Bobbie said and they laughed.

'You want to stay married to me then?'

'Certainly. My God. I have my respectability to consider.

Besides . . .' She got up. 'I can only say this because I am on the verge of having had too much whisky. I want you.'

'Now?'

'Yes. For beginners. But probably every night.'

'You think?'

'Oh yes. It's too light down here, let's go to bed. And in the morning you can go to her hotel and . . . I don't know, tell her whatever you have to.'

'She has her mother's family in York. She's half English.'

'Then you can be apologetic and gracious but it is too late and you are married and the awful English woman would never divorce you because you have a child and a hugely successful business and . . .'

She stopped there because he kissed her and when she put her arms around his neck he picked her up and carried her to bed.

Dryden had thought that going home would be wonderful so it wasn't. He had forgotten how loud the silence was in his house and in his life. Vinia had gone back to Joe and everything was just the same as it had been before except that he didn't have Bobbie at all and stupidly night after night he expected her. By the summer he had stopped expecting her and had gone back to the whisky bottle for comfort. He wanted to see his child but he made himself not go. Major Stillman was, according to Tan, making big alterations at the factory and he was making a good job of things and Phyllis reported that Mrs Stillman looked very happy. Dryden had no intention of getting in the way of that happiness, however dearly it cost him.

He gleaned small scraps of information about his child but night after night when he went to bed he reminded himself that the little boy was in Durham, being looked after by people who loved him. He was there. And it was enough. It was enough and he would not let himself spoil his child's security or well-being. If Bobbie had decided she no longer wanted him he had his work and his house and sometimes he could even bear to go to Joe and Vinia's house for Sunday dinner.

Saturday nights were a sweet alcoholic haze except that just lately the weather had been too hot to sit inside and there was nowhere but a yard for him to sit outside so he had taken, in late evening, to putting half a bottle of whisky in one pocket and a glass in the other and walking out of the village towards the view of Weardale and lying down in the heather on the tops and enjoying a couple of hours before the night came down to meet the land.

One August late evening as he lay there he saw somebody walking away from the road towards him, a lovely blonde woman.

'Is that you, Sadie,' he said, 'or are you a bloody apparition?'

'I saw you go past the house. You did it last week.'

'So?'

'I own this.'

'You own the moor?'

'I own this bit of it and my grandmother's house and all the land around it.'

Dryden looked at her as she sat down.

'It wasn't me in the picture,' he said.

'It couldn't have been, could it?'

'Who was it then?'

'The man with the jewel in his ear.'

'The ruby.'

'You met him?'

'I did, yes, several years ago. Tommy went to him. I'm sure he did.'

'Can I have a drink?'

'There's only one glass.'

'I don't mind sharing.'

Dryden poured her some whisky and she sipped it and then gave it back to him. By the time the bottle was empty the evening was dark and the ruin of her grandmother's house stood out as a black shape against the skyline.

'Did you ever think about having it rebuilt?' he said.

'I like the house I have,' Sadie said and she got up. 'Do you want to come back with me?'

'No.'

'It's Saturday. I'm not doing anything.'

'You don't do anything any night,' he reminded her.

Sadie looked at the view though there wasn't a lot to see in the dark.

'Joe's wife went back to him,' she said.

'Aye.'

'He always loved her.'

'He did,' Dryden agreed, getting up.

'And you did?'

'Yes, I did.'

Sadie set off towards the road.

'I have whisky at my house,' she said.

'And isn't that the best offer I've had all week,' Dryden said.

He caught up with her. It wasn't far to her house and it smelled of clean dry washing and bread baked that morning. Dryden looked at the picture of the gypsy in the field at the farm.

'The man has no jewel in his ear. How do you know it's him?'

'My grandmother told me about him,' Sadie said, whisky bottle in one hand and glass in the other.

'What a terrible liar you are,' Dryden said.

'You believed me.'

'Just pour me some whisky, Sadie,' Dryden said. 'It is me.'

'I know. She told me how you came to her and how she looked after you when your son had died. You have another son.'

'How do you know that?'

'I know everything,' Sadie said and she poured whisky into a glass for herself and she smiled into his eyes and the hours ceased.

WITHDRAWN

NOV 17 2004